PRA[ ]
BESTSELL[ ]

"*Dead, Bath,* [ ]
missed cozy m[ ]

"Fans of the series will be invested in seeing just what
Katie's next step will be in her life, while mystery readers
will enjoy unpredictable plot twists and her suspenseful ef-
forts to ingeniously MacGyver her way out of jeopardy."
—Kings River Life Magazine

"Fun plot, fanciful characters, really fabulous crafts. A pal-
ette of colorful characters and enticing crafts. Bartlett put
her art and soul into this mystery!"
—Laura Childs, *New York Times* bestselling author
of the Cackleberry Club Mysteries, the Scrapbooking Mysteries,
and the Tea Shop Mysteries

"Ms. Bartlett has established a plucky, intelligent heroine
in Katie Bonner and has surrounded her with a cast of fas-
cinating multidimensional characters."
—Ellery Adams, *New York Times* bestselling author
of the Books by the Bay Mysteries and the Book Retreat Mysteries

"A co-op of artisans, one disgruntled artist, and a desperate
artifice—the perfect canvas for murder. Lorraine Bartlett's
characters come alive in this tightly crafted, suspenseful
plot that grips the reader's attention right up to the satisfying conclusion."
—Kate Collins, *New York Times* bestselling author
of the Flower Shop Mysteries

"Wonderful. . . . Bartlett starts the new Victoria Square
series with a can't-miss hit!"
—Julie Hyzy, *New York Times* bestselling author
of the White House Chef Mysteri[ ]

Berkley Prime Crime titles by Lorraine Bartlett

Yule Be Dead

LORRAINE BARTLETT
with GAYLE LEESON

BERKLEY PRIME CRIME
New York

BERKLEY PRIME CRIME
Published by Berkley
An imprint of Penguin Random House LLC
375 Hudson Street, New York, New York 10014

ISBN: 9780425266007

First Edition: November 2018

Printed in the United States of America
1   3   5   7   9   10   8   6   4   2

Cast of Characters

Katie Bonner: owner-manager of Artisans Alley, the anchor on Victoria Square

Andy Rust: owner of Angelo's Pizzeria and Katie's boyfriend

Francine Barnett: owner of Afternoon Tea

Margo Bonner: Katie's former mother-in-law

Ray Davenport: former homicide detective and owner of Wood U on Victoria Square

Nick Ferrell: co-owner of Sassy Sally's Inn on Victoria Square

Carl Fiske: bartender at The Pelican's Roost

Nona Fiske: owner of The Quiet Quilter; aunt of Carl Fiske

Godfrey Foster: lint-art vendor at Artisans Alley

Vance Ingram: vendor at Artisans Alley and Katie's second-in-command

Seth Landers: attorney and Katie's friend
Dana Milton: owner of It's Tutu Much dance studio
Ida Mitchell: crafter at Artisans Alley
Rose Nash: jewelry vendor at Artisans Alley and Katie's
  friend
Don Parsons: co-owner of Sassy Sally's Inn on Victoria
  Square
Detective Schuler: homicide detective with the Sheriff's
  Office
Rhonda Simpson: crafter at Artisans Alley
Susan Williams: crafter at Artisans Alley

One

For several seconds after her former mother-in-law had ended their call, Katie Bonner stared at her phone. What kind of sick joke was this? When Katie's husband, Chad, had been alive, one hour with Katie had been too much for Margo Bonner—and that hour had been used to make passive-aggressive digs at the woman who could never be good enough for her darling Chad.

And now—*now?*—after Chad had been dead for nearly two years, Margo would be "passing through" and wanted to spend a couple of days with Katie? Why? And even stranger, why had Katie agreed to host the persnickety woman in her tiny one-bedroom apartment? She could've said no, could've made up an excuse, could've suddenly booked a one-way ticket to Bolivia.

But she'd found herself saying, "Sure, that'll be fine."

Fine.

Why in the world . . . ?

Because of Chad. Because I still miss him, too.

Katie sighed as she pushed away from her desk. She grabbed a peppermint from the jar before heading out of her office at Artisans Alley, her long skirt swishing as she walked. She, and the rest of the vendors, was dressed in nineteenth-century garb for the Dickens Festival, the Alley's second annual celebration of the holiday season. The other merchants on Victoria Square had also adopted the custom—and it was paying off in spades.

Since Katie had taken over running the former applesauce warehouse now known as Artisans Alley—Chad's pet project—it had grown from being an unorganized, failing group of artisans to a profitable configuration of artists and vendors. Maybe that was another reason Katie hadn't refused Margo's offer. She wanted her former mother-in-law to see what she'd done with her son's legacy.

"Katie, Vance just called," Rose Nash said, the spryest seventy-something-year-old Katie had ever met. Today, she was manning cash desk one, a cute bonnet covering her blonde curls, her blue eyes sparkling with pleasure. "His church's choir will be here to sing on Saturday from one until four. Oh, I can't wait to hear those heavenly voices filling the Alley with song."

Katie smiled. The customers loved it, too. "That's great. I was just going over to the tea shop for a minute. May I bring you back anything?"

"Oh, no, thanks. It's . . . um . . ." Rose scrunched up her softly wrinkled face. "I've heard complaints about the food, and they don't seem to be doing much business lately."

Rose had a point. 'Twas the season, and all the other businesses in Victoria Square were bustling. From what Katie could see as she walked across the parking lot, there wasn't a single customer inside the tea shop. Something was definitely going on there. Two months ago, the tea shop seemed to have been thriving. Now, when it should have been at its busiest, the place was as dead as Jacob Marley.

Although the bell over the door tinkled merrily when Katie walked into the shop, no one came out to greet her right away. It gave her the opportunity to consider the display case. There were some blueberry scones, but they looked slightly burned around the edges. Some miniature chicken salad croissants looked okay, but she wondered how long they'd been sitting there.

Francine Barnett finally emerged from the back of the shop, sliding her palms down the front of her soiled white apron. "Hi, Katie. How are you?"

"I'm fine, thanks. Will you be open late for the lighting of the big Christmas tree on the Square on Saturday night?"

"I don't think so." Francine looked as though she'd been through the wringer. Her light brown eyes were red rimmed, as though she'd been crying, and black circles were evident on her pale skin.

"Is anything wrong?"

She sighed. "It's that obvious, huh?"

Katie chose her words carefully. "Probably not to anyone but me. You always seem lively and upbeat, but today . . ."

"Today I look like I've been crying my eyes out? That's because I have, dear. When we bought this place, Vonne swore to me that she'd help me run Afternoon Tea—that together we'd make it a grand success. And we did for a few months. Then Vonne got bored with it. It's too much for me to handle by myself, Katie."

She began to cry, and Katie hurried around the counter to put an arm around her and lead her to one of the tables. She pulled out a chair and eased her into it.

"Everything will be all right," Katie said. "May I get you some tea?"

Francine laughed through her tears. "See? You're better

at this than I am. Why don't you buy the shop? I'm sure you could make a success of it."

"Don't be ridiculous. You're just upset."

"I'm not," she said. "I've actually been considering putting the tea shop up for sale now for weeks. I remember your telling me one time that you'd once considered running a bed-and-breakfast. Wouldn't a tea shop be the next-best thing?"

Katie had wanted to serve afternoon tea at her B and B, the English Ivy Inn. But she'd been rudely awakened from that pipe dream when Chad invested nearly all their money into Artisans Alley and then died in a car accident, leaving her to make the best of "their" investment. She looked around the shop. There were so many things she could do to spruce up the place: fresh paint in a light pink with burgundy trim . . . delicate floral curtains . . .

"Katie!"

She snapped out of her reverie and apologized to Francine. "You caught me woolgathering."

"I caught you considering the possibilities."

Katie inclined her head. "You did. But I'm not sure buying a tea shop is a viable option for me right now."

"Of course it is! Look how you've turned around Artisans Alley in such a short amount of time. You'd have no problem here. You'd simply take over the lease, buy out our inventory and equipment—"

"Which might not be as easy as you make it sound," Katie said. "Getting a bank loan is no small feat."

"I know, but at least say you'll consider it."

"I . . . Have you talked with Vonne about this? Is she willing to give up the shop?"

Francine scoffed. "I don't know where Vonne's head is these days, but she certainly isn't concerned with the day-to-day running of this shop. I'm the one who put up the capital to open this place, and I'm the one who's going to sell it."

The thought gave Katie pause. Could she make a go of the tea shop? What would the vendors at Artisans Alley say? Would they think she was abandoning them?

The bells over the door signaled a new arrival.

Francine dabbed at her eyes with a napkin. "Thank you for listening, Katie. Let me greet this customer, and I'll get you your tea."

Katie recognized the man: Detective Schuler of the Monroe County Sheriff's Office. He strode over to meet Francine with his thumbs tucked into his belt, and appeared to be ever so full of self-importance. Sure, it was great that he'd been promoted from deputy, but that promotion had come only because Ray Davenport had retired from the force.

"I'm sorry, Ms. Barnett, but this is not a social call," he said, jerking his head in the direction of the tables. "I think you should sit down for this."

Naturally, that soothed Francine's nerves as well as you might imagine it would.

"What is it? What's wrong?"

"Is there somewhere we can speak privately?" Detective Schuler asked.

"Say whatever you came to say in front of Katie. It's not like all of Victoria Square won't hear whatever it is by sundown anyway." She glanced at Katie. "I'm not saying you'd mention it, but gossip just seems to spread around this place like warm butter."

Katie nodded her understanding.

"All right, then. Well . . . it's Vonne."

"I figured as much." Francine shook her head. "What now? Reckless driving? Another DUI? Can I even bail her out of trouble this time?"

"Um . . . actually . . ." Detective Schuler's bravado seemed to have left him. "Well . . . there was an accident. I'm sorry to be the one to tell you, but Vonne is dead."

~~~~~~~

Katie was shaken as she left Afternoon Tea . . . so shaken, in fact, that she ran headlong into Ray Davenport.

"Whoa, there!" He'd dropped the bag he was carrying in order to grasp Katie's shoulders to steady her.

To her dismay, Katie saw that the cinnamon bun he'd been carrying had fallen onto the pavement. She picked it up. "I'm sorry, Ray."

Ray had retired as a homicide detective in the Sheriff's Office some five months before, and he was now operating Wood U, a gift shop featuring wood products, on Victoria Square. When Ray and Katie first met, they'd had the antagonistic relationship of investigator and murder suspect, but they'd eventually become friends. Now the stocky man was looking down at her with concern, his bushy brows drawn together like a chubby caterpillar.

"Are you all right?" he asked. "You're pale as a ghost."

"Let's talk while we walk." She held up the destroyed, sticky cinnamon bun. "I'll get you a replacement."

"That's not necessary." He seemed to realize that his hands were still resting on Katie's shoulders, and he removed them, took a step back, and retrieved the cinnamon bun. He dropped it into the bag and then in the nearest trash can. "I probably didn't need it anyway."

"I beg to differ. And, as a matter of fact, I need one, too. Come on."

Ray fell into step beside her. "So, are you going to tell me what has you so addled?"

"I dropped into the tea shop for a snack because, well . . . I was supposed to meet Andy for lunch, but he got busy . . . and then I got busy . . . and then—"

". . ."

"What?"

Katie explained that Detective Schuler had come into the

tea shop just moments ago to inform Francine of Vonne's death. "Naturally, she closed the shop, and Schuler took her to Rochester and the morgue to make a positive identification."

Ray shook his head. "What a shame. I was afraid her reckless driving would catch up with her one day. Some people never learn."

"So Vonne had a bad driving record?" She recalled Francine's comments about DUI and reckless driving to the detective.

"When I was on the force, I seem to recall she was about one citation away from losing her license for good."

By then, they'd reached Angelo's Pizzeria. Going to a pizzeria for a cinnamon bun might sound odd, but Andy Rust—who also happened to be Katie's boyfriend and landlord—made the best cinnamon buns around. In fact, he was known on Victoria Square as the Cinnamon Bun King.

Ray opened the door for Katie and then followed her into the pizzeria.

Andy's blue T-shirt emphasized his muscular torso, and his eyes lit up as he stepped out from around the counter and gave Katie a peck on the lips. "What brings you by?" He gave Ray a quizzical look. "And did you eat that cinnamon bun already?"

"No, he didn't. I wasn't watching where I was going, and I knocked it out of his hands," Katie said. "So, I'd like two to go please."

"Coming right up." Andy got them the cinnamon buns, and Katie paid for them.

"I have to get back to work," he said, "but I'm looking forward to seeing you tonight." He gave Katie another quick kiss, glanced at Ray, and then went into the back room.

Out on the asphalt apron outside the shop, Ray assured Katie again that replacing his cinnamon bun hadn't been necessary.

"It certainly was," she said. "Would you care to eat with

me in my office? Or we can go back to your shop, if you'd rather. I'd just like to talk with you for a minute."

"Let's go to Artisans Alley. Your coffee is better than mine."

Katie was relieved that Rose wasn't at her post when she and Ray strode into the Alley's main showroom and down the aisle to the vendors' lounge. Rose must have taken a break to check her booth. Katie got the coffee quickly, so she'd be safely back in her office before Rose noticed her return. She didn't feel like explaining to Rose—or any of the other Artisans Alley vendors or patrons—why there had been a sheriff's cruiser at Afternoon Tea.

Katie doctored the cups of coffee: milk for both and two sugars for Ray. He liked his coffee sweet. She slipped into the cramped office where Ray sat on the chair near her desk. He'd spread paper towels out for their cinnamon buns.

"What did you want to talk about? Is it Vonne?"

Katie shook her head. "No. I don't want any news of Vonne's accident coming from me. Francine made it clear that she doesn't like the fact that news spreads so quickly in the Square."

He shrugged. "That's small-town life."

"I wanted to talk with you about your in-laws."

His bushy brows shot up. "I must admit, I wasn't expecting that. What do you want to know?"

"Did your relationship with them change after Rachel died?"

"No. Her parents have always been supportive and involved in the girls' lives, and Rachel's death did nothing to diminish that. If anything, it made their bond with them stronger."

Of course. Ray had three teenage daughters. His situation was much different than hers.

After a pause, he said, "I can't help you if you won't talk to me, Katie."

She smiled slightly. "It's Chad's mom . . . Margo. She

and I never got along, but she called me this morning, said she was going to be in the area and wants to spend a couple of days with me."

Ray's lips twitched. "You and a woman you don't like in a teensy apartment. I'm trying to decide whether or not I'd like to be a fly on the wall for that."

Katie scoffed. "Trust me, you would not. Why? Why, after all this time, would she want to visit me?"

"You're her last tie to her son."

Tears pricked the backs of her eyes, and Katie quickly blinked them away. But, then, not much got past Ray.

"I'm sorry," he said. "I didn't mean to make you feel worse."

"You didn't. I simply hadn't looked at it from her point of view."

He patted her hand. "Give the woman a chance. She's reaching out to you for a reason. You owe it to yourself— and to her and even Chad—to spend some time with her."

Oh yeah? Then why did it feel so wrong?

Two

~~~~~~~~

The sun set way too early in December, and it had been dark for more than an hour before Katie made it back to her apartment. Soon after, Andy took a break from the pizzeria and joined her for what she knew would be far too short a time.

Katie snuggled against Andy's chest as they sat on her sofa staring at the blinking lights of the tabletop Christmas tree that sat by the window. Katie rented the place above Angelo's Pizzeria from Andy, and at a very reasonable price. It could accommodate the occasional overnight visit of a lover, but was not fit to billet a guest. And Katie knew it would be she—and her cats, Mason and Della—who'd be sleeping on the couch. And then there was the whole bathroom problem. To reach it, one had to traverse the bedroom. Could Katie hold her water all night long? The thought was disquieting.

"I heard about Vonne . . . and that you were there when Francine got the news," Andy said, his tone sympathetic.

"Yeah. It was a horrible situation."

"Why didn't you tell me about it?"

Katie sighed. "Francine was already bemoaning the fact that everyone in Victoria Square would know her business before sunset. I didn't want to be the talebearer."

His full lips tightened. "Did you tell Ray Davenport?"

"Yes, but that's because he was there when I came out of the tea shop."

"You trusted him with the news but not me?"

"Andy, it wasn't like that. It's tragic that Vonne died in an accident, but that's not what I wanted to talk to Ray about." She blew out a breath.

He pulled back and spread an arm across the back of the couch. "Let's hear it."

"Chad's mother is coming to stay with me for a day or two."

"And you felt the need to divulge this information to Davenport because . . . ?"

"Because he, too, is a widower with in-laws. Of course, he has daughters, so his relationship with his in-laws is very different from mine with Margo Bonner."

"What advice did the wise old widower have to offer?" Andy asked, his tone tinged with sarcasm.

"He reminded me that I'm Margo's only tie to Chad and said I should give the woman a chance."

Andy frowned. "I suppose that's good advice. The holidays are coming up. Maybe your former mother-in-law is feeling especially nostalgic and wants to see you in order to feel closer to her son." He pulled her close to him once more. "I want to feel closer to you. I've missed you."

"I've missed you, too. You're so busy lately."

"It's the holiday season and we're both swamped. I feel like I see more of Erikka than I do you."

He was talking about Erikka Wiley, his assistant manager. Stunning Erikka with her jet-black hair, big brown eyes, and voluptuous figure. Erikka, who spent part of every single day elbow to elbow with Andy. She was a sweet girl. Katie knew she shouldn't feel jealous of her. But for some reason she did.

Katie buried her hands in Andy's dark, wavy hair and pulled his mouth down to hers. She needed to put Erikka out of both their minds. She was succeeding until Andy's phone buzzed.

He reluctantly extracted himself from their embrace and looked at the screen. "Sorry, Sunshine. I have to take care of something downstairs. I'll be back as soon as I can."

Katie had heard that before too many times. Andy would go downstairs and one emergency would turn into two and she probably wouldn't see him the rest of the night.

One of her cats—Mason—eagerly jumped onto the spot Andy vacated. She picked up the cat and placed him on her lap, absently petting him.

"We've got problems, buddy."

Mason closed his eyes and opened his mouth, but no sound emerged.

"Do you remember your grandma? She called you *that animal*." The memory of the older woman's dismissive tone made Katie shudder. "The three of us will have to be on our best behavior."

Oh yeah?

"Then again, maybe if you heave a hair ball in one or both of her shoes, she'll go away and leave us alone."

Mason made no comment and purred quietly, as though sensing her restlessness.

Katie recognized the need to do something. She needed to bake. She'd make a double batch of sugar cookies. She could take some to Francine as a gesture of sympathy, save a plateful for Andy as a gesture of love, and a take a tin to Ray and his girls as a gesture of friendship and to thank him for lending an ear.

She kissed the cat's head, gently placed him on the floor, and went to wash her hands. "Time to get baking, Mason!"

~~~~~~

Before heading to Artisans Alley the next morning, Katie stopped off at Wood U to give Ray the tin of cookies. When she walked in, he was bent over his check-out counter—balding pate glimmering in the overhead light—working on something that he quickly threw a cloth over when he spotted her.

"What is it?" Katie asked.

"It . . . it's, uh . . . not ready for anybody to see yet."

"Oh. All right." She placed the cookies on the top of the wooden surface. "This is just a little something for you and the girls . . . a thank-you for listening to me about my former mother-in-law yesterday."

"That wasn't necessary, but I thank you." Ray slid the tin over and opened the lid. He sniffed deeply. "These cookies smell delicious. Mind if I have one now?"

"Please go ahead."

"Coffee?"

She shook her head. "I can't stay long."

"Could you stay for just a minute?" He took a star-shaped cookie from the tin and replaced the lid. "It's my turn to ask for advice."

"Of course."

"Something's going on with Sasha," Ray said.

As Katie suspected, Ray's need for advice concerned his girls. Now that Rachel was gone, he often found himself at a loss to understand his daughters. And, while Katie had no children of her own, because she was a woman, Ray seemed to trust her to help him figure out what was going on with the alien beings who lived with him.

"She thinks she's getting fat or something. I've tried to tell her that she's as skinny as a two-by-four turned sideways, but she doesn't believe me. She'll hardly eat anything at all anymore. I'm . . ." He rubbed his forehead with his free hand. "I'm afraid she might be developing an eating disorder."

"I'm not all that familiar with eating disorders. One of my friends in college had a . . . well, I think she might've been bulimic. She'd go on eating binges and then . . . well, you know."

He nodded. "Sasha doesn't do that, as far as I know. She just refuses to eat. She eats as little as she possibly can. Do you think I should have her talk with her school counselor?"

"How long has this been going on?"

"About a week, but I want to nip it in the bud."

"Why don't you let me talk with her and see if I can get a feel for what's going on with her?"

Ray frowned. "If she knew I'd told you, she'd kill me."

"Then how about I invite the girls to go Christmas shopping with me? Although it would need to be tonight, since Margo will be here tomorrow morning. I could buy them dinner and it would give me a chance to see what I can find out."

"That sounds fantastic. You're a genius, Katie Bonner. I could kiss you!" His eyes widened as he realized what he'd said. "Figuratively speaking, of course. I mean . . . you know what I mean."

Katie laughed. "I know what you mean, Ray. But don't get your hopes up. Sasha might not level with me."

"I believe she'll come closer to talking with you than to anyone else."

Knowing the girls always stopped by Ray's shop on their way home from school, she told him to have them drop by Artisans Alley. "Hopefully, they don't already have plans. If they do, we can always—"

"They won't. I generally don't allow them to go out on school nights. But I can make an exception this time."

"Good. I'll let you know what I find out." She turned to go.

"Wait," Ray said.

Katie turned back to him.

"I thought you should know—I talked to Schuler." Was it pertinent that he couldn't voice the former deputy's new rank? "It seems Vonne Barnett's death was no accident."

Katie's jaw dropped. "What?"

"Word is that the accident was staged. The ME says she was killed by a blow to the back of the head and then placed in the car."

Katie felt her legs wobble and she gripped the worktable for support. Ray put down his cookie and came around the side of the table to place a stool under her.

"I'm sorry," he said. "I shouldn't have blindsided you like that."

"N-no. It's all right." She lowered herself onto the stool. "I'm just stunned. Poor Francine. To lose a child in an accident is one thing, but to find out your child was murdered . . ." She shuddered.

Ray rested a hand on her shoulder. "I really wish I hadn't told you. But I knew you'd find out sooner or later."

"No. I'm glad you told me. I made some cookies for Francine, too—not festive, no sprinkles, just round sugar cookies. But now the thought of taking them to her seems frivolous."

"It's still a nice gesture, Katie."

"I don't know. When someone dies, people take casseroles or pies to the family—not sugar cookies."

"When Rachel died, we had casseroles coming out our ears. The girls and I would have been very happy with sugar cookies."

She smiled. "You're just saying that."

"I'm not. We had to donate the majority of those casseroles to a homeless shelter."

Katie stared into Ray's watery blue eyes for a long moment. As a widow, she understood his grief at the loss of his wife—the mother of his children. She stood. "I'd better go. Don't forget to send the girls over."

"I won't. And thanks again. This means more than you know."

~~~~~~

Katie had just finished updating the profit-ratio spreadsheet—and things were looking mighty fine indeed—and was sitting in her office munching on a peppermint as a reward when Rose knocked on the office doorjamb. She scrunched up her face and shook her head, setting her blonde curls to bouncing.

"I wish you wouldn't do that," Rose said. "It's bound to be murder on your teeth."

Katie motioned the older woman inside and asked her to shut the door. "That's a funny choice of words. As it happens, Ray Davenport told me earlier that Vonne Barnett over at Afternoon Tea didn't die in the accident. She was murdered, and the car wreck was staged."

Rose gasped as she lowered herself onto the chair by Katie's desk. "Is he sure?"

"He said someone from the Sheriff's Office told him."

"They wouldn't make something like that up," Rose said, and worried the bow attached to the collar of her red silk blouse.

"I never heard of Vonne having any enemies. Did you?"

"The only people I can think of who didn't care too much for Vonne would be . . . you know . . . romantic rivals. She could be quite the flirt, and she'd made it clear lately that she was in the market for a husband in a big way."

Katie frowned. "Really? I hadn't heard that."

Rose inclined her head. "I don't know if there's any truth to it or not, but I understand Vonne even got too friendly with Liz Meier's husband, and Liz let her know she didn't appreciate it."

"Was Vonne drunk at the time?"

"I don't know. But the word is Vonne *did* like her alcohol."

Francine had asked the detective if Vonne had been stopped for DUI again.

"I wonder if Francine knows Vonne was murdered," Rose murmured.

"I'm guessing yes. I mean, surely they'd have told her before they'd tell an ex-member of the Sheriff's Office like Ray Davenport. Wouldn't they?"

Rose raised her bony shoulders. "The open sign is on over at the shop. How could Francine be working if she knew someone had murdered her daughter?"

Katie frowned. "How could she be working when her daughter has just died, period? Since business hasn't been good lately, maybe she feels like she has to. I think I'll go check on her. Do you want to come?"

"Yeah. I'll see if Vance can man the cash register. But before I do, there's something you need to know."

"How well should I brace myself?"

"Not much, I wouldn't think," Rose said. "It's Godfrey Foster. He's complaining about the ballerinas."

The ballerinas Rose spoke of were from It's Tutu Much, the dance studio on the north side of the building. Quite a few of the pupils were practicing for a performance of *The Nutcracker*. How a group of charming little girls could be bothering Godfrey was beyond her. But, then, if cute kids were going to be an aggravation to anyone, it would be Godfrey. Back in September, he'd made such a stink about the odor emanating from the nail salon that Katie had been determined to kick the guy out. But Godfrey begged to stay, offering to pay not only a year's rent in advance, but ten percent more to keep his booth of dryer lint art going.

Several vendors had come to her to plead his case, which made Katie suspect he might have paid them to do so, since it seemed his friendships with other vendors were few and far between. She'd let him stay, and so far, he hadn't caused any more trouble—but his mere presence still irked her.

"And what are the tiny dancers doing to perturb dear Mr. Foster?" Katie asked.

Rose's lips twitched in an obvious effort not to laugh. "They took a coloring book page and stuck different colors of chewed gum onto it, signed it *Goofrey*, and left it in his booth."

Katie burst out laughing. "I'd love to see that. Do you have it?"

Rose joined in the laughter. "No. Godfrey threw it away. It was all I could do not to laugh while he was telling me about it."

"We'll tell him that if it happens again, he needs to hold on to such an item as evidence."

"He might even be able to dig that one out of the trash," Rose said.

"Uh . . . no, thanks. I don't want to come within fifty feet of anything that has been in Godfrey's trash. Are you ready to go to the tea shop now?"

"Sure. Let me go get Vance."

Vance Ingram's booth featured small wooden furniture and he was Katie's unofficial second-in-command. He'd helped the former owner run the place and knew just about everything there was to know about Artisans Alley. Once Rose had enlisted the skinny Santa Claus look-alike, and Katie retrieved the cookies she'd made for Francine, she and Rose donned their coats and battled the bracing wind as they crossed the parking lot to Afternoon Tea.

A woman sat at a table in the far corner of the room reading a paperback and sipping a cup of tea, but she appeared to be the tea shop's sole customer.

Francine sprayed a cleaning solution onto the counter

and wiped it up with a paper towel. "Hello, ladies, and welcome to Afternoon Tea. Would you like to try our blackberry ginger tea?"

Rose wrinkled her nose, but Katie answered for both of them. "Um, sure. To go, please."

Francine poured the hot tea into two lidded paper cups, returned to the counter, and gave them a total.

Katie proffered the tin of cookies. "I made these for you. I thought you might need something comforting in your time of sorrow."

Francine accepted the tin. "That was nice of you. Thanks." Curiously enough, she didn't seem all that sorrowful.

"I'm surprised to see you back at work so soon," Katie said, offering a ten-dollar bill.

Francine rang up the sale. "I have bills to pay."

"I'm sure there are . . . other things . . . you need to be doing," Katie said. "If you feel the shop absolutely must be open, then I'd be glad to hold down the fort for the day."

"You're sweet to offer, but I know you have your own work to do. Of course, if you were to *buy* the shop, that would take a load of responsibility off me." She looked at Rose. "I'm trying to get Katie to buy Afternoon Tea. I think she could make a great success of it, don't you?"

Startled, Rose looked from Francine to Katie, back to Francine, and back to Katie again. "Um . . . what?"

"Oh yes. Now that Vonne is gone, I'm absolutely putting the shop on the market. I simply can't do this by myself. I'm trying to get Katie to assume ownership. She could take over the lease, buy out the inventory and equipment, and go right to work." She turned to Katie with a smile. "What do you say, Katie? You know you'd love it . . . the way you enjoy baking and all."

Katie's eyes widened. "Well . . . I'll consider it."

"Don't take too long. I wouldn't want someone to buy the place out from under you."

Katie thought about Sassy Sally's at the east end of the

Square, the bed-and-breakfast she'd wanted to buy and renovate herself. Actually, she and Chad had planned to buy the old mansion before Chad had invested their savings in Artisans Alley. She'd missed one opportunity. She didn't want to miss another. And given her success with Artisans Alley, it seemed as if turning around seemingly lost causes might be her specialty.

But how would the Artisans Alley vendors feel about it? Would they see her buying the tea shop as a betrayal? And what about the Victoria Square Merchants Association? Katie was their president. Would the association feel that she was spreading herself too thin if she tried to continue to operate Artisans Alley as well as a tea shop? Would she be?

Rose lightly touched her arm. "I should be getting back."

"Yeah. Me, too. Francine, I'm nearby if you need anything."

"Just please give my offer some serious consideration. I'll make you a good deal on the place."

Katie nodded. "All right."

"And thanks for the cookies."

Rose was quiet as she and Katie left the tea shop. Katie thought it best not to press the matter. On the one hand, she wanted Rose's honest opinion. But on the other hand, she wanted to make the decision on her own. She cared about and respected her friend's and the other vendors' opinions, but she had to do what was best for her.

The sound of a door opening to her left caused Rose to grab Katie's arm and propel her past a parked car toward the other side of the Square. "Let's go this way. My, isn't the wind bracing? Good for clearing our heads."

"It is." As a matter of fact, Katie usually power walked around the Square at least twice each morning, which not only was good exercise but gave her a peaceful time to think, although she hadn't taken time to do so today. Still, Rose's behavior was odd. "But what are we really doing?"

"We're avoiding Nona Fiske."

Nona was the fussbudget who owned The Quiet Quilter next door to the tea shop. She was someone best to be avoided most of the time, but Rose was like a woman on a mission.

"Why are we avoiding Nona?" Katie asked.

"She accosted me at the grocery store yesterday and told me she thinks one of the new Artisans Alley vendors is knocking off her quilt patterns."

"Oh my goodness." Katie finally raised the blackberry ginger tea to her lips. "Hey, this isn't bad."

Rose tentatively raised her own cup and took a sip. "No, I guess not. So, are you going to do it?"

Katie was saved by responding when Ray Davenport stepped outside Wood U and flagged them down.

"Hey, Katie, have you got one second?"

"Sure." Katie looked at Rose.

"I'll go back to the Alley before Vance has my hide for saddling him with the cash register for so long," she said. "I'll see you later."

Katie mounted the steps and entered Ray's shop.

"Sasha called from school—she needed me to email one of her teachers my permission for her to go on a field trip tomorrow," he said. "Anyway, I went ahead and told her you'd like to take her and Sadie Christmas shopping after school, and she was really excited about it."

"Good. I'm looking forward to it, too." She took another taste of the tea. "Ray, when you were a cop, you had to deal with a lot of people who'd just suffered loss, right?"

"Every day, it seemed. That's one of the reasons I was ready to retire. Why do you ask?"

"Rose and I just came from Afternoon Tea. Francine is there . . . working . . . acting as if everything is fine."

Ray rocked back on his heels. "Well, everyone processes grief differently. It's possible she appears indifferent in public but grieves in private."

"I suppose. Rose told me that Vonne was a big flirt. And

since you're one of Victoria Square's eligible bachelors, I wonder if she ever made a play for you."

The color rose in Ray's cheeks. "She did. I shut her down. She wasn't my type."

"Rose thought she was in the market for a husband."

"That's the impression I got," Ray said. "She wanted somebody to take care of her." He was quiet for a long moment, as though mulling something over before he spoke once more. "The latest news—and please keep this to yourself—is that Vonne was pregnant when she died."

Three

For months, Katie and Andy made sure to make time for each other by getting together for lunch at Del's Diner at least every other day. That day, after trading her Dickens costume for street clothes, Katie slipped into the booth at Del's, feeling as if she'd just finished the one-hundred-yard dash. She shrugged out of her coat and placed it on the seat next to her.

Andy, who'd been waiting for her to join him, grinned. "Has the day been that bad already?"

"As a matter of fact, it has." She told him about Ray telling her that Vonne's death hadn't been an accident—leaving out the information that Vonne was pregnant and that Rose told her any enemies Vonne had were likely romantic rivals. "Rose seems to think Vonne was actively seeking a husband. And since you're the most handsome bachelor on

Victoria Square, I have to wonder if she didn't have her sights set on you."

Andy gazed around the restaurant and raised a hand. "Hey, Sandy, could we order please? I have to get back to work soon."

"Sure, hon. Be right there."

"Can I take that as a yes?" Katie asked quietly. She'd been joking, but Andy obviously didn't want to talk about Vonne.

Sandy came over to their table, removing the notepad and pen from the pocket of her black apron. The portly blonde woman with a sweet face had apparently noticed no tension between the two of them.

"What'll it be, guys?"

Katie ordered a grilled cheese sandwich, and Andy decided on a cheeseburger and fries. Sandy said she'd get their order in right away, and then she left to see to other customers.

"Well?" Katie asked.

"What?"

"You know what. What aren't you telling me about you and Vonne?"

He blew out a breath. "Okay. We went out once. Once. It was no big deal."

"Why didn't you tell me about it?"

"It was before you and I started seeing each other. Vonne and I ran into each other at The Pelican's Roost, and then I took her to dinner. But, again, it was no big deal."

For some reason, it felt like a big deal to Katie. Probably because Andy didn't want to talk about it.

"Come on, let's talk about something else," Andy said. "What's going on at the Alley today?"

"The ballerinas—at least, that's who Godfrey said it was—antagonized him with chewing gum art and called him Goofrey."

Andy laughed. "How much did you take off the dance studio's rent for that?"

"Nothing . . . yet," Katie said with a grin. "Rose and I went over to talk with Francine. Francine is trying to talk me into buying out Afternoon Tea—I'd change the name, of course. I mean, I will if I decide to take Francine up on her offer."

"It sounds like you might be seriously considering it."

"I am. But I already have so many obligations to Artisans Alley and the Victoria Square Merchants Association . . ."

"True." He took her hand. "But you need to think about you, Katie. You need to do something for yourself for a change."

"Maybe. I always wanted to serve tea at the English Ivy Inn. Owning a tea shop would at least allow me half of my dream, and the financial risk would certainly be a lot less. But what would it mean for us?"

Andy shrugged. "I don't see the problem."

"I'd be twice as busy."

"Has our relationship suffered since I started making cinnamon buns?"

Truthfully, yes. But they'd made sure to carve out time for each other. Would lunch every other day, and the occasional sleepover, be enough?

There wasn't time to contemplate that thought as Sandy arrived with their lunches.

Andy smothered his fries with ketchup and launched into a soliloquy on how much better his December pizza sales had been over November—and that he was stepping up production on the cinnamon bun side of the business as well.

"In fact, I'm thinking of trying some new recipes. Cinnamon pumpkin and apple cinnamon—the apple cinnamon was Erikka's idea. What do you think?"

"I think they both sound delicious."

Andy continued to talk about possible future plans while Katie ate her sandwich without much enthusiasm. She had a lot to think about, and none of it was very pleasant.

~~~~~~~~

When Katie returned to Artisans Alley, some of the vendors were huddled in the lobby and were obviously in a snit.

"What's going on?" Katie asked.

"There was a man in here, and he stole one of Susan's dolls!" Rose exclaimed.

"It was Arthur Henderson," Susan Williams said, glowering down at Katie. At six feet tall, Susan towered over Katie anyway, but the boots she wore with her Dickensian costume gave her an additional three inches of height. Susan made pretty dresses for American Girl and other dolls, basing them on Disney princesses as well as every holiday across the twelve-month calendar.

"Are you sure?"

"Of course I'm sure." Susan anchored her hands to her hips. "Why would I make something like that up?"

Katie looked around the lobby. "Where is he now? Maybe he's still shopping and intends to pay for it."

"None of us have seen him since he took the doll," Rose said.

"Has everyone checked their booths to see if he put the doll down somewhere else?" Katie asked. "We have to be absolutely certain Mr. Henderson stole something before we go slinging accusations."

"We've looked around," Vance said, "but we can do a more thorough search."

"Thank you." Katie was grateful for Vance's calm thinking. If she ended up buying the tea shop, he would be an excellent assistant manager at Artisans Alley.

"Come on, everyone. Time to get back to work. Susan, I'll help you look for the doll," Rose said.

The group dispersed and Katie went back to her office. So far the day had been filled with just a little too much drama and she was ready for some quiet time. That meant paperwork—which never seemed to end. But finally the day wound down. Vance had agreed to close and lock the Alley while Katie skipped out early to pick up the two youngest Davenport sisters for their shopping foray to Greece Ridge Center. Sophie, the oldest, was still at school—the prestigious Culinary Institute of America—but was expected home soon for the upcoming winter break.

The perky young blondes practically bounced as they walked through the mall. It was obvious their mother's death had left a hole in their lives they very much needed filled—if only temporarily.

"How about a hot chocolate break?" Katie suggested.

"Sounds great," Sadie said.

Sasha looked away. "I'm not really very thirsty."

Or was it that she didn't want to ingest the calories?

Katie ordered two hot chocolates to go and the three of them settled at one of the tables in the food court, putting their shopping bags on the floor.

"Thanks for this, Katie," Sadie said. "I'm really glad we're getting to shop without Dad around. He's almost impossible to shop for anyway, but when he's with us . . . ugh." She rolled her eyes, making Katie laugh.

"I know, right?" Sasha chimed in. "But wait until you see Dad's present to you, Katie. You're gonna love it."

"Sasha!" Sadie scolded her sister, but Katie was barely aware of their conversation. Ray was giving her a Christmas gift? She hadn't even considered getting something for him. And now she'd have to think of something . . . something suitable . . . something that wouldn't send the wrong message . . . something that—

"Katie."

Her thoughts were interrupted by Sasha.

"I'm sorry," she said. "I got distracted." It also crossed her mind that maybe she should get something for Margo, too. And what would that be?

"Well, I'm sorry I told you about Dad's present," Sasha said. "Sadie's right—it was supposed to be a surprise. I mean, it still will be. I didn't tell you what it is."

"Sasha, that's enough. You're going to keep on until you tell her everything."

"No, I won't."

"Yes, you—"

"Oh, hey!" Katie exclaimed, before the sisters' argument escalated further, and pointed across the way. "That boutique seems to have some really pretty clothes, and I'd love to have something new to wear to all the upcoming parties. Let's check it out."

Katie headed for the boutique, and the girls fell into step on either side of her. Once inside, Katie saw that the clothes were designed with teens in mind. But that was okay—it stopped the girls from bickering, and the two of them might find something they'd like.

Sadie made a beeline for a short green dress. She flipped through the hangers until she found her size and then held it up to her thin frame. "What do you think?"

"That color would look gorgeous on you," Katie said. "Try it on." She looked at Sasha. "Anything catch your eye?"

Sasha shook her head.

"Aw, come on." Katie looked around the boutique. "You'd look stunning in that pink sweater over there. Why don't you try it on?"

"No, thanks. I need to lose weight before I buy anything new."

"Oh, good grief," Sadie muttered.

"You're beautiful, Sasha," Katie said. "Why on earth are you concerned about your weight?"

Sasha looked down at her hands. "There's this girl at school—she's super skinny—and she's been paying a lot of attention to Adam."

Katie remembered Ray saying that Adam was a boy Sasha had been enamored with. Had their relationship graduated to dating? She also realized that insecurity and relationships were virtual roller coasters to teenagers. To everyone, she supposed. She decided a show of solidarity was in order.

"You know, sometimes I feel insecure, too. Just the other day Andy told me he feels like he's been spending more time with Erikka, his assistant manager, than with me." She shrugged one shoulder. "And you guys have seen Erikka— she's gorgeous."

Sadie scoffed. "Both of you stop it right now. You're both pretty, and if the knuckleheads you're with don't appreciate your looks and the fact that you are way more than your looks anyway, then maybe you should both start looking for someone else."

Katie smiled. "Wow. Well said, Sadie."

Sadie shook her head. "I don't get why some women act so desperate. Like that Vonne who died in the car accident. She was desperation personified."

In the car accident. Was Ray protecting his daughters from the truth?

"You've got a point there," Sasha said. "That woman was calling our dad every night for a while. He got to where he wouldn't answer the phone—and wouldn't let us answer it, either—because he didn't want to talk with her."

"Right. We had to use the answering machine to screen the calls. I mean, why? Like our dad would be interested in any woman other than our mom anyway, but why would she throw herself at a guy who obviously had no interest in her?" Sadie shook her head. "I'd never do that. I'm independent. I'll never need anyone. If I want to include someone in my life, that's one thing. But if I have to chase after him, then he doesn't deserve me." She held up the dress. "I'm going to try this on. Be right back."

"She's made an excellent point," Katie told Sasha.

"Yeah. Sadie's as headstrong as they come. I guess I'm more of a people pleaser."

"I think you have a terrific figure. Do you really feel like you need to lose weight?"

Sasha nodded. "I just feel . . . ugly."

"Well, you aren't. You're stunning. But if you think you need to get healthier, why don't you walk the Square with me weekend mornings and when school lets out for winter break? I've been neglecting it lately, and you could be the inspiration I need to get back at it."

Sasha's smile was tentative. "Well, I guess I could."

"Great. Then I'll see you Saturday. How about seven o'clock?"

"Works for me."

Sadie reappeared, looking resplendent in the frilly frock. She did a three-sixty turn to show off for her audience.

"You look terrific," Katie said, and Sadie blushed.

"Are you going to buy that?" Sasha asked.

"Are you kidding? I can't afford this. But if Dad wants to know what to get me extra special for Christmas . . ." Her blue eyes practically sparkled.

"I dunno," Sasha said, taking a gander at the price tag. "He might think it's pretty frivolous. Like, when would you ever wear it?"

Sadie frowned. "Prom?"

Sasha laughed. "You gotta find a guy first."

Like she had? Katie wondered.

"I might just go by myself."

"And who would you dance with?" Sasha asked.

"Everybody."

"There you go!" Katie said. She liked these girls more and more. They were bright, and funny and . . .

Maybe it wasn't such a good idea to get too attached to them. And why did she suddenly feel that way?

~~~~~~

It was late by the time Katie dropped the girls home and returned to her apartment. She was a bit tired after the long day, but she still had work to do. Margo would arrive the next day, and there couldn't be a speck of dust anywhere.

"Please don't shed a single hair while Margo is here," Katie told her cats, Della and Mason.

The pair looked nonplussed and assumed the attitude that they'd shed right on Margo herself if they got the urge and the opportunity presented itself.

Katie put on some lively Christmas music, diffused some gingerbread essential oil she'd bought at Gilda's Gourmet Baskets, and got out her cleaning supplies. She needed to scrub the bathroom from top to bottom, clean the kitchen, dust . . . It was as if spring had come early to McKinlay Mill. She always kept a neat home, but not even Martha Stewart could undergo the scrutiny of Margo Bonner and come out unscathed.

Katie started with the bathroom, cleaning the toilet and the sink, while two furry little faces watched from the doorway. Then she tackled the bathtub before scrubbing the floor. She put out her prettiest guest towels and gave the cats a stern warning not to claw them up.

Next came the kitchen. She sprayed oven cleaner in the spotless oven before starting on the countertops. By the time she'd wiped down the cabinets, it was time to finish with the oven. She took some pretty Christmas dish towels from a drawer and placed them on the magnetized hooks on the oven. She wished she had oven mitts to match the towels, but the plain red ones she had would have to do.

After dusting the living room, Katie lugged the vacuum cleaner out of the closet. She plugged it in and ran it over the living room floor. Then she moved the sofa. That was more of a job than she'd expected it to be. Too bad Andy was still working. She could've used his strong arms.

Her phone rang, and she answered without looking at the screen. "Hello?"

"Um . . . hi."

It was Ray.

"Am I interrupting anything?"

Katie laughed, realizing how breathless she'd sounded when answering. "Actually, yes. I'm moving the sofa. But I've got it to where I can vacuum behind it, so you're giving me a break before I have to push it back into place."

"Do you need me to come over and help you?"

"No, but I appreciate the offer," she said. "I'm guessing you're calling for an update."

They hadn't talked when Katie dropped off the girls earlier.

"Yeah, they're in their rooms now, so I thought we could talk. But if this is a bad time for you . . ."

"It's not. I'm simply trying to get everything shipshape before Margo gets here." She laughed again. "Maybe I need another lecture from Sadie on not caring what other people think."

"Oh boy. She gotcha, huh?"

"Sasha and me both."

"Well, Sadie has never shied away from a soapbox or a debate in her life," he said. "And if she lectured you, she did it for your own good and because she cares about you. Take it from one who's been there."

"You're raising some terrific girls, Ray."

"I had a lot of help. Can't take credit for most of their good qualities."

"Do I need to have Sadie lecture you?" Katie asked.

He chuckled. "Touché."

"Sasha did say she's concerned about her weight. It's something to do with Adam and a girl at school who's been flirting with him. I invited her to come walk with me on Saturdays and when school lets out for winter break."

"They told me about the walking. They're both planning to take you up on your offer, and they're going to enlist Sophie, too."

"Good. I need the accountability lately and will enjoy the company."

"They enjoy your company, too. Thanks again for your help."

"Anytime."

"Talk to you soon," Ray said, sounding cheerful.

"Yeah," Katie agreed, and they hung up.

Katie pushed the sofa back into place. She finished vacuuming the apartment and then returned the machine to the closet. When she flopped onto the couch wondering what she should do next, Mason and Della joined her. Della, the tabby, climbed onto her lap while Mason, her black-and-white cat, lay against her thigh.

Her thoughts turned to Francine's offer. "What do you think, guys? Should I open a tea shop?"

The cats responded with thoughtful purrs.

"What would we name the place? Afternoon Tea is too bland. What about Tealightful?" She laughed. "Just Tea Zing? Subtle Tea? The Tea Cozy? Or what about The Tea Cottage?" She groaned. "I need to do something. I'm turning into a crazy lady who talks to her cats."

She still hadn't made up her mind about taking over the tea shop. It was a huge responsibility, especially given her duties at Artisans Alley. But, truth be told, the Alley was almost running itself now. It wasn't necessary for her to be as hands-on as she had been in the beginning. It was possible she could do both . . . especially if she brought in a full-time manager for the tea shop.

It wouldn't hurt to drop by the bank to see about getting a loan. And she'd have plenty of time to do that before Margo arrived. She just needed to draw up a business plan. But first she should see if Vance could be at Artisans Alley the following morning to unlock the doors.

Although it was just past nine, Katie took a chance and dialed Vance's home number. He wasn't home, but his wife, Janey, said she felt sure he wouldn't mind.

"He usually gets there about the same time you do anyway."

"Thanks, Janey. How're you feeling?" Janey had MS, but it had been in remission for nearly a year now.

"I'm still doing fine. I appreciate your asking. By the way, I hear that Francine is selling the tea shop."

Katie hadn't intended to broach the subject of the tea shop with Janey, but now she confirmed that the rumor was true. "In fact, she's trying to talk me into buying her out. If I do, I'd need Vance to help out a bit more at the Alley. And of course I'd pay him for it."

"Are you seriously thinking of buying it?"

"Yes. Of course, it's a long way from being a done deal. I wonder what the vendors would say if I diversified."

"I can only speak for Vance," Janey said, "but he believes you can do anything you set your mind to. In fact, I used to be envious of you because Vance speaks so highly of you."

Katie pictured Janey with her pretty face and Dolly Parton–like figure.

"There's no need for you to ever be envious of another woman. Vance adores you, and you know it."

Janey giggled. "I do know it. Still, he would encourage you to buy the tea shop if that's something you want to do."

"I don't want the vendors at Artisans Alley to feel like I'm letting them down."

"Honey, they wouldn't be in business right now if it weren't for you. You kept that place afloat when Ezra died."

"It wasn't easy." Katie shivered at the recollection of the poor old man dead at the bottom of the Alley's main staircase.

"I know it wasn't. And if they're honest with themselves, they know it wasn't, either. Just know that if you buy the tea shop, Vance and I will be two of the first ones through the door."

"Aw, that's sweet. Thanks, Janey."

"You're welcome. I have to admit, I've kinda missed it. My friends and I stopped going there a couple of months ago because of Vonne."

"Oh? What did she do?"

"Well, she and Francine hired Vance for a handyman job at their home. After that, Vonne started calling Vance wanting him to do other work. He refused. When I asked why, he said she'd behaved inappropriately."

"In what way?" Katie asked.

"I'm not sure, but she wouldn't quit calling. I finally had to put that woman in her place and tell her to find somebody else to do her work." Janey blew out a breath. "I hate to speak ill of the dead, but I wonder if Vonne didn't cause a lot of people to stop going to the tea shop."

"I suppose you've heard the police suspect foul play."

"I did hear that. Do they know who killed her?"

"I don't think so." Katie thought back to Rose's inclination that it was some woman who saw Vonne as a rival for her romantic partner. After talking with Janey, Katie was more convinced than ever that Rose just might be right.

Four

The next morning, Katie wanted to look her best when facing both the loan officer and her former mother-in-law. She pulled her hair up into a French twist, applied a little more makeup than her usual mascara and lip gloss, and put on the navy suit she hadn't worn since leaving Kimper Insurance. The hem of her skirt brushed the tops of her tall, dove gray boots. Pearl studs given to her by Chad on their first wedding anniversary completed the look. She felt that she looked every inch a successful businesswoman as she left the apartment.

Her confidence remained intact as she was ushered into the office of Sandra Harrison, loan officer. Sandra, who sat behind her walnut desk, also wore a suit—hers was a black-and-white houndstooth. The woman's hair was cut in a chin-skimming bob that barely moved when Sandra stood to shake Katie's hand.

Unfortunately, Katie's confidence took a nosedive after Sandra looked at her proposal and "ran the numbers."

"But that's impossible," Katie said. "Are you sure you can't make me a better offer than that?"

Sandra leaned back in her chair and folded her well-manicured hands atop the folder containing the business plan Katie had prepared the night before. "I'm sorry, but based on the amount of equity you have in Artisans Alley, these are the best terms we can provide you."

The terms were crap and Sandra had to know it, but Katie was still trying to be professional. "I've got a proven track record. You can clearly see from the financial statements I've provided that I completely turned Artisans Alley around. The place was on the verge of bankruptcy when I took it over."

"Yes, but that's only one business. And running a . . . a flea market . . . is entirely different from operating a successful tea shop."

Katie's jaw dropped. "A flea market? I'll have you know that Artisans Alley is a far cry from a flea market. It's a co-op of talented professionals working together under—"

"Yet you will agree that it's an entirely different type of business, Ms. Bonner. You have no experience with food service."

Katie's mouth tightened. "Would you be this condescending if I were a man?"

Sandra slid Katie's folder across the desk. "I'm sorry if you feel I'm being sexist with the loan terms presented, but you're wrong. We don't discriminate."

"According to a popular website, female business owners get offered higher interest rates and shorter terms for smaller loans than their male counterparts. What do you say to that?"

"Look, just as this bank isn't a 'good old boys' club' where we throw money at any male who comes in and asks for it, neither is it a sisterhood where I'll give our best terms to someone at high risk of default merely because she's a woman."

"I didn't ask for the best terms. I merely asked for decent terms."

"And I made you the fairest offer you're going to get. If you don't believe me, go to another bank and see if you fare any better."

"I'll do that." Katie snatched the file from the desk, grabbed her coat, and stormed out of Sandra Harrison's office.

~~~~~~

Katie realized as she left the bank that she had plenty of time to get to the airport before Margo's flight arrived. She'd anticipated being at the bank longer . . . discussing the empowerment of women in business . . . signing the loan papers. She contemplated heading back to Artisans Alley to get a little work done but in the end decided to go on to the airport and have lunch there instead. It would give her the opportunity to clear her mind and formulate a new plan of action.

When she strode toward the sandwich shop, she was surprised to hear a familiar male voice call her name. She turned and smiled broadly when she spotted her friend Seth Landers sitting at a table alone.

"What a nice surprise," she said, walking over to the table and into his warm embrace. "What are you doing here?"

"I came to pick up a client, but his flight was delayed, so here I am. What are you doing here?"

"Are you ready for this?" She looked straight into his warm brown eyes. "I'm here to pick up Margo, Chad's mom."

"I thought you two despised each other," Seth said.

"Despised is a strong word." It was fairly accurate, but Katie hated to admit that, especially now that Chad was gone. "I haven't seen her since Chad's funeral."

"So, why now?" He shook his head. "Wait. I'm keeping

you from your lunch. Put in your order, and then come back and tell me everything."

"Deal."

Katie returned five minutes later with a ham-and-cheese sandwich and an iced tea. Seth stood to pull her chair out for her. Not only did Seth have impeccable manners, he was magnificently handsome—sandy hair, always fashionably dressed, the build of a professional trainer—and he was like a brother to Katie. That he was also an attorney didn't hurt matters, either.

Once she was seated, and Seth had returned to his chair, he returned to the question of the purpose of Margo's visit.

"All she told me was that she was going to be in town and would like to stay with me for a couple of days."

"That's how she worded it—a couple of days?"

Katie nodded.

"Then that could literally mean two days . . ."

"Or it could mean a week," Katie said. "Yeah."

He grinned. "All right."

"It isn't funny," she said. But as she looked into his teasing eyes, she had to concede that she could find a teensy bit of amusement in the situation. "It's crazy. She called me the day before and invited herself to stay with me. Ray Davenport thinks she's feeling nostalgic and wants to feel close to Chad."

"That makes sense. Or maybe she has a gift—something Chad left for you—that she just discovered and wants you to have."

At that, Katie did laugh. "If the Margo Bonner I know had found something Chad had left behind, she'd keep it for herself."

"Maybe she's changed." He nodded toward her outfit. "Is that why you're dressed up today—to impress the mother-in-law?"

"Former mother-in-law, and no, I'm dressed like this

because I went by the bank this morning to see about a loan—fat lot of good it did me."

"A loan? I thought Artisans Alley was doing well."

"It is! Really well. So much so, in fact, that I'm considering assuming ownership of Afternoon Tea."

"I heard Francine was selling."

"I believe she's been considering it, but now that Vonne's gone . . ." She trailed off and took a sip of her tea.

Seth leaned closer. "What have you heard about that situation?"

"I've heard that she didn't die in a car accident," Katie said.

"She didn't." He lowered his voice. "Also—and this was told to me by a friend who works with the medical examiner—she was pregnant."

Katie didn't bother to feign surprise at that piece of news. "Do you think that's a motive for her murder?"

"It's a strong possibility," Seth said. "And my . . . friend . . . does, too."

"Tell me more about this friend," she said with a smile. "I get the impression this person is more than that."

"He is. We've been out a time or two . . . and we're seeing each other again tonight. I'm making dinner for him." He dabbed at the corners of his mouth with his napkin. "And how are things going with you and the cinnamon bun king?"

"Fine." Katie thought she'd said it like she meant it, but apparently, she had not.

"Uh-oh. What's wrong?" he asked.

She shrugged. "We're both just so busy these days that we rarely have time for each other . . . and yet we both keep taking on new projects. At first, Andy seemed content to run the pizzeria, but then he added cinnamon buns to the menu." She sighed. "Sure, they're terrific and a wonderful moneymaker for Andy, but now he's busier than ever."

"You still get together for lunch at least every other day, don't you?"

Katie shook her head. "More often than not, one of us gets caught up at our job and can't make it. And now I'm considering assuming ownership of the tea shop." Her shoulders slumped. "Maybe at this point in our lives, our careers are more important to us than our relationship."

"Aw, come on. Don't say that." Seth reached over and gave her hand a squeeze. "The guy's crazy about you. I'm sure you'll be able to carve out more time together after the holidays."

"I hope so," Katie said. "But please, if you meet Margo, don't mention Andy in front of her."

"Why not?"

"I don't want her to know I'm involved with anyone. She'll only be in town for a day or two—"

"You hope . . ."

"—and what harm will it do to let her think I'm still being faithful to Chad's memory?"

"Katie, it could do a lot of harm," Seth said. "You're a strong, healthy woman who lost her husband almost two years ago. It's perfectly natural for you to move on."

A clipped female voice came over the intercom announcing the arrival of Flight 4021.

"That's my client," Seth said, gathering his trash onto the black serving tray. "Promise me you'll be up-front with Margo."

"I'll think about it." She would . . . for about thirty seconds. Margo Bonner was devoted to her only son. She'd never forgive Katie for . . . well, for moving on with her life.

Sometimes Katie felt the same way.

~~~~~~

Katie's first thought upon seeing Margo stride through the security barrier was that the woman still carried herself like a 1950s movie star. She wore a black ankle-length coat and patent leather pumps. Her shoulder-length silver hair was pulled up on one side and secured with a pearl-encrusted clip. She clutched her red—or, rather, her rouge—Hermès Kelly bag in her left hand.

A handsome younger man—in his early to mid-thirties—pulled a cheetah-print carry-on bag as he walked beside Margo. Katie strode forward to meet them.

Margo turned to the man, smiled warmly, and patted his arm. "Thank you for being such a darling. Katie can take it from here."

"My pleasure," the man said. He winked at Margo and transferred the handle of the suitcase over to Katie. "I hope you enjoy your stay."

Katie watched his retreating back as he headed off to luggage claim.

"I know. Handsome, isn't he?" Margo asked, her smile just a tad smug.

"Yes. Who is he?"

"Doug something-or-other. He sat beside me on the plane." She raised a brow. "Oh. Did you want me to introduce you? He's single." She looked Katie over with an appraising eye. "Although I think *I* might be more his type. Still, I can call him back here if you'd like to meet him."

"Of course not. I just wondered how you knew him," Katie said. No one she'd ever sat near on a plane had offered to lug her carry-on around for her. "Do you have additional luggage?"

"No. I packed light."

"You look fantastic," Katie said. "I'm sorry I haven't done a better job of keeping in touch."

"Well, neither have I. So . . . what have you been up to?"

On the drive back to Victoria Square, Katie told Margo all about Artisans Alley and its transformation and how proud she thought Chad would be of it. Margo was noncommittal, but Katie had expected as much. Margo wouldn't comment on whether Chad would be proud of something until she saw it for herself.

Katie also told her about the tea shop and indulged herself in a little rant about how she'd been treated at the bank that morning. Margo didn't comment on that, either. Her lack of conversation made a million and one thoughts tumble through Katie's mind. Among them: Was the woman tired from her flight? Feeling sad to be visiting Victoria Square knowing her son wasn't there? Did she already regret coming to visit? What was she thinking about Katie? Did Margo resent her for being the one alive? Did she wonder why her son had to die instead of Katie?

When they parked in front of the pizzeria, Margo frowned. "Oh, I'm not hungry, dear. But if you are . . ."

"Um . . . no. My apartment is above the pizzeria."

"Oh."

That tiny *oh*. How could the woman say so much by saying practically nothing?

~~~~~~

After showing Margo the apartment—which took all of about five minutes—Katie got her former mother-in-law settled into the bedroom and then took her over to Artisans Alley. At least, that was something of which Katie was proud.

As they toured the Alley, Margo met Rose, Vance, and Ida Mitchell. Naturally, they were taken with Chad's charming mother. Godfrey Foster, whose copies of fine art paintings rendered in colored dryer lint sold at ridiculously high prices, stuttered like a schoolboy and offered Margo any of his works free of charge. Margo tactfully declined the offer, saying she wouldn't dream of taking advantage of his generosity in such a way. When he insisted, she said she'd be back to look them over later in the week.

"Right now," she said to Katie, "I'd love to see Chad's studio."

Katie had left Chad's Pad—a storeroom Chad had stayed

in illegally during their brief separation—as it was. She
never sold any of his paintings, though. They were there as
a tribute. She showed his mother the studio and then stood
by the door as Margo went from one painting to the next,
lovingly caressing each frame.

Chad painted mostly florals and landscapes, but Margo
paused in front of a depiction of a woman with her back to
the viewer. The woman wore a long white dress and stood
in the midst of a wheat field, her dark hair falling to her
waist in bouncy curls.

Hearing Margo's muffled sob, Katie hurried over to put
an arm around the older woman's shoulders.

"It's me," Margo said softly. "I used to tell Chad about
standing in the wheat fields when I was a teenager watching
for Daddy to come home." She covered her mouth with her
hand. "I never knew he painted this." She turned and clung
to Katie while she wept.

A moment later, the sound of a throat being cleared from
the doorway got the women's attention. Embarrassed, Margo,
turned away.

"I'm sorry for interrupting," Ray said. "Rose told me
you were up here. I didn't mean to intrude."

"That's all right, Ray," Katie said. "Is something wrong?"

"No . . . not at all." He dug a handkerchief from his
pocket and took it over to Margo. "I promise, it's clean."

She laughed. "I'll take your word for it." She dabbed at
her eyes and then extended her hand. "Margo Bonner."

"Ray Davenport. It's a pleasure to meet you."

"It's a pleasure to meet you . . . and to find out that chiv-
alry is alive and well in McKinlay Mill."

This from the woman who had Doug from the plane
carrying her suitcase. Did every man end up eating out of
this woman's hand?

"So, why were you looking for me, Ray?" Katie asked,
more sharply than she'd intended.

"Oh . . . yeah. Sophie's coming home tomorrow, and she

wants to prepare a meal for the family. She specifically asked me to invite you. I think she's hoping you'll take over the tea shop and will consider her as an intern."

"I appreciate your asking, and I'm flattered that Sophie thought of me, but Margo just arrived in town and—"

"Would your wife mind the extra company?" Margo asked.

"Sophie's my daughter," Ray explained. "I'm a widower."

Margo pressed Ray's handkerchief back into his hand, caressing the back of his hand briefly with her other hand. "Thank you again. Katie, we don't have plans for tomorrow evening, do we?"

"No. Are you sure you'll be up to going out for dinner?"

"Of course!" She beamed at Ray. "Tell your darling daughter that Katie and I will be there. Is there anything I can bring?"

Before Ray could answer, Katie said, "Well, I'll leave you in Ray's capable hands. I need to change into my Dickens costume."

Why did it irritate her so much that Margo and Ray were hitting it off? Margo was close to Ray's age, and Ray was bound to be lonely for female companionship. As far as Katie knew, he hadn't dated anyone since Rachel died. And if he had, she'd certainly have heard about it—Francine had been absolutely right about there being no secrets in Victoria Square.

At least, not for long.

Five

~~~~

Katie had barely gotten back to her office and changed into her costume when Nona Fiske, owner of the Square's The Quiet Quilter shop, barged through the door.

"You've absolutely got to do something about this!" The seventy-something woman stood there, arms akimbo, face looking like the tragedy theater mask, and not a dyed brown hair out of place. How did such a petite woman manage to look so formidable?

"About what?" Katie asked as she took a peppermint from the glass jar on her desk and sank into her chair.

"About Rhonda Simpson! She's stealing my patterns and putting them on her dish towels and pillowcases!"

Rhonda Simpson was one of the Alley's newest vendors. A crafter, she sold embroidered pillowcases, dish towels, bath towels, bibs, napkins, and other household items.

Whether she was stealing Nona's patterns—could one even own a quilt pattern?—remained to be seen. Still, Katie didn't feel like arguing with Nona. She ran a hand over her brow. "I'll talk with Rhonda about it."

"Today?"

"Yes."

"Thank you. I'd appreciate your taking care of this as soon as possible. She won't want to see me in court." With that, Nona spun around, and the tail of her black wool coat clipped the edge of Katie's desk.

Katie gasped as her favorite bone china teacup fell to the floor. "Oh no!" she wailed, and hopped up from her chair, tears already pricking her eyes. The "Black Magic" patterned cup and saucer—sole survivor of beloved Aunt Lizzie's wedding china—had been given to her by a distant cousin mere weeks before. It had arrived broken—and then been inexpertly repaired. And now—thanks to Nona's carelessness—was hopelessly smashed. When she closed her eyes, she could still see the deep pink roses set against a band of black shattered on the floor.

"Now, don't worry about that," Nona said cavalierly.

Katie opened her eyes to see the older woman sweeping the pieces of the broken cup and saucer into her purse. "What are you doing?"

"I'm taking this to my nephew. He used to work for a fine porcelain, ceramics, and pottery repair and restoration firm in Manhattan." She shook her head. "Now, due to circumstances he had no control over, he tends bar over at The Pelican's Roost. He can have this fixed up in no time. He's great at repairing bone china, porcelain . . . anything like that really."

"But—"

"One of us will let you know when it's done," Nona said, and hurried out the door.

Katie sank back into her chair and tried not to cry.

Rose rushed in and closed the door. "Goodness, what went on in here? I thought I heard glass breaking. Did she throw something at you?"

"No."

"Did you throw something at her?" Rose asked, eyes widening.

"No. She knocked my teacup off the corner of my desk."

Rose's face crumpled in sympathy. "Oh no. Not the one that belonged to your great-aunt."

"Yeah. I knew I should have taken it home, but I like looking at it during the day. It reminds me of my aunt every time I see it."

Rose nodded sympathetically. "Speaking of tea and such . . . have you thought any more about taking over the tea shop?"

"I don't know." The words emerged on the tail of a sigh. "The bank doesn't seem to think I'm a worthy loan candidate."

"Oh, what do they know?" Rose sat down and smoothed her blonde curls.

"They know they aren't going to give me very good loan terms."

"Well, then we'll just have to figure out something else . . . that is, if you decide you want the tea shop." She paused. "*Do* you want it?"

"Until I was turned down by the bank, I was very enthusiastic," Katie said. "Now I'm not sure I want to take on more than I can handle."

"True. But you might be able to handle more than you think."

Katie rolled her eyes. "Talk to me after Margo leaves."

"That bad?" Rose asked.

"Not yet. But, then, she hasn't been here a full day." Katie frowned. "And what's up with Godfrey? He nearly tripped over his tongue when he met Margo. He even offered to give her one of his pieces of dryer lint art."

"Are you serious?" Rose raised her hand to her chin. "I knew he was trying to date, but I never thought the stingy fellow would resort to giving away his art."

Katie frowned. "He's trying to date? Since when?"

"Didn't you know? His wife left him about a couple of months ago."

"That was one piece of gossip I hadn't heard," Katie said. "Maybe Francine is wrong about all of Victoria Square knowing everyone's business in a matter of hours."

"Yeah, but you keep to yourself more than the rest of us do," Rose said. "Godfrey has been trying to keep it quiet, but it's old news around here. It seems, though, that he wasn't the only one interested in your former mother-in-law."

"Really?"

Rose nodded, her mouth quirking into an odd smile. "Ray took Margo over to Wood U to give her a personal tour of his shop."

Katie felt her face tighten, but she said, "Good for him. They'd make a nice couple."

"Wouldn't they, though? I'd like to see Ray find himself a new love. It seems like Margo could be perfect for him." She glanced at her watch. "I'd better get back to work. Sorry about your cup."

"Me, too. Nona took it with her. She seems to think her nephew can fix it, but I find that hard to believe."

"Well . . . let's hope he can." Rose didn't sound as though she held out any more hope for that than Katie did.

After Rose pulled the door closed behind her, Katie took another peppermint from the jar, unwrapped it, and bit it in two.

Margo, Margo, Margo!

She felt like Jan from the old television show *The Brady Bunch*, saying, "Marsha, Marsha, Marsha!" And she could really sympathize at that moment with poor little Jan, the middle sister who felt that she couldn't compare to her older sibling. Katie had always felt second-rate around Margo.

She hadn't thought she'd feel that way after all this time, especially given the fact that she and Margo were no longer "family." But she did.

Margo came sweeping into town looking elegant and vulnerable, and she immediately won over everyone she met. Katie certainly hadn't won over the residents of Victoria Square that quickly—especially not Ray Davenport. It seemed to have taken him forever to warm up to her. And vice versa. She finished crunching the mint.

Feeling disheartened, Katie woke her PC. Nona could be a bitter pill. Katie knew where her loyalties lay—with her new vendor, Rhonda—and started researching copyright law pertaining to quilt patterns.

~~~~~~

Near the end of the day, Katie went looking for Rhonda Simpson. Rhonda was a pleasantly plump married mom of two young boys. Her long blonde hair was piled onto her head and tucked beneath a red bonnet. Her Dickensian dress was red and trimmed in white lace and red-and-green plaid, and she wore a plaid caplet trimmed in faux fur. She looked darling, and Katie told her so.

Rhonda gave her a wide smile. "You look lovely yourself in that green velvet. Didn't someone write a song about that once?"

"I believe that was blue velvet. My aunt Lizzie used to listen to it."

"Ah . . . right." She spread her left hand out to encompass her table. "Are you looking for something?"

"I might come back later and find something for my mother-in-law—former mother-in-law, I mean."

"Oh, Margo! Isn't she a treasure? She's as sweet as she can be."

Of course. Another person conquered by Margo the Magnificent.

"Have you seen her lately?" Katie asked, realizing she hadn't seen Margo since she'd disappeared with Ray shortly after they'd arrived.

"Not for about an hour or so."

A flurry of pink came by the booth, and a group of ballerinas twirled past. One got dizzy and slammed into Katie, causing her to stumble into Rhonda's table.

"Sorry!" came an unapologetic voice.

Giggles trailed in the wake of the sugarplum fairies . . . or whatever they were supposed to be.

Katie righted the things she'd upset when she slammed into one of Rhonda's tables, and her eyes dropped to a set of tea towels with a little Dutch girl pattern. "There's another reason I came up to talk with you."

"Let me guess. Nona Fiske?"

Katie nodded.

"Rose told me she's been complaining about me," Rhonda said. "I've been nothing but nice to that woman, and I've never stolen a thing in my life."

"I know. Nona can be so difficult. Anyway, I wanted to let you know that I researched quilt pattern copyright. Basically, there's no such thing."

Rhonda breathed a sigh of relief. "That's good to hear."

"In the article I read, it quoted the Copyright Act of 1976, title 17 of the United States Code." Katie took the scrap of paper upon which she'd jotted her note from her pocket. "'Section 102: (b) In no case does copyright protection for an original work of authorship extend to any idea, procedure, process, system, method of operation, concept, principle, or discovery, regardless of the form in which it is described, explained, illustrated, or embodied in such work.' The quilting site where I read the article emphasized that the majority of patterns are not copyrighted and that patterns are generally not copyrightable."

"I'm in the clear, then?"

"I believe so," Katie said. "If Nona gripes to me about it again, I'm going to suggest she talk with Seth Landers about it."

Rhonda's blue eyes widened. "You don't think she's planning to sue me, do you? I mean, even if her lawsuit has no merit, I don't have the money to go to court. Christmas is coming up, and—"

Katie held up a hand to interrupt. "Don't worry about it. If Nona actually would talk with Seth about it, he'd set her straight in a hurry." At least, she thought he would. She thought maybe she should give Seth a call and make sure she was right.

"Thanks, Katie."

"No problem. If you see Margo, could you let her know I'm looking for her?"

"I sure will."

Katie walked down the aisle away from Rhonda's booth and came face-to-wart—er, face—with Ida Mitchell. Why had she never had that thing removed? "Hi, Ida. By any chance, have you seen Margo? She's—"

"I have! Isn't she the most charming woman?" Ida asked.

Katie managed a tight smile and a brief nod.

"The last time I saw her, she was upstairs. I think she was in Chad's Pad," she said. "By the way, you need to talk with that dance instructor. Those little ballerinas are menaces. They came by my shelf earlier and messed with all my lace."

"Did they tear anything up?"

"Well, no. But they handled everything, put my lace on their heads, made mustaches with it, and then just dropped it back onto the shelf. It took me half an hour to get everything back in order."

Knowing how little stock Ida actually had, Katie thought that seemed unlikely. "Okay. I'll look into it. On the bright side, they're only here for extra rehearsals for *The Nutcracker*. Hopefully, they'll have their performance soon and go back to their regular dance class hours." Katie headed for the stairs.

"Fine. But the little monsters had better not come back to my shelf if they know what's good for them."

Katie ignored Ida's parting shot and continued to the staircase. She passed Godfrey on the steps and nearly gagged at the smell. She'd noticed the scent of sweat on him earlier, but now it was worse. Much worse. She needed to speak with him about the odor before he ran off all the Artisans Alley customers, but she couldn't address the matter here on the stairway. She'd try to catch him later either in his booth or in the vendors' lounge. She definitely wasn't going to call him into her office and have that terrible smell permeate the air in there. People might think it was her who reeked!

Katie located Margo in the midst of Chad's paintings. She'd snagged a folding chair from somewhere and brought it into the room where she could gaze at her son's artwork. She started when Katie placed a hand on her shoulder.

"I'm sorry," she said. "I've lost track of time. I didn't mean to disappear on you."

"That's fine," Katie replied. "I get lost in these paintings sometimes, too."

"He loved you so."

Katie wasn't sure she'd heard her correctly. "Excuse me?"

"I said he loved you, Katie. He truly did. I know he was irresponsible with your savings and that he made some bad decisions, but he loved you." Margo swiped a tear from her cheek.

"I know," Katie said softly, swallowing the lump that had formed in her throat. "I loved him, too."

"I know you did." She patted the hand Katie still had resting on her shoulder. "You made him happy . . . happier than he'd ever been. Thank you for that."

Katie couldn't trust herself to speak again. Not for a few minutes. Together they stared at the painting of the young woman in the wheat field.

"I just wanted to let you know that we'll be closing at the top of the hour."

"Understood."

Katie went back downstairs and found Godfrey was still in the vendors' lounge. Unsurprisingly, he was the only one in the room. He was stuffing a piece of sponge cake into his mouth and washing it down with a bottle of cola. Cake crumbs floated in the bottle.

Katie stayed as far away from the table as she could without having to shout at Godfrey. She didn't want anyone else to hear what she needed to say to him, but she was afraid she'd be sick if she got too close.

"Godfrey, I'm sure you're unaware of this . . ." She was fibbing to save his feelings. How could he *not* be aware of it? "But . . . you . . . Did you take a shower this morning?"

"Of course I took a shower!" Cake crumbs and indignation flew from his lips. "But this ridiculous costume you insist upon makes me sweat like a prostitute in church. Normally, Lucy would take the damn thing to the dry cleaner's for me, but she . . . well . . . she hasn't been around much lately. I guess you heard we've separated?"

"I did hear that. I'm terribly sorry."

"We're trying to work things out."

"I hope you do. But, in the meantime, if you could leave early and take your costume to the cleaner's today, that would be great."

"So you want me to sacrifice the additional sales I'd make for the day in favor of going to the dry cleaner's?"

"You're not supposed to be monitoring your booth; you're supposed to be walking security."

"Who's going to do my job? You? After all, it's *your* sensitive nose that's offended."

Katie managed to bite her tongue. "I'd be happy to take over for you for the rest of the day." She glanced at her watch. "There's only about forty-five minutes left. And you've already been away for almost half an hour. We should both get a move on."

Katie kept her promise and walked the Alley's second floor, helping customers and keeping an eye out for suspicious activity. And, she noted, Godfrey's booth didn't have a single browser the entire time.

~~~~~~~

Since McKinlay Mill was a good twenty or so minutes away from the heart of Rochester, the sky wasn't saturated with light pollution and the stars shone brightly overhead. "It's beautiful here," Margo commented as she and Katie strolled toward Katie's apartment.

"It is, especially this time of year when stepping into Artisans Alley makes me feel as if I've gone back in time," Katie said. "The only thing the area lacks is an assortment of good restaurants. You have to go all the way to Greece, although there are a couple of taverns near the lake." She racked her brain to think of somewhere else Margo might be interested in dining.

"If you don't mind, I'd rather stay in this evening. I'm tired from the trip, and I'd like to simply get comfortable and catch up with you." She nodded toward the pizzeria. "And the aromas coming from that place are divine."

"All right." Katie tried to hide her onslaught of panic. She couldn't let Margo see she was involved with Andy, especially after their talk about how much she and Chad had loved each other. Margo would think that Katie had certainly moved on in a hurry. How much love could there have truly been there? But Katie *had* loved Chad. It wasn't her fault that he was gone and that she'd been able to get on with her life. Still . . . "Pizza it is."

Squaring her shoulders, Katie opened the door to the pizza parlor. Maybe Andy wouldn't be there. Maybe he was out running an errand. Maybe—

"Hi, there! Welcome to Angelo's!" With a broad smile, Andy came out from behind the counter.

"He's certainly friendly," Margo murmured to Katie. "And handsome, too."

Andy shook Margo's hand. "So, this is the famous Margo Bonner."

"I told Andy you were coming," Katie said. "He's my . . . landlord." She saw Andy's smile disappear. "And friend. He's been a great friend to me."

"Yep." His face tightened. "Katie, old buddy, old pal, could I see you for a minute?"

"Sure, go ahead," Margo said. "I'll place our order. It was a pleasure meeting you, Andy."

"You, too." He took Katie's elbow and propelled her past the order desk and into the back room. "What the hell was that? You introduce me as your landlord? And then your friend? Is that all I am to you?"

"Of course not, but she's Chad's mother."

"Chad has been dead for nearly two years. Surely, the woman understands that you've moved on and aren't living your life like a nun."

"Yes, but I don't want to flaunt my new boyfriend in her face," Katie said. "We just came from Chad's Pad, where she told me how much her son loved me. She'd never have said something like that when Chad was alive. She was so sweet to me, Andy. I can't hurt her by letting her know you and I are together . . . not yet, anyway."

"What about hurting me?"

"She'll be gone in a couple of days, and I'll make it up to you. I promise."

Lips pursed, Andy merely shook his head before he stormed back into the building and disappeared into his office.

A contrite Katie joined Margo at the counter.

"Was that about your rent?" Margo asked quietly. "Because, if it was, I'll be glad to help you out if you need money."

"I'm fine. That was about . . . um . . . caulking the tub."

Margo eyed her former daughter-in-law. "If you say so, dear."

Six

~~~~

For the thousandth time Katie wished that the stairwell to her apartment had better light. She supposed she could talk with her landlord about it—again—but she'd better let him cool off for a while first. At the landing, she juggled her purse and the pizza box as she sorted through her keys to open the door. Once she was inside, Mason and Della raced to meet her—that is, until they eyed the visitor who accompanied her; then they both backed off.

"Oh," Margo said with derision, "you have two of them now." She sidestepped the cats and went into the kitchen. "I didn't see but one of them when we were here earlier."

"Della can be a little shy until she gets to know you."

Margo shucked her coat, placing it on the back of one of the chairs at the tiny table before she searched the cabinets until she found the plates and took out two. "You keep your home tidy, Katie. I always admired that about you."

"Um . . . yeah . . . thanks." Katie placed the pizza box on the table. "I'll feed the cats, and then we can eat."

"Couldn't you feed them after?" Margo wrinkled her nose. "Because of the smell?"

Okay, some cat food had a strong aroma—but Mason and Della lived there—Margo didn't. Still, Katie forced a smile. "I'll take their dishes into the bathroom. Otherwise, they'll drive us bonkers while we eat."

"Well, we can't have that," Margo said a little too sweetly.

Katie held her temper in check. "Right." There was the persnickety Margo that Katie was more familiar with than the woman who'd beguiled everyone in Victoria Square. She took the cats' dishes, a can of food, and a bag of kibble to the bathroom while Margo opened drawers looking for silverware.

Well, I did tell her to make herself at home, Katie thought, fuming.

When Katie emerged from the bathroom, Margo had doled pizza slices onto plates, and placed napkins and a fork at each setting, and she was pouring sparkling water into glasses.

"Is water okay?" she asked.

"Water is great. Thank you." Katie washed her hands at the sink before sitting down at the table.

"So, tell me more about this tea shop," Margo said. "Is it something you'd really enjoy doing, or are you considering taking over the shop in order to help out the woman whose daughter died?"

"I honestly believe it's something I'd enjoy. Otherwise, I wouldn't even consider it."

"I hope not." Margo cut into her pizza with her knife and fork. "I was always afraid you could be a bit of a pushover, especially where Chad was concerned." She smiled rather wistfully. "I was guilty of giving in to Chad on more than one occasion myself."

Katie said nothing. She knew Chad was always golden, as far as Margo was concerned.

"You seem to put others' needs and desires ahead of your own," Margo continued. "And that's very noble, but you don't want to make a bad decision in order to help someone else out of theirs."

"That's true . . . but I really think I could make a success of the tea shop. Look at what I did for Artisans Alley," she said, indulging herself in a bit of a brag.

"I never got to see it when Chad was so over-the-moon for it, but it is charming. And everyone I spoke with told me how you'd saved the place from financial ruin. They all admire you."

"Maybe so, but you're the one who walked through the Square and charmed them all effortlessly—even the curmudgeonly Ray Davenport."

Margo chuckled. "I found Raymond very kind, and his shop is delightful. He does wonderful work there. And that boy he mentors came in while I was there—what a little sweetheart. Anyway, I'm looking forward to meeting the rest of Raymond's family tomorrow."

"You'll love the girls. They're fantastic kids." Katie sipped her water and sobered. "Back to Francine, though. I can't imagine how she's holding up so well after losing her daughter."

Margo swallowed a bite of pizza. "People deal with grief differently. I practically shut down after Chad died. I was suffocated by my despair. My last ray of sunshine, my last shred of hope was taken away when he left this world."

"It crushed me, too." Katie was about to say that she and Chad had been working on a reconciliation, but she didn't know whether Chad had even confided to his mother that they were living apart. They hadn't done so for long, and there was nothing official about their arrangement.

"I know how acutely you felt Chad's loss," Margo said, "but it was so hard for me. It still is. I lost him in so many capacities: my baby . . . my little boy . . . my young man

who made me so proud . . . my son who would one day
bless me with a grandchild to cherish." Her voice broke,
and she took a drink of her water as though to hide that raw
emotion. "I'm sorry. I didn't intend to lay this burden on
you here at the dinner table. It's just that I'm so alone now.
You're young—you can move on, Katie. I can't. You'll have
another husband someday—if you want one. I'll never have
another child."

Acute compassion flooded through Katie and she reached
over and patted Margo's hand. "I realize it's a small consolation, but you still have me."

Margo smiled, her eyes shining with tears. "That's not a
small consolation at all."

The pizza became their chief concern, and Katie decided
to change the subject to something much less volatile—the
joys of living in a small town and her hopes and dreams for
the future of Victoria Square. Margo listened and actually
seemed interested in what Katie had to say.

Katie made a pot of chamomile tea and they chatted for
a while longer before they washed the dishes. By then, it
was after nine.

"I hope you don't mind if I say good night. It's been a
rather long, tiring day."

"Not at all," Katie said. "Let me just get the cats' food
and water from the bathroom."

Katie, too, prepared for bed, and the cats had followed
her back to the living room to share her temporary bed.

For a long time after she'd turned out the lights, Katie
stared up at the ceiling and thought about Chad, Margo,
Francine, Vonne . . . and Andy.

~~~~~

Margo was sleeping soundly on Friday morning as Katie
quietly made her way to the bathroom. She got ready for
work and left her former mother-in-law a note telling her

she'd fed the cats—as if Margo would care about that—and that she would be at Artisans Alley whenever Margo felt like joining her.

After power walking around Victoria Square twice, Katie entered through the side entrance of Artisans Alley, headed for her office, and donned her Dickensian skirt and shirtwaist. As soon as she was settled in with a cup of coffee, she called Seth and was surprised when the attorney answered the office phone himself. "Did you give your receptionist the day off?"

"No, but she doesn't come in this early. What's on your mind this crisp, wintry morning?"

"It won't officially be winter until the solstice," Katie pointed out.

"Whatever. And you're calling in reference to?"

"Nona Fiske."

"Ugh. That's not the response I was expecting."

Katie laughed. "What response *were* you expecting?"

"I don't know—just not Nona Fiske. Why is she on your mind?" Seth asked.

"Nona has been harassing one of my new vendors—Rhonda Simpson—about the patterns Rhonda uses on her dishcloths and other household linens. She says Rhonda is copying her. She's even threatening to sue."

"Well, if she were to sue, I feel confident the judge would rule it a frivolous filing and throw it out before it progressed very far," Seth said. "Plus, if the case did proceed to court, Nona could be fined if her case is without merit and it's determined that she filed a baseless suit."

"That's what I was hoping you'd say. I don't know why she wants to torment poor Rhonda. It's not like Rhonda is producing quilts—they aren't in direct competition."

"Maybe she's jealous." He blew out a breath. "With Nona Fiske, you never know what motivates her."

"I'll say." Feeling better about the situation, Katie changed the subject. "So, tell me about your dinner last night."

"It turned out very well. I prepared roast chicken with Asiago polenta and chocolate cheesecake parfaits."

"As delicious as that sounds, I'm a little more interested in your date," Katie said. "Was he impressed with your culinary skills?"

"I believe so. This morning he asked me to go to Toronto with him for the weekend."

"Wow! This is getting serious!"

They shared a laugh.

"I'm happy for you," Katie said. "You deserve someone wonderful."

"Let's not get ahead of ourselves. I don't want to jinx it. How are you and Andy doing?"

Katie sighed. "Not great." She told him what had happened at the pizzeria the night before. "I mean, how was I supposed to introduce Andy to Margo as my boyfriend when Margo was being so nice to me and telling me how much Chad had loved me?"

"Katie, Chad has been gone for a long time. I seriously doubt Margo expects you to live like a nun."

Hadn't Andy used the same analogy?

"I know, but . . . but the timing just wasn't right."

"Take this for what it's worth, kiddo, you aren't doing anyone any favors—especially yourself—by being dishonest."

Was she being dishonest or just keeping the truth to herself? In this case, was it the same thing?

No matter what she did—or said—someone was likely to be hurt. Why had she chosen to favor Margo's feelings over Andy's? Katie didn't love Margo, but she did love—

Did she love Andy?

Sometimes Katie wasn't quite sure.

~~~~~

Not long after she'd talked with Seth, Vance stopped by Katie's office. The tall, skinny Santa Claus look-alike held a cup of coffee, and his demeanor suggested he wanted to chat.

"Come on in and shut the door," Katie said. "You look like you've got something on your mind."

He did as she'd suggested and then sat on the chair next to her. "Janey told me you're thinking of assuming ownership of Afternoon Tea."

"I am considering it, yes."

"Well, I wanted to stop by and tell you that she and I support you a hundred percent."

Katie couldn't help grinning. "Aw, thanks, Vance."

"What's holding you back?" he asked.

The grin was short-lived. "Financing, a fear of spreading myself too thin, not wanting to appear disloyal to the artists and vendors here at Artisans Alley, fear of failure . . . Shall I go on?"

Vance chuckled. "I think you've about covered it. Just don't sell yourself short, Katie. When you took over running the Alley, it was on the verge of bankruptcy. Afternoon Tea is in much better shape, at least as far as the equipment and furnishings are concerned."

"Janey told me you'd done some handyman work for Francine and Vonne."

"Very little, and it was at their home, rather than their shop."

"And Vonne did something to make you uncomfortable?" she asked, fishing.

"Damn right she did. The woman made a play for me—despite knowing I'm devoted to Janey."

Katie shook her head. "I feel as though I didn't know Vonne at all. I never would've thought she'd do something like that. But from everything I've heard since her death, it seemed she just went man-crazy."

"Before she . . . um . . . got too flirty, Vonne confided to me that the man she'd dated off and on for several years prior to her moving to McKinlay Mill got married a few months back. Vonne was bitter and resentful of this man's marital bliss and was determined to show him that she could find someone who'd love her, too."

"Wow, that's sad."

"It is," Vance agreed. "But Vonne was too attractive and smart to throw herself at anyone and everyone in order to spite an ex-boyfriend. I told her that, as a matter of fact, and I'm afraid she took it as an overture."

"I'm sorry. She must've been miserable. I wish I'd known and that I could've helped her in some way."

Vance shrugged. "I don't know, Katie. Had you been nice to her, she might've made a play for you, too."

Katie merely shook her head. Vance obviously didn't know Vonne was pregnant at the time of her death. "I'm definitely sure I wasn't her type."

Vance laughed. "These days, you just never know."

Katie's phone rang. Vance stood, gave her a little wave, and left. Katie answered to find that it was Ray calling.

"Katie, Sasha was throwing up in the bathroom last night."

"Oh no. How is she this morning?"

"She's fine. When I asked her about her being sick, she said she saw something gross in her science book and it gagged her. She said it was no big deal. I think it *is* a big deal. I believe she forced herself to throw up her dinner."

"Surely not. Maybe she did gag over one of those photographs—they put some disgusting things in those science books, you know," Katie said. "I'm afraid I might've put the idea of Sasha forcing herself to throw up into your head when—"

"And I'm afraid you've got your head in the sand. I was one of the best police detectives on the force. I know guilt when I see it, and I know when someone is lying. I thought you were going to help me with this."

"I am. Calm down, Ray. Do you want me to talk with Sasha about it?"

"No. Not yet." He muttered a curse. "I just don't know what to do."

"Let's both think on it, and we'll talk later. All right?"

"Yeah . . . all right."

After ending the call, Katie stared at the cluttered surface of her desk for long moments before she logged on to her computer to learn more about anorexia.

~~~~~~

It was nearly ten when Margo arrived at Artisans Alley wearing navy slacks and blazer, a blue-and-white-print blouse, and black ankle boots. Her makeup was flawless, and not a hair on her head was out of place. And yet she said she felt dowdy, since she wasn't in costume like Katie.

"Believe me, you look stunning," Katie said.

"Thanks, but I'm sure you're merely being kind. If I planned to stay longer, I'd have to invest in one of these Dickensian costumes, but I suppose it would be pointless, since I'll be leaving in a couple of days."

Katie was relieved to hear that Margo didn't feel she'd be in town long enough to warrant a costume. She'd been afraid to ask the woman how long she'd planned on staying.

"I haven't had breakfast," Margo said. "Have you?"

"Not yet."

"Then let's walk over to that tea shop you've been telling me about."

Katie frowned. "Technically they don't open until eleven thirty, but Francine arrives hours before that to bake and get the dining room ready for the day. I have to warn you that the food hasn't been up to par lately."

"That's all right. If I don't see anything that appeals to me, we'll go elsewhere."

"It's a deal."

Katie slipped out of her costume and they headed for the exit.

While they were en route to Afternoon Tea, Nona Fiske came rushing out of The Quiet Quilter to intercept them.

"Did you talk to her?" Nona demanded.

Ignoring her question, Katie said, "Good morning, Nona. Have you met Margo yet?"

"No, I—"

"Nona, is it?" Margo extended her hand. "It's a pleasure to meet you. I'm Margo Bonner."

"Bonner?" Nona echoed.

"Yes. I'm Chad's mother."

"Oh. Well. It's nice to meet you. I . . . I'm Nona Fiske. I own The Quiet Quilter."

Quiet? Usually, Nona was anything but quiet.

"I'm sure your shop is charming," Margo said. "I'll look forward to coming by and checking it out . . . hopefully, later today."

"Yes, well . . ." Frowning, Nona turned her attention back to Katie. "Have you spoken to Rhonda Simpson yet about copying my patterns?"

"Yes, I have."

Before Katie could comment further, Margo jumped in. "Rhonda is simply as sweet as sugar, isn't she?" She continued before Nona could reply. "I believe if I were you, I'd try to form a sort of alliance with her. I mean, someone who likes her Sweet Sue pillowcases would probably love to have a Sweet Sue quilt, don't you think? You could work out a way to sell them as a set, or you could at least promote each other."

Nona's frown deepened. "Hmm . . . I'd never thought of that."

"It's worth considering. You could both possibly make considerably more money if you utilize each other as assets."

"I'll think it over." Nona said good-bye and headed back to her shop at a much slower pace than her arrival.

"Sorry if I overstepped," Margo told Katie. "I was in

human resources for years, and sometimes I had to get pretty creative when it came to encouraging people to get along."

"You didn't overstep at all," Katie said. "I just hope it works. Your approach beats lawsuits and name-calling all to pieces."

Margo merely smiled and opened the door to Afternoon Tea.

Francine was setting silverware on lacy paper place mats but immediately abandoned the job and hurried to greet Katie and Margo. "Welcome, ladies!"

"Hi, Francine. I'd like you to meet Margo Bonner."

"Margo, the pleasure is all mine," Francine said, sizing Margo up. "Are you thinking of going in on the tea shop with Katie?"

Both Katie and Margo started at the rather impertinent question.

"Oh no. I'm most definitely retired. I'm only here for breakfast."

"What about you, Katie?"

"I know you're not officially open for the day, but I'd like some breakfast, too."

"I meant about the shop," Francine persisted.

"I'm still considering it."

"All right. But don't take too long. I've had other inquiries, you know."

"Oh? Are any of them serious?" Katie asked.

Francine hesitated. "Well . . . of course."

Katie nodded, not sure she believed the woman. She changed the subject. "Have Vonne's arrangements been finalized?" Katie asked.

"They have. I'm having a very small memorial service on Sunday."

"I'm so sorry for your loss," Margo said with sympathy. "Katie told me about your daughter."

"Thank you."

"I wish I'd been a better friend to Vonne," Katie told Francine. "I'm only now discovering all she'd been going through."

"What Vonne had been going through?" Francine scoffed. "Like what?"

"I understand that her longtime boyfriend married someone else," Katie said. "I imagine the fact that he could move on from her so quickly hit her hard."

"The guy was never that crazy about Vonne to begin with." Francine shook her head. "Charles wanted a woman with a good education and a successful career . . . someone he'd be proud to take home to his parents and show off at corporate events. I tried to tell Vonne that for years, but she simply wouldn't listen to me."

"And how did she take it when you said I told you so?" Margo asked.

"She didn't like it one bit. In fact, that's when Vonne dumped the entire tea shop in my lap and started running wild."

"Ah." Margo nodded. "I take it Vonne inherited her coping skills from her father. I feel certain you're able to keep a clear head, Francine."

"Vonne took on everything from her father. She didn't have any of my traits at all."

A delivery truck pulled up outside the door, and Francine scurried to intercept the driver. "If you see anything that appeals to you," she said to the room at large, "please let me know."

Five minutes later, Katie and Margo left with cups of hot tea and two blueberry muffins.

"Was Vonne Francine's stepdaughter?" Margo asked as the women headed back to Artisans Alley.

"I . . . I don't know." Katie had never thought to question the nature of the women's relationship. Everyone recognized them as mother and daughter.

"I just think it's odd that Francine was adamant that

Vonne had none of her traits. It made me think that she was Francine's husband's daughter from a previous marriage or something. Francine clearly doesn't behave like a woman who lost a child. As a matter of fact, she doesn't act like a woman who'd even lost a friend," Margo commented.

No, she didn't, which piqued Katie's curiosity about the woman. Why was she so insistent about selling the tea shop? Where was the grief she felt at losing a daughter—be it natural or stepchild? Why was she acting so out of character, if indeed her actions and reactions were out of character?

Katie wished she knew.

Seven

~~~~~~

The parking lot was half-full of holiday shoppers, and many of them were bustling about Artisans Alley when Katie and Margo returned.

"My goodness. Is it always so busy on a weekday morning?" Margo asked.

"No, but this is definitely what's known as the Christmas rush. It's make-it-or-break-it time for retail."

Margo looked around at the shoppers loitering around various booths and choking the aisles. "If you wouldn't mind, I'd like to spend more time in Chad's Pad. I've got books I can read on my phone."

"Of course," Katie said. "I don't have a lot to do today, so we should be able to leave around noon and go do something fun. Would you like to go antiquing?"

"I'd love to, but don't make any concessions on my account. Go ahead and do whatever you need to do, Katie. I realize my visit hit you out of the blue. It wasn't my intention to disrupt your life."

"You aren't. But I want us to do something fun today."

"All right. Come find me when you're ready."

They parted and, after shedding her coat, Katie went directly to her office. Once there, she sat before her desk and lifted the lid from her tea, then retrieved the Artisans Alley checkbook from her locked cabinet drawer. Bill-paying was the priority of the day, and it shouldn't take too awfully long.

As she sorted through the envelopes in her inbox, she considered the possibility that Vonne could be Francine's stepdaughter. Maybe Francine and Vonne's father married late in life, and that's why Francine wasn't particularly close to Vonne. But, then, Katie had heard Vonne call Francine Mom. Still, many stepchildren did the same.

There was a perfunctory knock at the door before Rose came in and dropped off the morning mail, but it took a few moments for her presence to register in Katie's brain.

"My dear, you seem to be a million miles away," she said to Katie.

"Not that far." Katie smiled. "Just down the street a bit. I've been wondering if maybe Francine and Vonne weren't actually related by blood and if that's the reason Francine isn't more upset over her death."

Rose shrugged. "I guess that's possible. Francine and Vonne weren't originally from McKinlay Mill, so I'm not familiar with their history."

"I wonder who would be."

Rose looked thoughtful. "Let me think on it. I'm sorry to say that Vance had to run Arthur Henderson off while you and Margo were out."

Katie groaned. "What did he do this time?"

"He stole one of the primitive animals from Joan McDonald's booth. A pig, I think."

"And Vance caught him with it?"

"Yes, but Arthur said he was carrying it downstairs to pay for it," Rose said. "But Vance saw him stuffing it into his pocket."

"I doubt he was going to do so, but since he hadn't left Artisans Alley yet, he has a valid argument that he was placing the item in his pocket in order to keep his hands free while he finished shopping. We have no proof that he didn't intend to pay for it before he left." She sighed. "I guess I need to call the vendors together and address this. Thanks, Rose."

As her friend left the office, Katie's phone rang. It was Andy.

"Hi, handsome."

"Are you this flirty with all your friends?" he asked sarcastically. "Or just your landlord friend?"

She blew out a breath and ignored the question. "I don't think Margo plans to be here much past the weekend."

"Not much past the weekend?" he asked, his tone softening. "I miss you and want to see you. Couldn't I take you and Margo to dinner tonight as your friend?"

"Ray Davenport invited us to his place for dinner tonight. His oldest daughter, Sophie, is home from culinary school and wanted to make a special meal. I'm certain it's because she's wrangling for a summer internship should I end up taking over the tea shop."

Andy didn't respond, and after a long moment Katie was afraid that their call had been disconnected. "Andy?"

"Yep. I'm here. So you can hang out with your friend Ray but not with me?"

"It isn't like that, Andy. Margo and Ray really hit it off yesterday. It would be good for both of them if they became friends."

"Yeah . . . whatever. Just call me when you have time to work me into your schedule."

"Maybe tomorrow we could all get together after the tree-lighting ceremony?"

"Maybe. See you."

Katie sighed and put aside her phone. Andy was obviously upset . . . and she supposed he had every right to be. But it wasn't like she'd invited Margo here. A little voice within her whispered that Katie could have been honest with Margo and the three of them could be having dinner tonight rather than Katie and Margo dining with the Davenports, but that still seemed wrong somehow. Wouldn't that make Margo feel like Katie had replaced Chad? No one would ever replace Chad in her heart. That didn't mean she couldn't make room in her heart for someone else, though.

She decided to try again to make dinner plans with Andy and Margo tomorrow night. Andy was too upset to converse with right now, but if, at the tree-lighting ceremony, she casually said to the two of them, "Hey, let's all go to Del's and grab a bite to eat," that just might work.

Feeling a teensy bit better, Katie attacked the stack of bills with renewed vigor. It had been a while since she'd taken off from work for a frivolous reason. She deserved the occasional break from the routine. But which Margo would accompany her? The friendly HR chief or the persnickety mother-in-law?

Katie crossed her proverbial fingers and hoped for the former.

~~~~~~

As Katie rounded the stairs just around the corner from Chad's Pad, she heard Godfrey's booming voice echoing from the rafters and cringed.

". . . fine painter. Did he get his artistic ability from you?"

From the doorway, Katie heard Margo's reply. "I'm afraid not. I'm doing well to draw stick figures."

"Oh, now, I'm sure you're being modest. A lovely woman like you—"

"Hey, Margo!" Katie interrupted. "If we're going to make it to that antique shop before they close, we'd better be going."

"Let me grab my coat and purse," Margo said. "Godfrey, thank you for keeping me company."

Godfrey beamed. "Anytime. I'll be around later if you'd like to talk some more."

The two women escaped Artisans Alley as quickly as they could.

"Thanks for the rescue," Margo said. "Good heavens, where does he get all that dryer lint? And why does he think I'd want to hang dryer lint art in my home?"

"I can't begin to fathom an answer to either of those questions, so let's concentrate on lunch. There's a new French place just outside town. Would you like to try it?"

"I'd love to."

The day was bright, the local soft rock station played holiday music, and it was only a ten-minute drive to the restaurant. They strolled into the lobby of the beautiful brick building where a lovely, understated Christmas tree adorned with red and gold balls and twinkling white lights welcomed them. A garland festooned with lights framed the archway. A hostess in a tight black cocktail dress greeted Katie and Margo and showed them to a table for two by a window, placing menus down before them. Katie took in the surroundings. All the linen-covered tables were round, and the bistro chairs were made of black wrought iron with ivory padded seats and as charming as all get-out.

"Your server, Albert," she said, pronouncing it Albear, "will be with you momentarily."

The hostess had barely returned to the lobby when Albert materialized by their table. He had a charming accent, but cynical Katie had to wonder if his name was really Jake and if his accent was affected for their benefit. Either way, Albert was a handsome young man who loved to talk.

"*Bonjour, mademoiselles.* How are you this lovely Friday afternoon? *C'est bien, aujord'hui?*"

"*Nous sommes très bien, merci. Et vous?*"

But, of course, Margo could speak French.

"*Mieux vaut maintenant que vous êtes là.*"

Margo laughed. "He says he's better now that we're here. Oh, Albert, you are *trop charmant.*"

Katie gritted her teeth, irritated that Margo knew that Katie would need her to translate the waiter's words. The fact that she *did* need Margo to translate was even more aggravating.

"*Merci, cherie,*" Albert said to Margo. "Do you know what you'd like to drink?"

"I'll have a glass of your finest cabernet. And I'd like to order the steak Diane, please."

"*Très bien, mademoiselle.* You'll be delighted with the chef's use of brandy sauce set aflame to produce just the *perfect* touch of caramel to the dish." He turned to Katie. "And for you?"

Katie ordered a glass of water and the chicken Basquaise.

"Another excellent choice. The chef uses the Espelette pepper so popular in the region of Basque for this particular dish. I'll bring your drinks out to you *à moment.*"

Margo grinned at Katie after the waiter collected their menus and retreated. "You should hire Albert if you decide to buy the tea shop. That man can make anything sound like the most exquisite thing you've ever put in your mouth."

"Yeah. Let's hope we won't be disappointed now that he's raised our expectations so high."

They weren't. The food was delicious. And Albert was continually solicitous, especially toward Margo.

As the women dined, their conversation naturally turned to Chad. Katie looked around at the rustic plastered walls, the Provençal prints, and sighed. "Chad would have loved this place."

"He would have," Margo agreed, and gave Katie an appraising look. "You know, I have other family . . . a sister I'm especially close to."

"Yes, I met Aunt Sylvia at the wedding. Chad told me some great stories about the things you and she would get into."

Margo managed a weak laugh. "Yes. We still have our adventures now and then. But the point I'm trying to make is that I'm okay. What about you, Katie? Have you dated anyone since Chad's passing?"

"Um . . . I've . . . dated . . . some."

"Are you telling me you haven't been out with that sexy pizza guy yet? Because if you haven't, why not? He obviously likes you."

Katie's eyes widened. "As a matter of fact, I . . . we . . . have dated." How much should she tell Margo? Should she confess that she and Andy had been seriously dating for quite some time? No. Not yet. "We're both too busy with work to devote a lot of time to a relationship." That was good. It was true enough.

"That's a shame. You're still young. Chad wouldn't want you to let life pass you by. You know that, don't you?"

She dropped her eyes to her plate and avoided answering Margo's question.

"He'd want you to be happy."

Katie swallowed down a sudden pang of emotion. "Yes, he would—as I would have if the situation were reversed."

Margo's smile was warm. "I, too, lost my husband at a young age. But I had a child to take care of, to nurture. You have cats. It can't be nearly as fulfilling."

Katie's thoughts drifted to the lyrics of a song that often played on the oldies station broadcast through Artisans Alley. Any love is good love, and her cats had certainly blessed her with their total devotion. They'd never lied to her. They'd never gone behind her back, taking the money she'd scrimped and saved to invest in a losing proposition. Chad was no saint, even if Margo wanted to believe that of her son. But Katie knew differently.

Still, she said nothing on that account.

Albert returned and, seeing that they were almost finished with their meals, said, "The crème brûlée here is divine. Are you up for dessert?"

Margo positively grinned. *"Mais oui!"*

~~~~~~~

The Rusty Key, Katie's favorite shop filled with antiques and vintage items on consignment, had always cheered her even though it seemed her dream of ever opening an inn of her own would never happen. She always felt at peace when studying the shelves filled with crockery, boxes of old cutlery, and cedar trunks filled with hand-embroidered linens. But as they browsed the antique shop, Katie's warm, fuzzy feelings about the new Margo were diminished by the reinforced realization that old Margo was still very much around.

The first thing that caught Katie's eye in the shop was a cream-and-taupe-striped Louis XIV–style sofa. "Isn't this lovely?" She ran her hand across the back and then took a seat. It wasn't the most comfy sofa she'd ever sat on, but a plump pillow at either end would help with that.

Margo scoffed. "Don't be ridiculous. That thing is absurdly tiny. And it certainly wouldn't keep that pristine appearance for long—especially not with those cats of yours." She shuddered. "It would be clawed all to pieces."

Katie bit her tongue, got up, and wandered over to a French farm scene painting. "This would be nice in a kitchen."

"A painting of chickens? Really?" Margo looked at the price tag. "Five hundred dollars? You could get something similar at a home goods store for under a hundred . . . *if* you wanted."

"I didn't say I wanted it. I merely pointed out that it would look nice in a kitchen."

"Not my kitchen."

And so it went for the next hour. It seemed to Katie that every item she liked Margo deemed as tacky, cheap, ugly, or worthless. Katie begrudgingly admitted to herself that Margo was knowledgeable about antiques. But, then, so was she. And sometimes she liked things merely for their aesthetic value.

On the way back to McKinlay Mill, Margo mentioned the old Webster Mansion.

"Chad sent me photos of it back when you and he were considering turning it into a bed-and-breakfast. I'd love to see it in person."

"Nick Ferrell and Don Parsons bought the mansion and turned it into a B and B called Sassy Sally's," Katie said. "It's gorgeous. I'm sure they'd be happy to show you around."

They were happy to show Margo around. Actually, Don took the grand dame on a tour of the property while Katie hung out with Nick in the kitchen.

Nick smiled. "You look tired. Are you okay?"

"I'm fine," Katie said quietly. "Just hanging out with Margo this afternoon reminded me of how critical she can be."

"That bad, huh?"

"No . . . actually, she's been nicer to me than she's ever been. I thought we were turning over a new leaf."

"You can, darling. But you know very well that people's personalities don't change. You just need to learn to take the bad with the good. At least, until she leaves." Nick poured them both a cup of coffee and they sat on the stools at the island.

As he stirred cream into his coffee, Nick said, "The grapevine is buzzing with news about your taking over the tea shop."

"The grapevine is getting ahead of itself." Katie ran her hand over the smooth marble countertop.

"So you aren't interested in the shop?"

She sipped her coffee. "I didn't say that."

He grinned. "You know you want it."

"I do . . . and I don't. I'm conflicted, Nick. Could I take on a project of that magnitude? I mean, I'm dealing with the day-to-day tasks of running Artisans Alley. How can I possibly do the marketing and promotion it would take to turn Afternoon Tea around—that is, provided I could get the funding to assume ownership?"

"You could make it work. I know you could." He sighed. "I have to say, though, Vonne did a number on the place— taking financial risks, making people so uncomfortable they didn't want to stop in, leaving poor Francine to take care of everything."

"How much do you know about Francine and Vonne?" Katie asked.

"No more than anyone else. Just that they came here from Batavia and that everything seemed great at first . . . until Vonne seemed to lose her mind."

"She did, didn't she? Do you think it was because the man she loved married someone else?"

He shrugged. "I suppose that could do it. But I still feel there must be more to the story."

"I agree. It's bothering me that Francine doesn't seem to be terribly upset by Vonne's death. And then she said something earlier today that made me think that maybe Vonne wasn't her biological child."

"You think she was adopted?"

"Possibly. Or a stepchild. I wish there was a way to find out." Katie drummed her fingertips on the countertop.

"Do you know where the funeral service is being held?" Nick asked.

"No. Francine intimated that it would be a small, private affair."

Nick pulled his tablet over from the edge of the island and turned it on. "I'm guessing the service would be in their hometown." He typed *Batavia Funeral Homes* into the search engine. He then investigated each one until he found one with Vonne Barnett's obituary. He turned the tablet toward Katie. "Here it is. Thomason Funeral Home."

Katie read the brief paragraph, which didn't at all convey who Vonne had been. "Do you think I should attend the service as head of the Merchants Association?"

"That's up to you."

She shook her head slowly. "I'd feel unwelcome. I mean, Francine made it pretty clear that—"

"Then order flowers. When you call, you tell the receptionist that you want to send flowers for Vonne's viewing—and then you say, Is Francine her mom or her stepmom?"

Katie laughed. "Nick, you're impossible!"

"Maybe. But I bet it'll work."

"I might as well give it a shot."

"Might as well."

"I hope it's not me you're shooting," Margo said as she and Don returned to the kitchen. "This place is lovely. And the furniture is exquisite! The paintings and vintage photos are just perfect for the walls, and the Oriental carpets are gorgeous as well. Everything is just perfect."

"Did you know that Katie picked out ninety percent of it?" Nick asked.

Margo's smile faded. "You don't say."

"I do. It was all stuff she'd picked out to furnish this place when she thought it might be hers—and Chad's," he amended quickly.

"Buying it lock, stock, and barrel sure made our lives easier," Don agreed. "And she offered it to us at just over cost—to pay the cost of her storage fees."

"Which was still a bargain," Nick agreed.

A bit of a sneer curled Margo's upper lip. "Judging by your current apartment, I had no idea you had such decorating style, dear."

Katie forced a smile and her gaze traveled to Nick, who merely shrugged. She'd had a long day, and she had a feeling the evening ahead might prove even longer.

Eight

As Katie and Margo were pulling out of the parking lot on their way to the Davenports' house for dinner, Katie looked toward Angelo's Pizzeria and noticed Andy and Erikka standing behind the sales counter. They were laughing, and Andy was pushing back a lock of Erikka's jet-black hair that had fallen across her cheek.

"They seem awfully chummy," Margo said.

"Yeah . . . they do." Katie tried to catch Andy's eye to wave to him, but either he didn't see her or else he was ignoring her.

"Who is she?" Margo asked.

"Erikka, Andy's assistant manager."

"I don't want to overstep, but if you're interested in that man at all, my advice would be to move quickly." She clucked her tongue. "It might be too late already. Oh, do you mind if we stop at a floral shop? I'd love to get the Davenports some flowers. Of course, I'd normally bring wine to a dinner party, but I have no idea what they're serving."

They stopped at the local grocery store, where Margo snagged a mixed bouquet of carnations, daisies, and baby's breath.

Once they were on the road again, Margo prattled on about the dinner party. Katie's mind was still on Andy and Erikka and their intimate behavior. In fact, Katie dwelt on Andy and Erikka until she and Margo arrived at the Davenports' house.

It was a small rental house with brick on the first floor and vinyl siding on top. The windows had black shutters, but there wasn't much to distinguish it from other homes on the street except the colorful, twinkling lights that flanked the door and porch railing. Electric candles had been placed in all the windows at the front of the house. Katie wondered which of the girls was the decorator. She seriously doubted it was Ray.

She knocked on the door, and Ray opened it to admit her and Margo. Inside, he introduced Margo to Sadie, Sasha, and Sophie. Sadie thanked Margo for the flowers and took them into the kitchen to find a vase.

In the living room, the beautiful Christmas tree gleamed in a corner where Katie recalled an overstuffed brown recliner chair normally sat. The chair had been pushed a bit too close to the tan sofa, but Katie could easily imagine the four Davenports cozily sitting on the sofa and chair watching a movie or listening to some music . . . or maybe simply reminiscing as they admired their decorations.

She wandered over to the tree. As she'd expected, many of the ornaments had been carved and painted by Ray, and others had been made by the girls. She spotted a tiny gingerbread cottage that had obviously been crafted by Ray. She couldn't tell if he or one of the girls had painted it, but whoever had, did a wonderful job. White "icing" covered the roof and framed the door and windows. Round red-and-white peppermint "candies" served as shutters to the house, and there was a red heart on the door.

Katie started when a hand was placed on her shoulder. She turned to see Ray standing beside her with a bemused grin on his face.

"Like that one, do you?"

"It's lovely," she said. "Did you paint it, or did one of the girls?"

"Actually, Rachel did. She was a gifted artist."

Katie merely nodded.

"What's got you down?" he asked softly.

"Nothing. I'm fine."

He arched a bushy gray brow. "Can't fool me, you know."

She shrugged. "It's nothing."

Before Ray could press her further, Sasha nearly knocked Katie off her feet when she surprised her with a hug.

"Sasha, not so rough," Ray scolded.

"She's fine," Katie said, embracing the girl . . . glad to find an ally somewhere in this world of wonderful, talented women that apparently included Margo, Erikka, and Rachel, but not her. She immediately felt guilty. It wasn't like her to compare herself to anyone else or to be self-pitying.

"I'm looking forward to walking with you tomorrow morning," Sasha said.

"I'm looking forward to having the company."

"Could we go on into the dining room please?" Sophie asked loudly.

"Of course," Ray said. Under his breath, he told Katie, "She worked hard on dinner, and she's very proud."

"Sophie, you've outdone yourself," Katie said, when she saw the dining room table.

The rectangular table was covered with a white tablecloth, and then a long red and gold brocade runner had been placed down the center. White linen napkins folded in a bishop's mitre stood in front of each place setting.

The young woman had prepared bruschetta chicken, and

each dish had been professionally plated with parsley and tomato garnishes. To the side of each red-floral rimmed white dinner plate, there was a matching salad plate with an assortment of greens, carrots, cucumbers, tomatoes, and black olives.

"Dessert is a surprise," Sophie said.

After everyone was seated, Sadie regaled them all with the story of Ray playing "Hail to the Chief" for Sophie on the piano.

Ray did his best to look wounded. "I told you it was 'Hail to the Chef.'"

"I didn't realize you played piano," Katie said.

"Ah, I bang around a little now and then."

"Don't let him fool you," Sasha said. "He's terrific. He can show you after dinner."

"I don't think—" Ray began.

"You must," Margo said. "I insist."

"Suit yourselves. Just remember, you asked for it."

After they'd polished off the delicious meal, Sophie enlisted the help of her sisters in the kitchen. They left the table and each girl emerged from the kitchen with a dessert tray. Sophie's tray contained mini strawberry tarts topped with whipped cream. Sadie's tray was filled with petit fours with delicate pink roses on the tops. And Sasha's tray was full of individual dishes of tiramisu.

"Katie, I want you to try one of each," Sophie said.

Katie looked at Sasha with her eyes wide. "Then I'll have to walk from tomorrow morning until this time tomorrow night!"

Sasha giggled. "That's all right. I'll still walk with you."

Katie tasted each dessert and declared them all to be fantastic. She had noticed that Sasha declined dessert and that she'd barely touched her dinner.

"Which is your favorite?" Sophie asked, interrupting Katie's thoughts.

"I can't choose!"

The young woman smiled triumphantly. "Good."

Ray caught Katie's eye and gave her a wink. Katie smiled, but she wasn't just inflating Sophie's ego. The girl was talented.

Margo pushed her plate away and thanked Sophie for a delicious meal before turning to Ray. "I believe you promised us a song or two."

"You guys go ahead," Katie said. "I'll clear the dishes."

"You'll do no such thing," Ray said. "You'll suffer through my playing just like everyone else. The girls and I will take care of cleaning up later."

Katie and Margo followed the rest of the family into the den. Though tidy, it was more lived-in than the living and dining rooms. An upright piano whose cabinet and bench seat had seen better days stood against one wall. An air hockey table was placed along the other wall. An entertainment center with a large television sitting on the top took up the wall directly across from the door. A navy sofa and matching chair that had likely begun life in the living room until they were too worn, along with a couple of beanbag chairs, completed the room.

Ray took a seat on the piano bench, raised the keyboard cover, and fluttered his fingers over the keys with a flourish. He waggled his bushy brows at his amused audience. "Requests?"

When no one answered right away, he began playing the Nat King Cole classic "When I Fall in Love."

Unsurprisingly, Margo knew the song. She moved to sit on the bench beside Ray and began to sing. It was all Katie could do not to roll her eyes. Of course, she sounded great. Katie should've known that she would. Margo didn't do anything if she couldn't do it well.

Katie was stunned when Ray joined in on the chorus. Unbelievably, the man could also sing. And, of course, he and Margo harmonized beautifully. When they were finished, Katie joined the girls in applauding the couple.

"Do another," Sasha said.

Ray played the bridge leading to the animated movie *Toy Story* song "You've Got a Friend in Me."

"I'm bowing out of this one," Margo said. "I have no idea what you're playing."

"We do," Sadie said. "It's our favorite." She and her sisters began singing with their dad, who did Randy Newman proud.

Katie enjoyed this song much more than she had the love song. It was obvious that Ray and his daughters had sung it together often, and they really hammed it up.

After that song, Ray said, "Let's do one where everyone can sing." He played "Deck the Halls."

Katie joined in on this one, although she was self-conscious because the room was full of talented singers and she didn't count herself one of them. Her phone vibrated, she looked at the caller ID, and then excused herself. She went into the kitchen to take the call.

"Hello?" She hadn't recognized the number and was afraid it might be important.

"Yeah, is this Katie Bonner?"

"It is."

"Yeah, I'm Carl, Nona's nephew. She brought me this cup you broke."

"Cup *I* broke?"

"Yeah, a teacup. I've got it fixed if you want to come and get it. I'm at The Pelican's Roost."

"I'll be there soon. Thank—" She realized he'd ended the call.

"Okaaay," she said aloud to no one.

She looked around the kitchen. There were dishes stacked in the sink, and those were in addition to the dishes and silverware that sat on the dining room table. The Davenports had a dishwasher, but Katie was pretty sure Sophie had brought out their best china to entertain her and Margo.

She checked to make sure the dishwasher was empty. It

was, so she rinsed the pots, pans, mixing bowls, and spoons and placed them in the dishwasher. She then filled the sink with warm soapy water and went into the dining room to get her first batch of plates. She couldn't possibly leave this work for the Davenport girls to do.

From the den, the sound of "The Entertainer" wafted into the kitchen. She hummed along as she washed the first plate and put it in the dish drainer.

"What are you doing?" Ray asked from the doorway.

"If you're here, who's playing?"

"Sadie. Answer my question."

"I'm playing hopscotch. What does it look like I'm doing?"

"It looks like you're washing dishes . . . dishes that I told you not to wash."

"Now, there's the Ray Davenport I know and love. Curmudgeonly, pushy, do-what-I-say . . . not this thoughtful guy who plays piano and sings."

"I'm a man of many talents," he deadpanned.

"Obviously."

He located a dish towel and began drying the dishes. "Is everything all right?"

"Sure. Why?"

"You looked down when you got here. Then you got a call, and you decided you'd rather wash dishes than come back into the den."

"The call was Nona Fiske's nephew telling me he'd repaired my teacup . . . the teacup that belonged to Aunt Lizzie and that Nona Fiske broke," Katie said. "I'm doing the dishes because I didn't want you and the girls to have to do it."

"We don't mind. We were happy to have guests."

"And I was happy to be a guest. You and Margo sang really well together."

"You think? Should we take our act on the road?"

"I don't know that I'd go that far. By the way, I noticed Sasha hardly touched her dinner."

Ray instantly sobered. "Yeah, I saw that, too. I'm going to ask Sophie to talk with her. Sasha really admires her big sister."

"After we talked earlier, I went online and researched anorexia. Sasha has a lot of the warning signs—she's refusing to eat, she's obsessed with her weight, you heard her throwing up . . ."

"Like I said, I'm going to have Sophie talk with her. If anyone can help her, Sophie can."

"I don't know if that'll be enough," Katie said. "I'm concerned that Sasha might need professional help."

"And I'll consider bringing in a professional if Sophie can't help. I know my girls. Don't write Sophie off without giving her a chance."

"That's not what I meant. I meant that—"

"It's all right." Ray took the plates he'd dried and put them in the cabinet. "The house hasn't been this lively in months. I'm enjoying it."

"Me, too."

"Good. You need to stop by more often."

Katie smiled.

"Margo, too, of course."

Her smile faded. "Of course."

"How long is she staying?" he asked.

"Not much longer." Katie went back to the dining room for the rest of the dishes. When she returned, she asked Ray if he'd heard anything more about Vonne.

"No. Have you?"

"I'm afraid not. I wonder if they can find the father by testing the baby's DNA."

"Not without having someone to compare it to," Ray said.

"It seems like Vonne made passes at several men in the weeks before her death, but no one knows who might've fathered her child. It's weird, don't you think?"

"It certainly is."

~~~~~~~

As she backed the Focus out of the Davenports' driveway, Katie asked Margo if she'd mind accompanying her to The Pelican's Roost.

"What's that?"

"A bar. The bartender there is Nona Fiske's nephew."

"That awful woman who owns the quilting shop?" Margo asked.

"That's Nona. She broke a teacup I had sitting on my desk. She scooped it up and said she'd take it to her nephew to have him repair it."

"A bartender who repairs bone china?" Margo scoffed. "Don't get your hopes up."

"I'm not. I mainly just want my cup back. But Nona did say that Carl had once worked in porcelain repair, so maybe he did fix the cup adequately."

Margo didn't comment further on the cup, but it was clear she thought it was a lost cause. "It was nice of you to clean up the kitchen. I'd have helped had you asked."

"I just didn't want Ray and the girls to have to deal with it, especially when Sophie had worked so hard on the meal," Katie replied. "And then Ray ended up helping with it anyway."

"He's an awfully nice man, isn't he? He invited me to lunch tomorrow."

Katie's hands tightened on the steering wheel. "How nice. Where are you going?"

"I don't know. He said he'd pick me up at Artisans Alley around noon."

She knew she should be glad for Ray and Margo, but Katie wasn't. She couldn't put a finger on exactly why she wasn't. Maybe it was because she knew that long-distance romances seldom worked out. Maybe it was because she didn't want Margo taking her place with Ray and his daughters.

What place? They were friends. They'd remain friends even if Ray and Margo got together. Wouldn't they?

Katie pulled into the parking lot at The Pelican's Roost. It was crowded, but Katie managed to find a spot close to the door. The thumping music jarring the walls of the establishment could plainly be heard as soon as they got out of the car.

"Do you want to stay here while I run in and get the cup?" Katie asked, wondering if maybe her former mother-in-law would prefer to pass on the whole Pelican's Roost experience. "I'll be right back."

"No. I'll go in," Margo said. "As a matter of fact, I'd rather like a glass of wine."

"Come to think of it, so would I."

The place was decorated with garlands and multicolored lights on top of its regular beach decor. The two women threaded their way through small groups and around couples either standing or sitting around tall tables to get to the bar. As they approached, the bartender—a lanky young man with shoulder-length straight brown hair—was serving a cocktail to a young woman. He winked at her and placed a finger to his lips.

Katie took another look at the cocktail recipient. She couldn't have been much older than Sasha. "How old are you?" she shouted above the din.

The young woman twisted her lips. "What's it to you?"

"Are you twenty-one?" Katie asked.

"Hey, don't be like that other broad that used to come in here," the bartender said. "She was always busting my chops."

"If you're serving drinks to minors, you deserve to have your chops busted," Margo said.

He rolled his eyes. "She looks legal to me. Now, what can I get you?"

"I'm looking for Carl," Katie said.

"Yeah, you found him."

Katie bristled. So this was Nona's nephew? It must be a family trait to flout the rules. "I'm Katie Bonner."

"Yeah." He took about two steps to his left and retrieved a bag from beneath the counter. He brought it back and set it in front of Katie.

The cup and saucer were both surrounded with bubble wrap, which she removed, then picked up the cup and examined it closely. Granted, the light was dim in the bar, but the cup repair looked exceptional. In fact, he'd repaired the previous break that Vance had bungled. It looked like new.

"Thank you," she said sincerely. "What do I owe you?"

"Nothing. Aunt Nona took care of it already. Anything else I can do for you?"

"Uh, I'd like a glass of white wine please."

"Make that two," Margo said.

"Yeah. Coming up."

Before Carl could get their wine, Godfrey Foster came up behind them.

"What luck," he said. "Finding myself here alone when two pretty, unaccompanied women come walking into the bar."

Both Katie and Margo murmured unenthusiastic hellos.

"Let me buy you a drink," he said.

"No, thank you," Katie said, rewrapping her precious set. "We couldn't possibly impose on you like that."

Carl set the glasses in front of them, gave them a total, and Godfrey handed him a credit card. "I'm too quick for you."

"We appreciate your thoughtfulness, Godfrey," Margo said. "Thank you. I can't get over the kindness of men in McKinlay Mill. You, Ray Davenport . . ."

"Ray?" Godfrey huffed, taking the card back from Carl. "You think Ray Davenport is kind?"

"I do," Margo said. "In fact, he's taking me to lunch tomorrow."

Godfrey shook his head ruefully. "Well, have fun." He

looked out into the crowd. "Excuse me. I see someone I need to speak with."

"Maybe he'll leave me alone now," Margo said, once Godfrey had disappeared into the throng.

"Maybe so . . . now that he knows you prefer Ray."

"Ray's a good guy."

"He is," Katie said.

"You could do worse."

"Excuse me?"

"I'm just throwing that out there," Margo said. "That family obviously thinks the world of you—Ray included."

Katie didn't know quite what to say to that. Fortunately, she was saved from commenting when she noticed another seemingly underage girl receiving a drink from Carl.

"He didn't card her," Katie said.

As they watched, another girl approached. This one wasn't as pretty as the other two had been. Carl asked to see this girl's identification and refused her a drink.

"That rat," Margo muttered.

"Wait, that's the only time he did the right thing!"

"But for the wrong reason."

"True." Katie had to agree with her there. "I wonder how the owner of The Pelican's Roost would feel about what Carl is doing. He could get this place shut down for serving drinks to underage girls."

"You're worried about the bar owner? What about the police? The owner of this bar could only fire him. The police could charge him with contributing to the delinquency of minors."

"He mentioned 'that other chick.' I wonder who he was talking about," Katie said.

Margo shrugged. "Want me to ask him?"

Katie was about to say no when Margo waved Carl over.

"Hey, handsome. Top this glass off, and I'll keep my lips sealed about seeing you serve that cute teenybopper a beer."

Carl rolled his eyes as Katie felt hers nearly pop out of her head. Who knew Margo could be so brash?

The bartender took Margo's glass and added more wine. "Don't think you can try to shake me down like that other old chick. This is a onetime favor."

"What other chick?" Katie asked.

"That one who had the car wreck. They say she was drunk as a skunk . . . but she didn't get that way here. I cut people off when they've had too much."

Somehow Katie doubted that. Was Carl merely covering? Did he believe he could be held responsible if someone left The Pelican's Roost intoxicated and then had an accident?

A group of young men approached the bar a few feet down from where Katie and Margo were sitting. Carl threw up both arms. "Dudes!"

After he'd gone to meet his friends, Katie quietly told Margo that to those not in law enforcement, the story was that Vonne had died in a car accident.

"Then either this young man doesn't know any better, or he wants everyone to think he does."

It was nearly midnight by the time Katie and Margo arrived back at the apartment. Not surprisingly, the parking lot was all but deserted. Erikka's car remained in the parking lot even though the pizzeria was closed. Andy's truck was gone. Had the two of them left together?

"Is anything wrong?" Margo asked.

"No, of course not. I'm just making sure everything looks all right before we get out of the car. Safety first!"

Katie waited until Margo was in the bathroom getting ready for bed before calling Andy's cell phone. She listened as the ringing continued. Five. Six times.

He didn't answer.

Nine

The next morning, Margo again slept in. Katie supposed that was her regular habit—go to bed and get up whenever she felt like it. Must be nice. Katie was up, had the cats fed, and had left a note for Margo on the kitchen table. She was ready to go walking with Sasha and Sadie by seven o'clock. She picked up her phone to call Andy, but there came a knock at the door.

Maybe it's him. Maybe he wants to make up and explain where he was last night.

Katie hurried to the door. It was Sasha. The girl looked darling in a pink track suit with her hair pulled up in a ponytail.

"Sadie said to tell you she's sorry, but she'd forgotten a project that's due on Monday. Ready to go?" Sasha asked.

"I'm ready."

"Dad's teaching one of his woodcarving classes this

morning, and he let me ride to the Square with him. I hope I'm not here too early."

"You're right on time."

As Katie and Sasha headed out to the Square, Katie noticed that Erikka's car was still in the parking lot but that Andy's truck wasn't. Not that the fact that Andy's vehicle wasn't in the parking lot this early on Saturday morning was unusual, but that combined with the fact that Erikka's car was there was worrisome.

"Last night was so much fun," Sasha said.

"Yes, it was. Thank you and your family for having Margo and me over for dinner."

"Sophie really wants to work at the tea shop. When do you think you'll be taking it over?"

"I haven't yet decided that I will," Katie said. "It's a big decision—there's Artisans Alley to consider, the Merchants Association, and financing."

"But you *do* want it, don't you?"

Katie hesitated before confiding, "I do."

Sasha beamed. "Then you'll find a way. I believe in you."

"How are things going with Adam?" Katie asked, eager to change the subject.

"Okay, I guess."

"You know, lots of guys are going to like you all your life, Sasha. Besides beautiful, you're sweet, funny, and thoughtful."

They walked around the Square talking about boys and the upcoming holidays. Sasha mentioned that the Davenports were going to spend a few days with their grandparents soon.

"All of you?" Katie asked, surprised that Ray would join them.

"Yeah. We have such a good time together. I wish you could come, too."

"Me, too." She gave Sasha a one-armed hug.

As soon as they reached Wood U, Sasha said, "I'm pooped. I'm going to stop here."

"Okay. I'll see you later."

The parking lot wouldn't begin to fill with shoppers for at least another hour, so Katie decided to walk another lap. She was surprised Sasha had tired so quickly until she realized the girl hadn't been eating enough. Sasha wasn't merely tired, she was weak. Katie hoped Sophie could get through to her younger sister.

When Katie entered Artisans Alley, she went in search of Vance and found him in the vendors' lounge making a pot of coffee.

"Hey, Vance. Would you do me a favor?" she asked.

"Of course." He grinned. "Provided it's not illegal or immoral."

"Well, there goes that." She laughed. "Seriously, would you mind telling all the vendors when they come in to stay put for a brief meeting before we officially open?"

"No problem. Do you have news about the tea shop you'd like to share?"

"Nothing that exciting. It's about Arthur Henderson. Rose told me he tried to steal a carving from Joan yesterday. I thought we could address how to best handle the matter." She sighed. "I hate to ban him outright. He's old, and he might truly be simply forgetting to pay for things . . ."

"But we can't afford to let him keep doing it," Vance supplied.

"Right. So if you'll corral the vendors, I'll be back in a few minutes to talk with them."

As soon as Katie was settled in her office wearing her Dickens costume and sipping a water—she wasn't quite ready for coffee yet—she called the funeral home in Batavia that Nick had helped her find.

"Good morning. Thomason Funeral Home," a softly distinguished feminine voice answered.

"Hi. My name is Katie Bonner. I'd like to order flowers for Vonne Barnett's memorial service. Um . . . I can't seem to recall if Francine is Vonne's stepmom or her biological mom . . ."

"It makes no difference, dear. I'll see that the flowers go to Ms. Barnett."

"But—"

The receptionist cut her off, asking what type of arrangement Katie would like and how much she wanted to spend. Katie completed the order without finding out what she wanted to know. So much for that idea.

She took a peppermint from the jar on her desk, unwrapped the candy, and crunched it between her molars. She tried Andy's number, but still he didn't answer.

Katie walked back over to the vendors' lounge, pleased to see that almost everyone was there.

"Thank you for agreeing to meet with me this morning," she said. "I'm guessing you're all as concerned about theft—not only by Arthur Henderson, but by others—during this, our busiest time of the year. I understand that yesterday, Arthur took a carving from Joan's booth."

She met Joan's eyes, and Joan nodded.

"It was returned to me, though," she said, "by Vance. When he saw Arthur putting the piece in his pocket, he was quick to get it back from him."

"He kicked up quite a fuss," Vance said. "Said he wasn't stealing anything and that he was putting it in his pocket to keep his hands free while he shopped."

"And that's what I wanted to talk with all of you about," Katie said. "If you'll recall, when we had that sticky-fingered teenager last spring, the investigating officer said that the shoplifter must be outside Artisans Alley with the item before we can actually accuse him or her of theft."

"That girl got away with one of my blown-glass swans," Ed Wilson said.

"And some of my lace," Ida added.

"I lost a couple of pieces of jewelry," Rose said glumly.

"And she was never caught," Vance said. "So, how can we be sure to catch Arthur Henderson outside the store?"

"I say that when the man comes into the store, we waylay him just outside the door," Ed said. "And we'll make him empty his pockets."

"That's not a bad idea," Katie agreed. "I think Ed has a good point. We certainly want to make sure our vendors don't lose any of their merchandise to Arthur or to anyone else."

Ed gave a self-congratulatory grin.

"But we need to expound on it," Katie continued, making Ed's grin dim a watt or two. "When anyone in Artisans Alley sees a potential shoplifting, or believes he or she is the victim of a shoplifter, call me or the person manning the cash desk to give us a description of the suspect."

Katie looked around the room, satisfied with the nodding heads. "At that time, we'll get someone to shadow the shoplifter—and someone to stand outside the main entrance. The person shadowing the suspect will let us know if the item is put down elsewhere so that the person outside doesn't cause any undue commotion or embarrassment."

"What if the person doesn't put the stuff down?" Ida demanded.

"Then the shadower will follow the suspect outside, and together, that vendor and the person on the door will confront the shoplifter. When the item is found in the shoplifter's possession, we'll call the police."

"Sounds like a good plan," Vance said.

"Is there anything else anyone would like to discuss while we're all here?" Katie asked.

"Yes," Godfrey said. "What are we going to do about those bratty ballerinas?"

Katie remembered the chewing gum art someone—supposedly the ballerinas, but that hadn't been proven—left in Godfrey's booth. "Are they causing trouble?"

"They're menaces! That's what they are!" Godfrey's face reddened. "They mess around my booth all the time."

"And they twirl until they get dizzy and run into things," Rose said.

"Yes. They knocked into me at Rhonda's booth on Thursday." Katie looked at Rhonda, who gave her a wan smile.

"They're awfully sweet, though," Rhonda said. "I think they're simply excited about their upcoming performance and the holidays." She glanced at Godfrey. "They're just little girls."

"We'll keep an eye on them, too," Katie said quickly, before Godfrey could go off on a rant. "If they're caught making any mischief, let me know, and I'll talk with the dance studio owner to see if she can rein them in a bit. Anything else?"

No one spoke. Katie clapped her hands. "Let's have a great sales day!" she called, which was received with hoots and applause. She smiled, but it was short-lived.

When Katie returned to her office, she tried Andy's number once again. He still didn't answer. She realized he should've been at work by now, and she started to get worried. Maybe something bad had happened the previous night.

She got up, grabbed her jacket, and—still wearing the Dickens costume—sprinted to the pizzeria. She was both relieved and irritated to see that Andy and one other member of his staff was there working.

"Good morning, Sunshine!" Andy called out to her. "Let me get these cinnamon rolls in the oven, and we'll talk. I'm trying out a couple of new flavors—cinnamon pumpkin and apple cinnamon. I'm eager to see what you think."

Katie stood in the front of the shop feeling like an idiot as Andy finished arranging the cinnamon rolls on a large baking sheet. He slid the rolls into the oven, washed his hands, and came to greet her.

He started to give her a kiss, but she turned her face away.

"Let's talk in my office," Andy said. "Jeremy, keep an eye on the rolls, and if I'm not back when the timer goes off, get them out immediately."

"Sure thing!"

Andy walked Katie back to his office and closed the door. She whirled to face him. "I've been trying to call you."

"I had to get the cinnamon rolls made."

"Last night, too?"

"I was busy." His face was devoid of emotion, and Katie wondered if he was a poker player.

"Did Erikka work all night? I see that her car hasn't left the parking lot since yesterday."

"It wouldn't start last night. I gave her a ride home."

"I see." Katie pressed her lips together.

"It wasn't like that."

"So, how was it? Did you merely drop her off and go straight home?"

He blew out a breath.

Katie tried to get around him. She desperately wanted to get out of the office and out of the pizzeria before she made a fool of herself.

Andy blocked her way. "I went inside and Erikka and I talked for a while . . . and we shared a bottle of wine . . . which is why I was late getting to the pizzeria this morning to start the cinnamon rolls. In fact, the apple cinnamon rolls were her idea. The cinnamon pumpkin was mine. I know how much you enjoy pumpkin."

Katie's hands clenched into fists. "Did you spend the night with her?"

"No. We talked until after midnight . . . that's all."

"Get out of my way," Katie said tightly. "I need to get back to work."

"Why are you so angry with me? You had dinner at Ray Davenport's house."

"With his family and Margo . . . who is having lunch with Ray today. I even planned to see if you were free to have dinner with Margo and me after the tree-lighting ceremony, but—hey—you've probably made plans with Erikka already." She hurried around him, not wanting him to see the tears burning in her eyes.

"You're being unfair."

Even though she knew what Andy said was true, Katie just kept going.

~~~~~~

When Katie walked back into Artisans Alley, the place was swamped. She was glad—she was desperate for a distraction. She stepped behind cash desk three and called out that she could help the next person in line.

A young woman with long curly brown hair and caramel-colored eyes came to the counter. Katie recalled that the woman had worked off and on at Afternoon Tea for its previous owners.

"Janine—hey, it's great to see you!" she said. "You haven't been at the tea shop lately."

Janine leaned over so she could speak quietly. "That's because Ms. Barnett let me go. She said she couldn't afford to keep me there. I'm working at a grocery store in Greece now, but I miss the tea shop."

Katie also lowered her voice. "Did you hear that Francine is selling the place?"

Janine nodded. "There's no way I could afford it, though. I don't have much of a credit history yet, and no bank would loan me the amount of money it would take to assume ownership of Afternoon Tea based on my salary."

"Would you mind giving me your phone number please?" Katie asked. "I'd like to talk with you about it when we both have more time."

"Sure." Janine wrote her name and number on a slip of paper and handed it to Katie.

Margo breezed up to the cash desk beside Katie, greeted Janine, and began wrapping her purchases. "If I'm going to be a fixture here at Artisans Alley, I should make myself useful, shouldn't I?"

Katie forced a smile. She knew Margo was just trying to be nice, but her presence could still grate on Katie's nerves.

Only a few more days, Katie told herself. *Only a few more days.*

~~~~~~

When the rush died down, Katie went back to her office, and Margo returned to Chad's Pad. Katie was reviewing the agenda for the next Merchants Association meeting when Ray Davenport poked his head into her office.

"Got a second?" he asked.

"Sure. Come on in."

He came inside, closed the door, and sank into the chair at the side of her desk.

"Thank you again for dinner last night."

He waved away her gratitude with a large right hand. "Yeah, yeah. Just remember you owe me one."

"I'll keep that in mind, but I'll have to take you guys out to dinner. My apartment isn't big enough to accommodate the whole Davenport clan."

"I don't mean for dinner."

"Oh, you mean for walking with Sasha? That was my pleasure."

"No, that's not what I mean, either," he said. "You seemed sad or out of sorts last night, and I thought—" He looked over his shoulder to make sure they wouldn't be interrupted. "I thought maybe you could use a break."

She frowned.

"From Margo," he added.

"No. It's fine." She smiled. "But I appreciate your looking out for me."

"Anytime."

"You know, I was wondering . . . did Vonne have alcohol in her system when she died?" Katie asked.

Ray turned down the corners of his mouth. "I don't know. But I can find out. Why?"

Katie told him about Carl, the bartender at The Pelican's Roost. "Apparently, he has a habit of serving pretty, under-age girls. When Margo called him on it, he told her not to be like that 'other old chick' who died in the car wreck. Carl seemed to think the old chick was 'drunk as a skunk' but also intimated that she either had blackmailed him or was threatening to. Even though Vonne wasn't that old, I got the feeling it was her he was talking about."

"*Old* might just be some peculiarity in the way Carl speaks. Although, lately, Vonne had been looking older than her years."

"I think her drinking and whatever was driving her to drink was the cause of that," Katie said.

"I'll see what I can do about having a deputy talk to Carl," Ray said. "If a vice cop catches him selling to mi-nors, he's going to be in big trouble. If he *was* talking about Vonne, then he might tell them everything he knows about her—maybe something, maybe nothing—in order to get a lesser charge."

There came a knock at the door. It was Sasha and Margo.

"We're ready," Sasha said.

"Care to join us?" Ray asked. "I'll have two beautiful women on my arm—might as well have three."

Katie laughed. "But you only have two arms."

"I'll let you have mine," Sasha offered.

"As wonderful as the offer is, I've got a lot of work to catch up on. Maybe next time."

She was still smiling as the trio headed off for lunch. Despite the way her day had started, it was getting better . . . at least, a little.

~~~~~

Margo and the Davenports hadn't been gone long before there was a knock at Katie's door.

"Come on in!" she called, half expecting it to be Margo, Sasha, or Ray, either having forgotten something or trying to cajole her into going with them again. Had the latter been the case, she'd have gone this time.

Instead, her visitor was Francine Barnett.

"Hi, Francine. What can I do for you?" Katie figured she already knew, but she'd hear the woman out.

Francine closed the door and took the seat Ray had so recently abandoned. "I didn't open the tea shop today . . . not that it would matter all that much anyway, given how slow business has been lately. I think you could really turn the place around if you wanted to. Have you made your decision yet?"

Katie decided to be frank with her. "I'm interested in acquiring the shop, Francine, but the first bank I approached wouldn't give me loan terms I was happy with, and I'm afraid the terms won't be any better from another bank."

"You don't know that. Not without trying." She straightened, to make herself even taller in the chair. "I know you've been checking up on me."

"What? Why would you think that?"

"The receptionist at Thomason's Funeral Home told me you'd asked her whether I was Vonne's mother or her stepmother. She thought it was an odd question." Francine narrowed her eyes at Katie. "If you'd wanted to know something about my relationship with Vonne, Katie, why didn't you simply ask me?"

"Um . . ." Katie faltered. The truth was that the nature of their relationship was none of Katie's business. She just wanted to know why Francine was being so cold in the face of her daughter's death. But she couldn't very well say that to Francine.

"It's not common knowledge, but since it's apparently so important to you, I'll tell you. Vonne was my late husband's biological daughter. My husband, Booth, and his . . ." She cleared her throat. "Distant cousin . . . were Vonne's parents."

Feeling awkward, Katie decided to change the subject. "Francine, may I get you some coffee?"

"No, thanks." She was in the midst of her story now and apparently didn't want to stop. "Booth and Nancy had grown up together and had always been fond of each other. They hadn't seen each other in about ten years when someone in their family got married—I don't even remember who. I was sick and didn't make the trip to Ohio."

So, Francine and Booth were married at the time that he got another woman pregnant. Pregnant with Vonne. Katie felt sick in the pit of her stomach.

"Francine, please, you don't have to tell me this."

"No, I want to. I've been living with it for a long time," she said. "I knew there was something different about Booth the moment he arrived home. He acted guilty . . . extra attentive to me. He'd get nervous every time the phone rang. He never did confess, though, until Nancy called and told him she was pregnant."

Katie took a peppermint from the jar on her desk, opened it, and popped it into her mouth. She didn't bite it in two like she normally did. She was hoping the flavor would help settle her roiling stomach, and she wished she'd never poked this hornet's nest.

"Nancy didn't know what to do," Francine continued. "She wasn't married, and she was afraid the family would disown her if they found out. That's when Booth finally sat down and spilled it all to me. And I, of course, came up with the solution."

"You didn't toss him out on his ear?"

Francine shook her head. "No. I decided that Nancy would come live with Booth and me until after the baby was born. The story would be that I was having a difficult pregnancy, and Nancy was coming to help out. In fact, Booth and I had been trying for years to have a baby and couldn't conceive. That must've been my fault."

"Oh, Francine—"

"Anyway, once the baby was born, Booth and I would raise the child as our own and Nancy could go back home."

"What incredible strength you had," Katie said.

"Yeah, well . . . it was even harder than I'd expected it to be. And then seeing how much Booth adored Vonne when she arrived made it even worse. I'd hoped to love her like she was my own, but she looked so much like Nancy . . . and Booth doted on her so much. And when Booth died, Vonne began acting more and more like her willful, degenerate mother." She shook her head. "And that's why she wound up dead."

"I'm so sorry."

"Well . . . it's good to get that off my chest." She rose from the chair. "I do hope you'll consider trying again for a loan to buy Afternoon Tea."

"It's a big decision, but I am interested. I need to do a little more research and talk with some people. You know, financing, et cetera."

Francine nodded. "I'd appreciate it if you could let me know sooner rather than later. I'd like to begin putting this entire twenty-five-year-long fiasco behind me."

Katie nodded and watched the older woman leave.

Francine considered Vonne's birth mother degenerate? She had only *hoped* to love Vonne?

Vonne was not one of Katie's favorite people, but she felt yet another pang of sympathy for the poor dead woman. She'd apparently been unloved and possibly unlovable.

And where did Katie stand? Was Andy up to something with Erikka? Had Ray taken a shine to her?

She felt more confused with every passing hour.

Ten

Francine had been gone less than a minute before Katie closed her office door and was on the phone calling Nick Ferrell.

"Katie, what's up?"

"Francine Barnett's hackles—that's what's up."

"Oh no. What did you do?"

"I did what you told me to do. I called Thomason's to order flowers and asked the receptionist whether Vonne was Francine's daughter or stepdaughter."

"So, what did she say?"

"Nothing to me. But she certainly clued Francine in that I was—in Francine's words—checking up on her."

"Ugh."

"Ugh is right. She just stormed out of my office."

"Are you angry with me?" Nick asked. "Because you sound angry."

"I'm not angry with you. It was a great suggestion. I thought it would work. I just wasn't prepared for how well it *did* work."

"Spill."

Katie made Nick swear to the strictest of confidences, and then she told him the tale Francine had relayed to her.

"Oh my gosh," Nick said. "That's horrible. I admire Francine's ability to put the past behind her—although it doesn't sound as if she entirely did—but I wonder if Vonne might've been better off with her birth mother."

"She very well might have been. In fact, Francine said she was just like Nancy and that she became more like her mother after Booth died. She said that's why Vonne wound up dead. She never did say what happened to Nancy, though."

"If only we knew Nancy's last name," Nick began.

"No. I'm staying out of it. I think I've done enough damage."

"I don't know that you did any damage at all, dear. It must've been horrible for Francine to have Nancy live with her and her husband while Nancy was pregnant with Booth's child," he said. "Francine would have been watching them every day, gauging their behavior, knowing Nancy was giving Booth something she never could."

"I'm not sure I could've done what she did," Katie said. "Had I been in Francine's shoes, I think I'd have kicked both Booth and Nancy to the curb."

"I wonder why she didn't. Did she love Booth that much? Did she want a child that badly?" He sighed. "And then to have little Vonne be born and cherished by Booth—maybe more so because she reminded him of her mother."

Katie chuckled. "Nick, you should be a novelist."

"Maybe I will write a book. I could change the names and dramatize Francine's story. It's like something right out of a Tennessee Williams play. By the way, did Francine mention the fact that Vonne was pregnant?"

"No. We didn't talk that much about Vonne—our conversation was more about Francine. And it was a fairly one-sided conversation at that—I mostly listened."

"Hmm. Do you think Francine even knew Vonne was pregnant? Maybe she *did* know her stepdaughter was pregnant and refused to help raise another child that wasn't her own."

"What are you saying?" Katie asked. "Surely, you don't think Francine—" She stopped, unwilling to put the dire thought into words.

"No, no, of course not. I'm just working on my novel now." He chuckled.

"Are you seriously going to write one?"

"I might," he said. "What else do I have to do during the winter when Sassy Sally's is having its slow season?"

A knock on Katie's office door interrupted her conversation. A second later, Andy poked his head inside.

"I'll look forward to reading that novel, then," she said. She told him she'd see him at the tree-lighting ceremony later that evening before she ended the call.

"Who's writing a novel?" Andy said.

"Nick. Maybe." She nodded toward the box he held. "What's that?" She could guess by the tantalizing aromas drifting her way, but she wanted to be as difficult as she could be.

"Peace offering." He pushed the door closed and placed the box on the desk.

Katie opened it to see . . . Actually, she wasn't sure what it was. It appeared to be meat stuffed into a pale green, elongated roll. She looked up at him. "What is this?"

Andy grinned. "It's a Yule log. I used food coloring to dye some pizza dough green—we have red, too—for this limited-time-only holiday treat. After turning the dough a festive color, I roll it out, fill it with sauce, pepperoni, sausage, mushrooms, and peppers. Then I roll it up, bake it, and cut it into six-inch Yule logs."

"Was this another of Erikka's ideas?" Katie asked.

"Nope. This one was entirely my own. Clever, huh?"

"It does look . . . interesting."

"Taste it," he urged.

Katie was more in the mood for an apology than a pizza Yule log. "In a minute." She closed the box. "Did Erikka get her car fixed?"

"It's in the shop right now getting a new ignition switch," he said.

She lowered her eyes to the box.

"Katie, you have to believe me, nothing happened between Erikka and me last night."

"You shared a bottle of wine."

He sat on the chair that had seen its third visitor in less than an hour, turned her chair to face him, and took her hands. "Yes, we had some wine. And we talked. That's it."

She was stubbornly silent.

"Katie, I'm sorry."

She still had no words. All she could do was imagine Andy and Erikka sitting on a sofa drinking wine and engaging in intimate conversation. Lovely Erikka, tossing back her wavy hair, laughing, wetting her lips in an invitation for Andy to kiss her.

Andy squeezed her hands. "I'd like to take you and Margo out to dinner after the tree-lighting ceremony if that offer is still on the table."

"I'll need to speak with Margo to make sure she hasn't already made plans with Ray."

"If she has, could we have dinner alone?"

She shrugged. "I guess so."

"What's it gonna take to get you over being angry with me?" Andy asked.

Katie finally met his eyes. "Maybe a bottle of wine and intimate conversation until the wee hours of the morning."

Missing her barb, or ignoring it on purpose, Andy said,

"I'll look forward to that as soon as Margo leaves. How are you two getting along, anyway?"

"Better than I expected. Margo is being nicer to me now—for the most part—than she ever was when Chad was alive."

"What else is going on in your life? Have you come to a decision about the tea shop?"

"If it were an ideal world, I could assume ownership of the shop and put someone else in charge of the day-to-day operations. But the world isn't ideal, and thanks to the bank, that may never happen."

"Let me float you a loan."

"I appreciate the offer, but I feel it's best that you and I not mix business with pleasure."

Andy rolled his eyes. "I'm already your landlord."

"See? That's plenty of business between us. Maybe on Monday, I can try another bank."

"Don't push me away," he said. "I'm here if you need me."

Or until you decide you'd rather be with Erikka?

Katie looked away, hating herself for having such thoughts . . . but they wouldn't go away, either.

"Come on. Try the Yule log. I want your honest opinion."

She blew out a breath and opened the box. It really did smell divine. "Do I pick it up, or should I get a fork from the vendors' lounge?"

"You might prefer a fork," he said. "Be right back."

When he returned, he had a plastic fork and some paper towels. "Here you go." He wrinkled his brow. "I should've brought Margo one, too. I'd like to get her opinion on the Yule log. I'm guessing she has a refined palate."

Katie gritted her teeth. He wasn't helping his cause by insinuating that Margo's palate was more refined than hers. Of course, it was possible he hadn't meant that at all and that everything Andy said today was being sifted through Katie's anger, but still . . .

She took the fork and cut into the pizza Yule log. As unflattering as it was to admit—even to herself—Katie hoped she wouldn't like it. No such luck. The thing was delicious, and she couldn't help her appreciation for the taste from showing all over her face.

Andy gave a triumphant bark of laughter. "That good, huh? Yeah!"

Katie swallowed and wiped her mouth with one of the paper towels. "Yes. It's wonderful. You've got a hit on your hands."

He kissed her cheek. "Thanks, babe. Later you can try the apple cinnamon rolls and pumpkin cinnamon rolls and tell me what you think of those."

~~~~~~

After Andy had gone back to the pizzeria, Katie ate the rest of the pizza Yule log. It really was delicious. She'd help spread the word about them to the Artisans Alley vendors. Maybe Andy could make up a flyer describing the holiday treat and place it in the vendors' lounge.

She dismissed that idea for the time being and allowed her thoughts to turn to the tea shop. What if she called it English Ivy Tea in honor of her dream bed-and-breakfast, the English Ivy Inn? At least, that way she could retain some small portion of her dream. But no, that ship had already sailed without her.

And she couldn't see herself simply giving up Artisans Alley completely. Sure, the vendors and artisans were capable of overseeing themselves for the most part, but Katie still liked to think it was important for her to be there.

Still, if she could hire someone to handle the daily operation of the shop with Katie acting as supervisor, then it might just work. And Janine could be the perfect person for the job. She already had experience at Afternoon Tea, and she didn't seem happy with her job at the grocery store, but it was a two-or-more person operation. What about the daily paperwork? They had a lot to talk about.

Katie opened her desk drawer where she'd stored the slip of paper Janine had given her with her cell number on it. She considered calling the young woman, but she didn't want to get either of their hopes up . . . not just yet. Still, it couldn't hurt to get Janine's take on her idea. If she turned Katie down flat, then Katie would know that wasn't an option.

She dialed the number and was pleased when Janine answered right away.

"Janine, this is Katie Bonner. I'm considering assuming ownership of Afternoon Tea. Nothing is final yet, and I'm not even certain I can manage the buyout at this time. But if I can, I wanted to see if you'd be interested in supervising the day-to-day operations."

"Oh, I'd love that!" Janine squealed. "It would be the next-best thing to owning it myself."

"I'm glad to hear that. I was going to wait to talk with you because I didn't want to get your hopes up in case the deal falls through, but then I decided I should see if you could do it because I think you're the perfect person for the position."

"I truly appreciate the confidence you have in me," Janine said. "As you know, I already have experience working at Afternoon Tea, but I don't know if you're aware of my educational background."

"Refresh my memory please," Katie said.

"I'm at the top of my class at Monroe Community College working toward an associate's degree in hospitality management and certificates in food management and culinary arts."

"That's impressive."

"Thank you," Janine said.

"Would working for me hinder your education?"

"Not really. A lot of my classes are at night anyway. "I'd be happy to drop my résumé off to you at your office in Artisans Alley."

"That'll be fine," Katie said. "But it isn't necessary. If I do assume ownership of Afternoon Tea—which, of course, I'd change the name—you're my only choice for supervisor."

"Wow, Ms. Bonner, that means so much to me!"

"Please call me Katie. Hopefully, we'll be working together soon."

"I hope so." She paused. "How soon will you know?"

"Within the next week or two," Katie said.

"I'll be crossing my fingers."

"I'll let you know as soon as I'm able to do so."

Things might still be up in the air for a few months, giving Janine more time for her studies before Katie revamped and reopened the tea shop. The idea made Katie feel invigorated and she got up, closed her office door behind her, and went to see if Rose and the other cashiers needed any help ringing up sales. Since there was a lull and they didn't seem terribly busy, Katie decided to walk security.

When she got upstairs, she noticed Godfrey diligently working on a canvas. Since no one was in his booth, she stepped inside to talk with him. Though sweating profusely as he worked, he didn't smell as bad today. But he wasn't wearing his Dickens costume, either.

"Hello, Godfrey."

"Did you and Margo enjoy yourselves at The Pelican's Roost last night?"

"I guess so. We weren't really there to have fun, though. We were there to pick up a bone china teacup that Nona Fiske had knocked off my desk and broken. Her nephew Carl repaired it."

"Carl, the bartender?" Godfrey looked up from his lint, seemingly surprised to find that Carl could do such delicate work.

"Yeah. Do you know him well?"

"Who, Carl? I know his name. I don't frequent the bars that much, Ms. Bonner. I'm not an alcoholic," he said defensively.

"That's not what I meant at all," Katie said quickly. "It's just that when Margo and I were there, we noticed Carl serving beer to pretty young girls without asking for their identification. We got the feeling it was something he maybe did often."

"Oh. Sorry I jumped to conclusions. Since the separation, I have indulged too much on more than one occasion, but it's not a problem . . . just a coping mechanism. And yes, I have seen Carl serve alcohol to underage girls before. But I keep my mouth shut. I don't want to cause trouble for anyone."

"I'd prefer not to cause trouble for anyone, either," Katie said. "But there's a reason underage drinking laws are in place. What Carl is doing could destroy one of those kids."

"It's none of my business."

"I wonder if Vonne Barnett made it hers," Katie murmured. "Do you know if she went to The Pelican's Roost often?"

"As I already told you, I don't go there regularly myself, so I couldn't say for sure . . . but I did see Vonne there a time or two."

"I can't help wondering if she's the old chick Carl was talking about." She told Godfrey what Carl had said that had made her and Margo think Vonne had been blackmailing Carl.

"That doesn't make sense," Godfrey said. "For one thing, Vonne wasn't old. Why would Carl refer to her that way? Second, if Carl thought Vonne would report him, then why wouldn't he merely stop the behavior? I mean, the police have to catch him in the act, right?"

"I imagine so." Katie shook her head. "No. That doesn't make sense. I was just trying to make connections where

there probably are none. Ever since the police ruled Vonne's
death a murder—"

"What? A murder?" Godfrey's eyes practically bulged.
"But I thought Vonne died in a car accident."

"Really? I thought everyone on Victoria Square had heard
the news by now. You must be as out of the loop as I am."

"Murdered." Godfrey slumped onto his stool. "Who
would've murdered Vonne? She was a sweet girl. I . . .
we . . ." He shook his head.

"You . . . what?" Katie wasn't sure she wanted to know.

"We went on a date . . . once. We'd both been drinking.
It was nothing serious. I just . . ." He ran a hand over the
lower part of his face. "So you . . . you thought maybe Carl
did something? Caused the wreck or whatever?"

Katie studied the man before her. "I believe anything is
possible." She nodded at the canvas, hoping to soften her
next question with a bit of flattery. "I've always loved van
Gogh's sunflowers. That's going to be . . . something special."

"Thanks."

"So . . . you took your costume to the cleaner's?"

"Lucy did. We had dinner together last night before I
went to The Pelican's Roost, and she offered to drop it off
for me."

"I'm glad. It sounds as if things might be on the mend."

He shrugged. "We shall see."

Did that mean he wants a reconciliation . . . or not?

"I'd better go. Lots to do," Katie said, and started off
down the aisle. Five booths down, she looked over her
shoulder to see that Godfrey had not gone back to his work
and still sat there, looking thoughtful. And why had Katie
brought up the subject of Carl, anyway? She was telling the
wrong people about his probable misdeeds. What she should
have done was call the Sheriff's Office, even if Ray said he'd
handle it.

As she trundled down the back stairs that ended in the

vendors' lounge, she pondered why she hadn't done so. Had she, too, wanted to report Carl's illegal behavior but not have her name tied to the accusation?

If so, she was no better than Godfrey Foster.

Eleven

The sky outside was already a deep blue when Ray, Sasha, and Margo strolled into Artisans Alley at nearly closing time. Katie stood with Rose at cash desk one, helping out as her wrapper. "Did you have a good time?"

"Wonderful. We just stopped in to see if you need me to help, dear," Margo said.

"We're good." Katie would've said that even if she'd been drowning in a sea of customers. Was Margo asking for Ray's benefit, or did she feel guilty that she'd been gone all afternoon? It wasn't as if Margo was a vendor and was expected to help out or anything. She was a guest, for goodness' sake.

"Okay. I believe I'll go up to Chad's Pad for a few minutes, then." She stood on her tiptoes to kiss Ray's cheek. "Thanks so much for a delightful afternoon." She hugged

Sasha. "And you're just a burst of sunshine, darling. See you both later!"

It was all Katie could do not to roll her eyes. Margo was acting like the three of them were the perfect little family from a 1950s sitcom. So . . . was the relationship between Margo and Ray developing into something more than friendship? It could be good for them if it did . . . she guessed . . . but she didn't necessarily like the idea.

"You're a burst of sunshine, too, Margo. I'm going to look at all the cool merch, so I'll walk upstairs with you." Sasha took off without a backward glance.

Ray stayed behind with Katie, as if he had something he wanted to discuss with her. She desperately hoped it wasn't his growing feelings for Margo. That discussion just might make her sick. She decided she'd launch into her conversation first.

She wrapped the candles her customer had bought in paper before placing them in a bag, while Rose accepted the woman's payment; then they both wished her a good evening. Before another customer could arrive, Katie scooted away from the register.

"Shouldn't we go find Sasha?" she asked Ray.

"Oh, I'm sure she's—" He broke off when he noticed Katie's expression urging him to go along with her. "You know, you're right. Hard to tell what that girl will get into."

She hurried Ray away from the customers and vendors to an unattended booth. "I doubt you've learned anything new since lunchtime—especially since you've been busy—but it appears just about everyone in McKinlay Mill thought Vonne was driving drunk when she died," Katie told him.

"Actually, I was able to slip away and call one of my friends at the Sheriff's Office. Although there was alcohol in Vonne's bloodstream when she was found, she was well below the legal limit of intoxication. Had she been driving— and you and I know she wasn't—she wouldn't have been impaired."

"I wonder why Carl assumed she was drunk, then. Do you think she'd been at The Pelican's Roost before she died?"

"Possibly."

"I thought it was common knowledge by now that Vonne was murdered, but so many people are still attributing her death to the accident. What's up with that—wishful thinking? No one wants to think there's a killer among us?"

"The medical examiner hasn't made the actual cause of death public yet. The Sheriff's Office hopes the killer will somehow trip him- or herself up."

"Oh." Katie tried to think of all the people she'd discussed Vonne's death with. She didn't think she'd mentioned the possibility of murder rather than an accident with anyone who didn't know already, except Rose. And Godfrey. Still . . . "I hope I wasn't a major contributing factor behind the news that Vonne was murdered, then."

"Nah. Too many people in Victoria Square knew the truth almost immediately. You know how quickly word travels around here. But the greater McKinlay Mill community still probably thinks Vonne died in an accident."

"People like Carl?"

"Right," he said. "By the way, my friend is putting a couple of vice cops on duty at The Pelican's Roost tonight. If Nona's nephew pulls his contributing-to-the-delinquency shtick tonight, he'll be arrested." He jerked his head toward the hallway. "Come on. We'd better find my daughter before she tries to buy out the place."

"How did Sasha seem at lunch?" Katie asked. "She got tired fairly quickly when we walked this morning."

"Maybe you're just more fit than you think, because she was fine."

"Did she eat well?"

"She did okay. I'm thinking Sophie probably got through to her."

"Good." Katie had her doubts, but she kept them to herself.

They found Sasha in Rhonda Simpson's booth. She'd found a set of tea towels beautifully monogrammed with the letter M.

"Look, Dad! Aren't these beautiful? I want to get them for Margo."

"Sure, kiddo. That'd be nice." Ray took out his wallet and gave Sasha the money.

"Better hurry," Katie warned. "They'll be closing the store in just a few minutes."

Just then Rhonda appeared—no doubt to tidy her booth before the next day's customers arrived, and to check up on her sales for the day. "Hey, Katie, have you got a second?" Rhonda asked.

"We'll see you tonight at the tree lighting," Ray said.

"Bye, Katie!" Sasha hugged her friend before hurrying away. "See you tonight!"

"What a sweet girl," Rhonda said.

"She sure is." They watched father and daughter head for the cash desks.

Rhonda spoke first. "Has Nona mentioned me to you lately?"

Katie rolled her eyes. "No, she hasn't. What now?"

"Actually, it's a good thing . . . I guess. She wants us to collaborate—to come up with some complementary items to sell in sets. She wants this done as soon as possible so we can capitalize on the holiday shopping season."

"I don't know which is worse," Katie said with a laugh, "having Nona working for you or against you."

"I think having her work against me, as in a lawsuit, is definitely worse than working with her. I can always stall if she doesn't like whatever designs I come up with." Rhonda shrugged. "Still, it makes sense. If someone especially favors a particular quilt or linen pattern, it stands to reason that they'd want a full set. It might be good for both of us."

"Well, good luck. I hope the venture is a success."

Rhonda gave her a thumbs-up, and Katie headed to

Chad's Pad, where she found Margo staring at her favorite painting—the one with the young woman standing in the wheat field.

"You did a great thing," Katie said to her former mother-in-law.

"What's that?" Margo said, dragging her eyes from the painting.

"You worked some kind of magic spell on Nona Fiske. She actually took your advice and is working with Rhonda Simpson."

Margo smiled. "Good. I'm glad the matter was amicably resolved."

"I could use you at the Merchants Association."

The older woman had turned back to the painting, and Katie wasn't sure she'd even heard her.

"You know, I want you to take that with you when you leave McKinlay Mill," Katie said.

"Excuse me?"

"I want you to have that painting. If you're afraid it'll get ruined in transit, I'll have it professionally packed and sent to you at home."

Margo gasped and pulled Katie into a hug. "Oh, thank you! Thank you so much."

Katie gently extricated herself from the embrace. "Do you and Ray have plans following the tree-lighting ceremony?"

"No. Ray and his daughters are going to watch a Christmas movie. They invited us to join them, but I didn't know what you might have planned. Besides, Sasha mentioned they'd watched the movie every year for as long as she could remember." A wistful expression flitted across Margo's face. "I know the movie is something they enjoyed with their mother, and I felt it would be best not to intrude upon such a private moment. It reminded me of some of our old Christmas traditions."

"I agree. Andy invited the two of us to dinner. We can go, if you'd like."

"I'd love it," Margo said. "By all means, call him and take him up on the offer."

~~~~~~

Back in her office, Katie paused while straightening her desk before leaving for the day and decided to call Andy. "Wha'cha doing?" she asked.

"Figuring out next week's cheese order."

"I meant later tonight. Is that offer of dinner for Margo and me still open?"

"Why, yes, it is," he answered, and seemed pleased about it. "I'm glad you're not angry with me anymore," he said.

Katie didn't know how to respond to that, since she wasn't sure she was completely over his night of wine and conversation with Erikka. Instead, she changed the subject to Vonne.

"What exactly have you heard about Vonne's death?" she asked.

"Not much. I did hear it was murder rather than an accident, but you already knew that. Why?"

"When I went to The Pelican's Roost to get the teacup Nona Fiske's nephew repaired for me, Carl—he's the bartender and Nona's nephew—indicated that he believed Vonne had died because she was driving drunk and crashed her car. I mentioned it to Ray because I thought it was common knowledge now that Vonne had been murdered and placed in the car to make it look like an accident."

"And?"

"And he said the medical examiner hadn't released that information to the general public. Andy, do you think I might've somehow compromised the investigation by talking about the murder?"

"Not unless you think one of your friends is the murderer." He chuckled. "I'm only kidding. Don't worry about anything you might've said. I'm confident the deputies would keep the most important details secret. You didn't spill any beans that might've led to the conviction of the killer. I'm sure of it."

Katie thought about the fact that Vonne was pregnant. She certainly hadn't divulged that information to anyone. The only other two people she knew of who were aware of her condition were Ray and Seth, and they'd both told her about the pregnancy, not the other way around. She hadn't even confided that piece of news to Andy.

Still, she felt uncomfortable about the whole situation. Here she thought she was being helpful by gathering information, and instead might be responsible for putting the investigation into Vonne's death into jeopardy.

~~~~~~

After closing Artisans Alley, Katie and Margo went back to the apartment to feed the cats and slip into warmer clothing for the tree-lighting ceremony. The Merchants Association had conducted a raffle at their November meeting, and Ray, the Square's newest retailer, had won the honor of officially lighting the tree.

There was an air of excitement as the two women approached the grassy area between the vacant shop beside Sassy Sally's and Wood U. Vance's church choir was standing beneath one of the wrought-iron gas lamps dressed in Dickensian costumes singing carols. One distinguished-looking gentleman was accompanying them on the violin, while a young woman played a flute.

"How delightful!" Margo exclaimed.

Katie smiled at Vance and Janey, standing side by side singing. She wondered where Vance Jr. was. She was sure he was there, but he was at the age that singing in the choir—not to mention dressing like a character from *A Christmas Carol*—wasn't how he wanted to be caught by his peers. He was probably lounging against a building somewhere with his face formed into a mask of boredom and apathy.

Nick Ferrell and his partner, Don Parsons, came up beside the women.

"Isn't this magical?" Nick asked. "I adore this time of year." He waved to one of the choir members—a broad-shouldered woman with a wide smile—who wriggled her fingers at him in response.

"So do I," Margo said. "I'm sorry I'll be leaving soon."

"You'll have to come back," Katie said, surprising herself by not only saying the words but meaning them. "I realize you won't be able to make it back this month, but we're here year-round."

"And if you don't want to stay in Katie's teensy little place, we'll give you the friends and family discount at Sassy Sally's," Don said. "No offense, Katie, but you have to admit, Margo would likely be much more comfy staying in a suite with us."

Margo laughed. "Thank you." She turned to Katie. "Really, I'd love to visit again."

Katie wondered if Don had mentioned Margo's staying at Sassy Sally's on her next visit because Nick had told him that she and Katie were getting on each other's nerves. Either way, he was right—it would be better for both of them if Margo had a room and Katie had her apartment to herself during Margo's next visit.

She noticed that Godfrey was talking with Francine Barnett and wondered what he was up to. Was he now moving in on the distraught mom? How creepy would that be after he'd dated Vonne? She inwardly chastised herself for jumping to conclusions. Had it been someone else, she wouldn't have been as quick to judge. It was possible Godfrey was merely expressing his condolences to Francine.

She heard the sound of Andy's voice drifting across the parking lot and turned to see him arriving with Erikka. They were laughing, and Erikka was looking up at him. They looked happy. They looked like a couple. It almost turned Katie's stomach. She plastered on a smile and greeted them.

"Hi," Andy said. "Margo, it's good to see you."

"Good to see you, too."

Vance's choir took a break from singing and began handing out cups of hot chocolate from a small red-and-white cart. The high school band moved into position and got ready to play.

Sasha hurried over to Katie and whispered, "That's him—that's Adam—on the snare drum."

"He's handsome," Katie said. And, admittedly, he was a cute kid, and she was sure Sasha was over-the-moon for him in his band uniform.

Sasha waved to him, and he winked at her. The band played "The Little Drummer Boy," which really accentuated Adam's skill on that snare drum.

"I wondered where you disappeared to," Ray said, approaching Sasha. "I should've known."

"Sometimes women like to hang around together and talk about you guys," Margo said.

Ray merely laughed and shook his head.

A local news crew arrived on the scene in their big van complete with a satellite uplink.

"It appears we've hit the big time," Ray observed.

"One of the reporters is doing the countdown to the tree lighting," Katie said. "And he'll be introducing you to the crowd, Ray."

Ray blew out a breath. "Great. I wish I'd never won that stupid raffle. I didn't know lighting the tree would be this big a deal."

"Oh, Dad, I'm glad you won! And we'll be with you. Don't be nervous."

"Who said I was nervous? I've been on TV dozens of times talking about one crime or another. This is child's play." Ray put his arm around his youngest daughter and pulled her close. "But I'm retired . . . and I thought that meant no more crime and no more TV."

"And it appears you can't escape from either," Katie murmured.

Ray frowned at her, and she shrugged.

About fifteen minutes later, the reporter introduced Ray, the newest shop-owner on Victoria Square, as the official tree lighter. Ray brought his daughters to the dais in front of the tree, said a few words—mainly about his beautiful girls and how happy he was to be a part of the Victoria Square community—and flipped the switch. The effect was breathtaking. The enormous Norway spruce sparkled with tiny twinkling lights from the bottom all the way up to the illuminated star that sat atop the tree.

"Wow. That's beautiful," Andy said, sneaking an arm around Katie. "Margo, would you and Katie please join me for dinner?"

"We'd love to," Margo said.

"Dinner sounds wonderful," Erikka murmured. "I haven't eaten since lunch."

"Well, dear, I believe you've caught that handsome news reporter's eye. Perhaps you should go over and say hello . . . maybe offer to buy him a coffee," Margo said. "See you later."

At that moment, Katie could've hugged the woman.

Twelve

The cab of Andy's truck was a little crowded with Andy driving, Katie sitting on the console in the middle, and Margo in the passenger seat. They drove to a steak house about fifteen minutes east of McKinlay Mill. Andy helped Katie out of the truck before going around to open the door for Margo. Once they were inside, the hostess showed them to a booth. Katie and Andy sat on one side, and Margo sat facing them. The decor was mainly wood, long-horned steer skulls, and cowboy regalia.

"I . . . um . . . I didn't know Chad all that well," Andy began, obviously struggling for something to say to Margo, "but he seemed like a really good guy."

"Chad was the best," Margo agreed. She opened the menu and perused it. "So, Katie tells me that neither of you has much time to devote to a relationship."

Katie's jaw dropped, and she, too, became very interested in the menu. How could Margo throw out a statement like that so casually? What would Andy think she'd been telling Margo?

Luckily, the waitress arrived before Katie could speculate further. The hostess had been dressed all in black and looked a bit too sophisticated for the steak house. The waitress in her cowboy hat, jeans, and suede vest was a better fit for the ambience.

"Hi, I'm Melanie!"

Katie started at the young woman's loud, perky voice.

"What can I start you off with to drink?" Melanie asked.

Margo asked for water, Andy ordered a pop, and Katie said she'd have water as well, although just then she could have used something a wee bit stronger. Melanie said she'd get those drinks right out.

Katie still had a death grip on her menu and wouldn't look at either Margo or Andy, although she noticed Andy seemed to be sitting awfully stiffly beside her. Margo either didn't notice or didn't care about their discomfort.

"When your lives are drawing toward twilight, you'll wish you hadn't worked so hard and that you'd concentrated more on the people in your lives," Margo said rather sternly. "You need to think about what you really want most out of life and go for it. Both of you."

That salvo led to a very awkward meal with small talk limited to how nice Melanie was and how good the steaks tasted.

When Melanie returned to ask if anyone was interested in dessert, Katie was quick to say that she'd pass. Andy did likewise, but Margo asked Melanie what she'd recommend.

"Well, our strawberry cheesecake is awfully good," Melanie said. "It's my favorite."

"I'll have a slice of that, then," Margo said. She grinned at Andy. "Surely, you'll indulge in just a bite or two, won't you?"

Andy nodded. "I guess so."

"Great." Margo folded her elegantly manicured hands and placed them on the table as Melanie gathered their dirty dishes.

"Anything else I can get anyone right now?" the waitress asked.

"No, thank you, dear." As Melanie left, Margo leveled her gaze at Andy and Katie.

Katie resisted the urge to duck behind Andy for protection, and she wondered if he felt the same way.

"I'm sorry if I made the two of you uncomfortable," Margo began, "but you obviously care about each other. I'd hate for you to allow your work to interfere with your relationship. My husband is dead—I'm saying this for your benefit, Andy, since Katie knows already. Anyway, Charles died when Chad was still young, and now—especially *now*—I regret that I didn't take more time for myself when Chad was growing up. I devoted my entire life to that child."

I can vouch for that, Katie thought.

"I didn't take time to find someone else to share my life with." Margo lifted one shoulder in a half-shrug. "Of course, it's not too late. But this is about you two, not me. Build your careers and your lives *together*, as a team. That's what Charles and I had, and it was so very special."

Andy visibly swallowed. "Um . . . thank you . . . for sharing that, Margo. I appreciate it. I'm sure Katie does, too."

Katie managed a slight nod even though she *didn't* appreciate it. She knew Margo meant well, but what did she think gave her the right to come to McKinlay Mill and meddle in Katie's love life, of all things? And Margo had wanted to visit the tea shop to see if she felt Katie would be making a wise decision if she invested in it. That was none of Margo's business, either. Chad was the one who had been Margo's child. When he was living, Katie had been nothing but a nuisance or a failure in Margo's eyes—or, at least, that's how she felt.

Melanie arrived with the dessert and three spoons. Katie noticed that Margo handed one to Andy, took the other, and placed the third spoon on the table. Was that an unspoken suggestion that Katie shouldn't partake of the dessert? Well, she'd be darned if Margo Bonner was going to dictate her food choices to her.

She grabbed the third spoon and took a heaping bite of the cheesecake. It wasn't half-bad.

Katie was delighted when it was time to head back home. Had she and Andy thought the cringe-worthy moments were all behind them, though, they were mistaken. As soon as Andy pulled up in front of the pizzeria, Margo asked Katie for her keys.

"I'll go on up to the apartment so the two of you can say good night."

Mouth agape, Katie dug through her purse and produced her keys.

Margo snatched them from her hand. "Thanks for a delightful meal, Andy."

"We'll have to do this again before you leave," he said.

Margo's smile was tentative. "Well, good night."

She got out of the truck and headed for the stairs.

"Wait!" Katie started to bolt from the truck and go after her former mother-in-law. After all, Margo didn't even know which key opened the front door.

Andy put a restraining arm around her. "The woman practically told us to make out. We shouldn't disappoint her."

"Oh, Andy," Katie chided.

"What?"

Katie sidled over the console onto the still-warm seat Margo had vacated.

"Did I say something wrong?" Andy asked, sounding just a little wounded.

"No. It's just . . . I feel so awkward. I was married to her son and now she's trying to play matchmaker for us."

"What's wrong with that? We've been together for more than a year. Are you ashamed of our relationship?"

"No, not in the least. But still . . . it's awkward." That was the best explanation she could come up with.

Andy leaned across the barrier between them, capturing her face and pulling her closer. "Kiss me, you fool."

"Fool?" Katie asked skeptically.

"Fool for love?" Andy suggested, and then leaned in to give Katie a very satisfying kiss. She responded in kind but realized that kisses were all they could expect until Margo departed.

And how soon would that be?

~~~~~~

Margo was in bed reading when Katie tiptoed through the bedroom to the bathroom to get ready for bed. "Hello, Katie."

"Hi." To her own ears, Katie's voice sounded small and guilty.

"Did you get a good-night kiss?"

She nodded and hurried into the bathroom, leaving Margo giggling in her wake.

Katie took her time getting ready for bed, and when she left the bathroom, Margo was sleeping. That, or she was feigning sleep. Either was fine with Katie.

Not yet sleepy, Katie stretched out on the sofa and thumbed through a magazine dedicated to the pleasures of afternoon tea. Margo was right. She and Andy needed to get their priorities in order if they wanted to have a life together. She wondered if Andy *did* see a future that included her. And did she see a future that included Andy? They'd carefully avoided that topic after Margo left them alone in Andy's truck.

However, the question of what the future held for her and Andy bothered Katie on way too many levels.

Finally, she turned out the light and closed her eyes.

Still, sleep would not come. The clock in the kitchen ticked on and on.

The longer she lay on the lumpy sofa, the more uncomfortable Katie became. She finally got up. A glance at the clock showed her that it was one o'clock. She paced the living room for a few minutes, but that seemed to make the cats restless. She finally decided to slip on her track suit, grab her pepper spray, and go for a walk. Maybe that would help clear her head and let her get some rest when she returned. And it would burn off those cheesecake calories. She'd only had the one bite—and that was to spite Margo—but she hadn't needed those extra calories.

She slipped into the bedroom, where Margo was now snoring softly, and took her track suit from the closet. She put it on, slid her feet into her sneakers, and headed out. Although she carried the pepper spray, she felt fine without it. She always felt safe on Victoria Square, no matter the time of day or night. Across the way, lights on at Sassy Sally's indicated that Nick, Don, and/or some of their guests were still awake. That was a comfort as well. She wondered what they were doing at Sassy Sally's—listening to carols, watching a movie, playing charades? Nick and Don were always up to something fun with their guests.

Katie's attention was drawn back to the magnificent illuminated Christmas tree, which had been placed on a dusk-to-dawn lighting mechanism. It gleamed so beautifully, making Katie feel as she always had when she was a little girl staring at the Christmas tree she and Great-aunt Lizzie would decorate. She felt a sense of tranquility—that everything would work out fine . . . that Christmas was on its way and that when it got here, there would peace on Earth and goodwill for everyone.

Everyone, except Vonne, she guessed. No goodwill for her this year. Katie had momentarily forgotten that there was a killer on the loose in Victoria Square. Yet she still didn't feel frightened. She was sure that Vonne's murder was personal . . . that it wasn't a random act. Poor Vonne. And her baby.

Katie tried to shake off her melancholy by resuming her walk, watching where she stepped, suddenly wary of black ice. She turned and strode past Sassy Sally's. The sound of music coming from the parlor made her smile. She turned the corner and considered Afternoon Tea up ahead. It was a charming building. And it was in a prime location. She would love to assume ownership of it. She hoped the bank she planned to visit on Monday morning would give her better terms than the first one. She paused when she got to the front of the building, thinking briefly about how she'd style the windows for greater appeal.

Arranging teas for individuals and parties and catering larger events appealed to her. Her gaze shifted to the bright white star at the top of the big tree across the Square, and not only did Katie wish upon that star that she might soon own the tea shop, but she crossed her fingers, too.

As she wandered away from the building and into the Square's vast front parking lot, the roar of a powerful engine cut the air. A bright light stung her eyes and she instinctively shaded them. She tried to get out of the way, but the driver steered the car in her direction. He was looking right at her. Katie dived to the left, but the car clipped her, sending her flying. She hit the tarmac at what seemed like warp speed, and then time wavered in and out.

Was she screaming?

Or did she hear sirens?

Or both.

Thirteen

A myriad of blurred images flashed before Katie's mind's eye. Distorted sounds wobbled in her ears and she wasn't sure whether any of it was real. Lights, voices—and pain . . . lots and lots of unrelenting pain hammering in on her from all directions. Unable to make sense of what was happening, Katie allowed herself to zone out. She was tired—so tired—until what seemed like eons later when a new voice managed to penetrate the fog around her brain.

"Ms. Bonner? Katie, can you hear me?"

Katie managed to open her eyes a crack, knowing the light was going to be searing, and squinted as she opened her eyes. Framed in the almost overpowering glow was the most beautiful man with the warmest brown eyes she'd ever seen, and the aura around him made him look divine. He must be an angel.

Somehow she managed a smile. "Hello."

But instead of "welcome to heaven," he said, "I'm Dr. Bhardwaj. You came through surgery just fine."

A frown settled across Katie's lips. "Surgery?"

"Yes. You have a broken fibula. We had to put a rod and a couple of screws in it."

"No," she said. Her brain was still fuzzy, but she knew she didn't want screws in her fibula. What was a fibula, anyway? Fibula . . . fibula . . . fibula . . . what a funny word.

"You're going to be fine. You're very lucky."

Considering how discombobulated she felt, Katie didn't feel lucky. She frowned.

"Do you remember what happened?" the handsome Indian doctor asked.

"No."

"You were hit by a car."

Katie's brow wrinkled. "I'm sorry."

He laughed and brushed the hair off her forehead. "You did nothing wrong. You were merely in the wrong place at the wrong time. I'll be back to see you again soon, okay?"

"Okay."

Okay?

Then the handsome face went away and yet Katie heard him talking to someone in that deep, angelic voice. Then she was rolling away, drifting as though on a tranquil ocean. Her eyes blinked shut. Dr. Angel would take care of her. Her and her fibula . . . whatever that was. But then . . .

"Katie, thank God." Someone to her left was talking. It was a man.

"Katie, I'm here for you, Sunshine." That was a man, too. He was at her other side.

"Let me see her, for goodness' sake!"

"M-Margo?" Katie murmured, unable to open her heavy eyelids.

"Yes, darling. And don't worry about a thing. I'm here, and I'll stay until you're a hundred percent again."

Oh no. The fabulous fibula-fixing angel has put me on a cart headed for hell!

~~~~~~~

The next time Katie woke—fully, this time—she realized she was in a hospital room. The room's floor and walls were a muted dove gray. The furniture was chrome with rust-colored cushions. The pictures on the walls were shades of orange. Katie supposed the room was meant to be soothing. Instead, she felt a slight sense of panic. There was an IV in her hand, and a clip on her finger fed information to a blood oxygen monitoring device.

The beautiful angel she vaguely remembered was gone. But her room was full of other people. Margo sat in a chair by Katie's bed. Andy and Ray were on a small bench sofa in front of the window. All of them were dozing, and Katie was glad for that small reprieve to try to remember what the heck had happened.

She'd been walking—and Dr. Angel said she'd been hit by a car. Hit. By a car. On purpose. Her eyes widened in horror. She remembered it now. The car had steered toward her and hit her on purpose! The driver had meant to run her down.

"Katie, you're awake!" Margo exclaimed.

Naturally, her proclamation woke the men, and they said her name in unison. Ray came to one side of the bed, and Andy hurried to the other—the side with Margo.

"Oh, Katie. I'm so sorry," Ray said, his voice tinged with guilt.

"Why were you out walking at that time of night?" Andy demanded. "Are you out of your mind?"

Because of the pain, Katie found it hard to focus, but her mind zeroed in on what Ray had said. "You're sorry? For what?"

"It's my fault. The driver who hit you—it was Carl Fiske."

That piece of the puzzle fell into place. That was right. It was Carl. Carl from The Pelican's Roost. She'd recognized him when he aimed his car in her direction.

"But why?" Katie frowned. "Why would Carl run me down? Was he drunk?"

Ray shook his head. "He was being pursued by the police . . . the vice cops I told you about."

"They caught him." Katie meant to say that the vice cops had caught Carl selling liquor to minors. Ray misunderstood.

"Yes." He squeezed her hand. "They caught him. If I have my way about it, they'll try the creep for attempted murder."

Katie frowned. Whatever medication they'd given her was still making her brain foggy.

"I'm so sorry," Ray repeated.

"This wasn't your fault," Katie said.

"You never answered my question," Andy said, his voice tinged with anger. "Why in the world were you out at that time of the morning?"

"I . . . I couldn't sleep."

The door opened, and the handsome doctor walked in. "Hi, everybody. How's our patient?"

"Not well at all," Margo answered, sounding worried. "I'm not even sure she understands what's happened to her."

Katie closed her eyes and wished everyone would go away and let her rest and clear her head for a few minutes.

Dr. Bhardwaj said, "If you'll excuse me, I'd like to talk with Ms. Bonner."

"Alone," Katie said quickly, eyeing the crowd.

The doctor nodded in understanding. "Yes, please, if you'll all wait out in the hall, that would be great."

Margo, Andy, and Ray filed out of the room, closing the wide wooden door behind them. Dr. Bhardwaj lifted Katie's wrist and checked her pulse. "Are they upsetting you?" he asked.

"No . . . not really."

He arched one dark brow.

"A little," Katie amended. "I'm just trying to get my head around what happened to me, and as soon as I woke up, they all started talking to me at once."

"You need time to rest and process," he said.

"Yeah," she agreed, "I do."

"I'll take care of it. Now, let's talk about your leg." He explained that she'd suffered a broken fibula and that it was the smaller of the two bones in the lower leg. He made sure she understood all about her injury, the surgery he performed, and the healing process ahead of her. "Any questions?"

Just one. "When may I go home?"

"Tomorrow."

"Thank goodness. I have so much to do. I—"

He shook his head. "No."

"No?"

"No work for a week to ten days. You need to rest and heal for at least that long."

"I can't!" Katie wailed, thinking of all the tasks that awaited her attention at Artisans Alley.

"You must."

She closed her eyes and willed herself not to succumb to tears.

"I understand that you're a strong, independent woman. But right now you need to let those people in the hall take care of you."

"You don't know what you're asking," she said, feeling weary.

"I know exactly what I'm saying . . . and so do you." He grinned. "I'll give you an hour's reprieve. I'll send them all to lunch to let you rest for a little while. See? I'm not such a bad guy."

No, but you aren't the angel I thought you were, either, Katie thought.

"Get some rest," Dr. Bhardwaj suggested, and patted Katie's hand before leaving her alone.

Closing her eyes, Katie drank in the quiet. Yes, she needed to rest, but the idea that Carl Fiske had deliberately tried to run her down haunted her thoughts.

Dr. Bhardwaj bought her the hour he'd promised, but that was all the well-meaning stooges gave her before they were once again driving Katie insane. When she pushed her hospital lunch tray away in distaste, all three were quick to offer something better. Andy said he could have one of his guys bring over a pizza, a Yule log, or one of the new flavors of cinnamon rolls she hadn't yet had an opportunity to try. Ray said Sophie would be happy to prepare home-made chicken soup for her. And Margo said she'd be glad to go down to the cafeteria and get Katie some yogurt.

"No, thank you. I'm not hungry."

"Darling, you have to eat something," Margo said. "And yogurt would be just the thing to knit your bones back together."

She didn't need her bones knitted back together. Dr. Bhardwaj had already taken care of that with a rod and some screws. But she conceded to allow Margo to go get the yogurt so the woman would get out of her hair for a few minutes.

Andy seemed to have a one-track mind and kept asking, "Katie, why were you out so late? Weren't you concerned for your safety?"

"I couldn't sleep," was Katie's response. How many times was she going to have to answer this question? "And no, I didn't think I had anything to be worried about."

"Was it me? Is it because I've taken your bed?" Margo asked, returning just in time to hear Katie's answer. "I'm sleeping on the sofa from now on. I insist!"

"Margo—no. I just have insomnia once in a while. Doesn't everyone?"

Whenever Ray could get a word in edgewise, he wanted to know if Katie could ever forgive him.

"Ray, there's nothing to forgive," Katie said. "You didn't run me down in a car."

"No, but I feel like I loaded a gun and handed it to that maniac. Carl ran you down because I had my friend send vice cops to watch him."

"If our roles were reversed, and you were lying in this bed, what would you tell me if I asked for your forgiveness?" Katie asked.

He looked away. "That's different."

"No, it isn't. You'd say, 'You aren't responsible for anyone's actions but your own.' Right?"

"Maybe, but—"

"Carl blames me because I commented on what he was doing. He figured—correctly—that I was the one who said something to get the deputies to check him out."

Margo put her hand to her chest. "It could've just as easily been me. Oh, Katie, in effect, you took a bullet for me!" She squeezed Katie's hand until Katie winced in pain.

"But here's the most important thing," Katie said. "Did Carl confess to killing Vonne?"

Everyone's attention turned to Ray.

He sighed and dropped his chin to his chest. "Not yet. They're still working on him, though. If he knows anything, it'll come out."

Katie didn't hold out much hope for that, and judging by Ray's posture, neither did he.

Fourteen

It was long past visiting hours when Andy, Ray, and Margo left Katie to finally allow her to rest. It was really stressful being watched like a pot on a stove for hours on end. Still, much as she wished sleep would come—it didn't. Not even the pain relievers she was given seemed to give her weary brain a break. Too many thoughts circled around in her mind. Carl Fiske and the way he'd steered his car right at her . . . She shuddered as she recalled the look on his face. He'd been so *angry* . . . his expression murderous. Was that furious visage the last thing Vonne ever saw?

And why had Vonne chosen to blackmail Carl in the first place? Katie was well aware that Afternoon Tea needed money, but a large part of the tea shop's declining fortunes could be attributed to Vonne in one way or another. Had she truly wanted to better the shop, she'd have left the men of Victoria Square alone and gotten back to work. Or was there something she needed money for that she didn't want Francine knowing about?

The word "abortion" kept circling around Katie's thoughts.

A light tap on the door drew Katie's attention, and then Rose stepped into the room carrying a tin decorated with the Stewart tartan, not Katie's clan McDuff tartan, but she knew Rose meant well. It must be cold outside because Rose had her red wool coat buttoned all the way, and her nose and cheeks were pink.

"Hi, dear," Rose said, her voice barely above a whisper. "How are you?"

"I'm fine."

Rose eyed the cast poking out of the bedclothes. "No, you're not. Some creep ran over you and broke your leg."

"Well, there is that," Katie said, with a slight smile.

"I brought you some shortbread cookies. It's past visiting hours, but the nurse allowed me to pop in for just a minute. Everybody at Artisans Alley sends their love and hopes for a speedy recovery. Is there anything you need?"

"No, thank you. I feel like an idiot for being out walking after midnight and getting myself into this predicament."

"Oh, you got yourself into it?" Rose asked. "I hadn't realized you'd been wearing your *Run Over Me with Your Car* sweatshirt."

"Well, my *Mug Me* shirt was in the wash." After sharing a laugh with Rose, Katie turned serious. "Thank you for holding down the fort today."

"Vance and Rhonda Simpson were tremendous help. We were swamped all day."

"That's good for business, but I wish I'd been there to help. I'll be out of the hospital tomorrow morning, and I plan on going to Artisans Alley and doing the paperwork I should've been doing today."

"The paperwork can wait," Rose said. "Vance can run the computer program that spits out checks—so there's no

reason for you to hurry back. You can stay home and rest."
Rose gave Katie a satisfied smile.

"Right . . . until Tuesday." She wondered if there was any
way she could get to the bank tomorrow. Most likely, Margo
wouldn't hear of it, and that's if Katie was released from the
hospital in time to make it there before they closed.

"Do I have to come to your apartment and sit on you?
Because I will. I don't want to—I'd prefer taking care of
customers at the Alley—"

"Point made." Katie held up both hands in surrender.
"One mother hen that I'll likely be stuck with now a lot
longer than I'd planned is more than enough."

"Go easy on Margo. Your accident has given her a
chance—maybe her last chance—to behave like a doting
mother. Let her have that."

"Yes, Rose," Katie said meekly.

"Now, now," Rose chided. She opened the tin and offered Katie one of the cookies. "They say a spoonful of
sugar helps the medicine go down, but I think a cookie
works just as well."

Katie smiled. "Yes, I'm sure you're right." She bit the
shortbread and chewed, glad her friend had come to visit.
It made a pleasant change from smothering guilt and ac-
cusatory questions. "Did anything happen at Artisans Alley today that I need to know about? Did Arthur Henderson
come in?"

"No. He wasn't there today, but the ballerinas squealed
and giggled and bumped into customers all day long. I'm
afraid you're going to have to talk with their teacher—
Dana, is it?—and have her take them down a peg or two."

"I already spoke to one of the teachers. She assured me
she'd keep them under a tighter rein. They aren't all bad little
girls, but they seem to have a ringleader. I realize they're just
children being children, but we're running a business, and
we can't have our customers being jostled and stepped on."

"Nor can we vendors have our merchandise at their mercy. They had their sticky little fingers all over Ida's lace again today," Rose said. "I believe they mess with her and Godfrey so much because it's so easy to get under their skin."

"True. I'll talk with Dana again on Tuesday." Katie sighed. "And, hopefully, they'll go back to their regular schedule of one class a week once their performance is done."

Rose patted Katie's arm. "Don't worry about it, dear. I shouldn't have brought it up while you're still recovering. Vance and I can handle it in the meantime. In fact, it'll be these kinds of situations we may have to handle on a daily basis once you buy the teashop."

Oh dear. Another subject that was bound to keep her awake for hours.

Rose stood. "Sleep well, Katie." She bent down and kissed Katie's forehead. "I'll see you soon."

Katie watched as Rose headed for the door and waved as Rose pulled it to.

The room was silent—what she'd hoped for all day. But now it was just as annoying as the buzz of voices had been earlier. Fumbling for the TV control, Katie flipped channels until she came to a rerun of *It's a Wonderful Life*. Soon after that, she was sound asleep.

~~~~~~~~

The next morning, Katie was somewhere between sleep and consciousness when she sensed someone by her bed. She felt her hand being lifted and pressed to firm lips. Her own lips curved into a smile. Her hand was gently placed back on the bed.

Katie opened her eyes, but instead of Andy by her side, she saw . . . "Ray?"

"Good morning."

"What are you doing?" Had he actually kissed her hand, or had she dreamed that?

"Looking at you. I'm glad you're still among the living. You could've been killed, and that would've broken my . . . my family's heart." He cleared his throat. "The girls adore you, you know."

Katie found herself pulling away. "Shouldn't you be at Wood U?"

"Sophie is minding the shop until I get back. It's good for her—she enjoys being in charge."

"That sounds like me." She sighed. "All I want is to go home and be in charge of my own life once again."

"I know. But if all goes according to plan, you'll be there later today. Right?" He moved around to the chair on the other side of her bed and sat down. They looked at each other for long seconds. Ray's expression was a mix of worry and . . . something else.

Katie broke the quiet. "So, do you know whether or not Carl ever confessed to killing Vonne?"

Ray shook his head. "He lawyered up and refused to say anything."

"Do you believe Carl did it?"

"One thing my years in the Sheriff's Office taught me was not to be too hasty in fixating on one particular suspect until concrete evidence is in hand. Everything they have on Carl Fiske with regard to Vonne's death is pure conjecture— there's not an iota of circumstantial evidence linking him to her murder."

Katie's eyes widened. "Are the deputies going to let him go?"

"No. They're holding him on attempted murder charges." His expression hardened. "And don't you worry your stubborn little head. I'll do everything in my power to protect you from that maniac."

She wished that made her feel better.

"I mean it, Katie," he said. "I won't let him get within a hundred feet of you."

Katie didn't trust herself to speak. Ray—and the entire Sheriff's Office, for that matter—could talk a good game, but she knew that no one could protect her if Carl wanted her dead badly enough.

Just then Andy and Margo burst into the room, and Katie's heart practically jumped.

Ray's eyes shot daggers at Andy. "Think of what Katie's been through. Could you try not to scare her?"

"Oh, please." Andy bent down to kiss Katie lightly on the lips. "Hi, Sunshine. How're you feeling?"

"I'm okay." Katie hazarded a glance at Margo to see what her reaction to the kiss had been and was grateful the older woman appeared to be unfazed.

"I brought you another track suit, dear," Margo said. "The one you were wearing the other night was ruined, of course. I thought about bringing jeans, but I thought fleece would feel better against your bruised leg."

"Thank you." Katie didn't say so, but she could tell this morning that her leg wasn't the only thing that suffered bruising. She knew the doctors had thoroughly checked her out, though, and that she hadn't sustained any other breaks. "How are the cats?"

"They're fine. I gave them a can of that foul-smelling food before I left the apartment."

Katie wondered if Della and Mason thought she'd left them . . . with Margo. What a horrible thought for her kitties! They knew the woman didn't like them. But Katie would soon be there to reassure them.

Margo smiled at Andy. "Andy was kind enough to take me to the grocery store yesterday evening when we left here, so your apartment is well stocked for your recovery."

"How thoughtful. I appreciate that."

"Well, it wasn't only for *you*." Margo chuckled. "Those cats and I will be there for the duration, too."

"Right." Katie remembered Rose telling her to give Margo a break, so she didn't groan at the thought of Margo "being there for the duration." She merely wondered how she could speed up that duration.

"Has Dr. Bhardwaj been in to see you yet this morning?" Margo asked.

"Not yet, but I'm sure when he gets here, he'll give me the all-clear to leave."

"I hope so." Margo set the zipped tote bag containing the track suit on the bench in front of the window. "If he does, I think you should be transported home by ambulance." She looked at the men. "Don't you?"

"Nah. That's an unnecessary expense," Andy said.

"I agree," Katie said, wondering for the first time how much financial responsibility for this hospital stay she'd be assuming. She had good insurance, but even good insurance had its limits.

"I can take her in my truck," Andy continued. "Ray, you won't mind driving Margo over, will you?"

"Oh, Andy, you don't understand," Margo protested. "Katie's going to need to stretch out that leg."

"She's right," Ray said. "There's not enough room in the truck. Margo, you can ride with Andy, and I'll drive Katie home. She can ride in the backseat of my car."

Andy's mouth tightened. Katie could see that he wanted to be the one to drive her home. It didn't really matter to her, as long as she got there. And she rather resented the fact that everyone was trying to make the decision without her input.

"It's my left leg that's hurt," Katie said. "If someone could bring me my car, I could drive myself home."

That certainly gave everyone something to fuss about until Dr. Bhardwaj showed up.

~~~~~

It was midafternoon by the time Katie had proven her skill with the crutches, all the paperwork was signed, and Katie was finally released. Her three caregivers decided that Margo and Andy would pick up her prescription from the hospital pharmacy and that Ray would drive her home. So, with her crutches in the front seat and her broken leg stretched out on the backseat, Katie felt utterly ridiculous on the ride home. She felt especially so when she was forced to converse with the back of Ray's head.

Ray parked the car outside the apartment, and things went from bad to worse, as far as Katie was concerned. He got out and came around to open the door for her.

"Turn forward and slip your arms around my neck," he instructed.

"I can get out and stand on my right leg just fine," Katie said. She turned forward and scooted until she could put her right leg on the pavement. She then raised herself up onto her good leg. "If you'd please hand me my crutches—"

"Nothing doing. There's no way I'm going to allow you to walk up those steps your first time using crutches." He slipped an arm around her waist.

"Back off, Ray. They gave me instructions on using them back at the hospital, and I did fine."

"Take it from me, it's harder than it looks," he said. "When I broke my leg, I hated having to rely on those stupid crutches. You'll grow to hate the damn things."

"I don't doubt it. But I hate being dependent on people even more than I hate being dependent on the crutches."

He scoffed. "Are you going to stand here in the cold on one leg like some kind of demented flamingo, or are you going to put your arms around my neck so I can carry you inside?"

"I'll stand here until we're both frozen solid before I'll consent to being carried like a helpless child."

"Katie Bonner, after what I've put you through, I should have to carry you up those stairs every day for the next six weeks."

"You haven't put me through anything. Get it through

that hard head of yours that you are not responsible for Carl hitting me with his car."

"Fine." He opened the passenger door, retrieved the crutches, and thrust them at Katie. "Here. Knock yourself out."

Katie slipped the crutches beneath her arms and managed to get to the stairs. It was tougher to do than she'd imagined, but she was determined not to let on to Ray that she was experiencing any difficulty. She placed both crutches under one arm so she could take hold of the handrail. She stepped up with her right leg, pushed down with the crutches, and then stepped up with her left. She winced at the pain and was glad Ray couldn't see her face. There was one stair . . . She tried not to think about how many more she had to go.

"Need any help?" Ray asked. To Katie's ears, his tone sounded mocking.

"None whatsoever." She placed her right leg on the next stair and pushed herself up. She was aware of Ray moving closer to her—he was probably afraid she'd fall—but she ignored him and concentrated on her task.

By the time she'd gotten to her door, she was perspiring, but she'd done it. And she'd done it all by herself.

Just then Andy and Margo arrived. Andy sprinted up the steps and put a supporting arm around Katie's waist.

"Good grief, Davenport. Couldn't you even help her up the stairs?"

"No," Ray said. "I couldn't." With that, he turned to leave.

Katie felt a small stab of guilt. "I didn't need any help. I got up here just fine on my own."

Andy kissed her cheek as he unlocked the door. "You're as stubborn as they come."

"Chad was, too," Margo murmured, following them into the apartment. "I'm sure that caused the two of you to butt heads on more than one occasion."

Katie didn't comment. Any time she and Chad had disagreed in front of his mother, Katie had always—without exception—been the one at fault.

She heard Ray's car pull out and was sorry she hadn't thanked him for driving her home. And she was sorry if she'd made him feel . . . what? Unnecessary? Unwanted? She made a mental note to thank him the next time she spoke with him. She would not, however, apologize for not allowing him to carry her up the stairs. She wasn't some simpering damsel in distress, and she never would be.

~~~~~~

Later that afternoon, Margo retired to the bedroom to read while Katie was supposed to be resting. She was actually trying to figure out how to get back to work on Tuesday. Andy promised to bring a pizza by later on and stay for dinner. Even the cats seemed overly solicitous, and had glued their furry little bodies against Katie's good leg and lap. Katie had the impish thought that maybe they were just happy not to be alone with Margo anymore.

Katie ruminated over the events of the day. Having Andy around with Margo underfoot was awkward. She was still uncomfortable with displays of affection between her and Andy in front of her former mother-in-law, but Margo either pretended not to notice or pretended not to care. She had to be pretending because how could she not care that her son's widow was kissing another man? She and Margo needed to have a conversation about that soon, but not yet. Katie wasn't up to it just then.

The doorbell rang. Katie had insisted on their leaving the door unlocked—after all, Carl Fiske seemed to be her only threat, and he was safely behind bars.

"Come in!" she called.

Francine Barnett bustled through the door with a canvas tote bag hanging from one wrist and a basket filled with goodies from Afternoon Tea in the other. She set the apparently heavy basket on the kitchen table. She wore a puffy blue down coat, hand-knitted scarf, and leather gloves, and though the room was cozy warm, she didn't take off any of her winter gear.

"Thank you, Francine," Katie said. "But you didn't have to bring me a gift."

"Don't say that just yet," Francine said. "I've brought you more than baked goods." She placed the tote bag on the floor in front of the sofa. "As soon as you feel up to it, take a look at that."

"What is it?"

"I thought I heard someone come in. Hello, Francine," Margo said, emerging from the bedroom. "How nice of you to drop by. May I take your coat?"

"No, thank you. I can't stay. I brought Katie a get-well basket and some reading material." She nodded toward the tote. "Hopefully, the ledgers in that bag will help you decide that you can't go wrong with assuming ownership of the tea shop."

"That's hardly uppermost in Katie's mind at the moment," Margo admonished, and moved to retrieve the tote.

"It's fine," Katie said, putting her hand on the canvas bag. "Maybe I'll feel like looking it over this afternoon. It's going to be awfully boring for me if I merely sit around this apartment and feel sorry for myself until my leg mends."

"That's right." Francine shot a triumphant glance at Margo. "I am terribly sorry that Nona Fiske's nasty little nephew tried to kill you . . . but I appreciate that you're always looking for the silver lining. Hopefully, deciding to buy the tea shop will be it."

Neither Katie nor Margo had a reply for that.

"By the way, thank you for the flowers from the Merchants Association, Katie. They were lovely. I'm sure Vonne would have appreciated them," she said rather briskly.

"I'm sorry we were unable to attend the service," Margo said.

"That's quite all right," Francine said. "I'd better get back to the shop. I need to get ready for tomorrow's customers— such as they are. Let me know if either of you need anything," she said, although without much sincerity.

"Thank you," they chorused, and watched as Francine left the apartment.

As soon as they heard Francine's tread on the stairs outside the apartment, Margo turned to Katie. "The nerve of that woman!"

Katie shrugged. "Well, she hasn't made any secret of the fact that she's desperate to have me buy the tea shop. My accident simply gives her another excuse to try to sway me in her direction." She affected Francine's voice. "Now, Katie, had you been minding your own business running a tea shop and hadn't been fraternizing with the clientele at The Pelican's Roost, this never would have happened to you."

Margo joined in the fun. "Katie, don't lose sleep over your love life. Lose sleep over a failing tea shop like I do!"

Both women laughed, but then Katie decided this, unfortunately, was the time to have that conversation about Andy.

"Margo," she said gently, "I know you encouraged Andy and me to get together, but—"

"But nothing. I did encourage you to get together. I meant it when I said you're young and that Chad would want you to move on with your life."

"Don't you feel like I'm cheating on Chad? Betraying his memory?"

"No. I know you loved my son," Margo said wistfully. "But he isn't here now . . . and you're barely in your thirties. Is that how you feel? That you're betraying Chad in some way?"

Katie's eyes filled with tears, and she nodded.

"Is that why you're keeping those two men at arm's

length—because you're afraid that if you love either one of them, you're being unfaithful to Chad?"

"T-two . . . men?" Katie echoed.

"Andy and Ray. They're both in love with you. You have to know that."

Fifteen

Later that afternoon, Margo retreated to the apartment's bedroom and Katie could hear the television in the background playing softly. Oh, how she needed some alone time, and yet . . . stuck on the couch with her leg hoisted on the coffee table—unable to hobble to the bathroom—she felt bored, Bored, BORED. She was supposed to be resting, but she was itching to do something—anything! She reached over and hauled closer the tote bag Francine had left hours before.

Katie opened the first ledger. It was from the spring, and the tea shop had been doing really well then. So why had it taken such a nosedive? Was it simply because Vonne had abandoned the shop, or was there more to it than that? Come to think of it, Vonne and Francine had seemed to be doing fine at that point relationship-wise as well. In fact, they'd seemed like a typical loving mother and daughter—not without conflict, but what mother and daughter are?

Katie finished thumbing through that ledger and opened another one. This one appeared to be more of a list of suppliers and what was bought from each. She flipped through the pages and was about to put the ledger back in the tote when an envelope fell to the floor. It fell faceup, and Katie could see that it was addressed to Vonne. The return address sticker gave the sender's name: Nancy Parks.

Was this *the* Nancy—Vonne's birth mother?

Feeling as though she probably shouldn't invade the dead woman's privacy but justifying the fact that she was doing so anyway because the letter might have a bearing on Vonne's murder, Katie picked it up, unfolded the letter inside, and read it.

She immediately wished she hadn't. Poor Vonne. It seemed no one had wanted her. Either Francine was the most stoic woman on the planet, or she wasn't mourning Vonne's death. And Nancy made it unbearably clear in the letter Katie held that she didn't want anything to do with her daughter. Katie read the most heartbreaking paragraph in the letter once again.

> *Booth, Francine, and I made our decision*
> *concerning you before you were even born. I'm*
> *sorry you're unhappy, but that's not my problem.*
> *I've built a good life for myself, Vonne, and I*
> *absolutely will not allow you to destroy it. My*
> *family knows nothing about you, and I'm keeping it*
> *that way. Don't ever contact me again.*

How harsh! How absolutely cold and unfeeling.

Katie felt compelled to share the contents of the letter with someone, but the only one she'd told Francine's story to was Nick. She reached for her phone and called him.

He answered on the first ring. "It's our dove with the broken wing! I meant to come and visit you today, but then we had guests arrive, and—"

"Don't worry about that, Nick. Believe me, I've had plenty of company—maybe a little *too* much."

"How are you, love?"

"I'm doing all right. But I did want to talk to you about something." She explained how Francine brought the tote bag with the ledgers and business information in another attempt to persuade her to buy the sinking business. "And, Nick, a letter fell out of one of the ledgers."

"Dum-de-dum-DUM! Now it gets *good*."

"No, now it gets bad. Really *bad*. I didn't know Vonne had such a miserable life."

"Read this letter to me immediately," Nick said.

She did. Afterward he was quiet.

"So, what are you thinking?" Katie prompted.

He sighed. "The same thing you are—that Vonne was more pitiable than any of us ever dreamed. Here we were thinking she was merely sowing her wild oats, and she was . . ." Again he sighed. "I have no idea what she was doing. Trying to be accepted maybe?"

"She wanted someone to love her." Katie's voice broke. "Tell me what to do about this letter. Should I give it to Francine? Put it back in the ledger where I got it? Give it to the police?"

"You should definitely give it to Detective Schuler and let the man follow up on it. I mean, what if Vonne didn't leave Nancy alone? You can tell how adamant Nancy sounded in that letter."

"Adamant? She was downright hostile."

"Right," Nick said. "She might've been desperate enough to kill Vonne to keep her away from her new family."

"I'd hate to think that Vonne's own mother would . . ." She gulped. "Would do that, but I'll call Detective Schuler right away."

"Do make that call. And, by the way, Don and I want to have you over for lunch as soon as you're able."

"I'll hold you to that." As Katie ended the call, she noticed Margo standing against the bedroom doorjamb.

"I'm sorry, but I couldn't help overhearing your reading the contents of that letter." She walked into the living room and sat on the armchair. "So, Francine isn't Vonne's biological parent."

Katie shook her head and explained the situation to Margo. "Do you think I should tell Francine about this letter?"

"No. You should do as planned and turn the letter over to the detective. If nothing comes of it, then Francine never has to know. She's been hurt enough by Nancy."

"That's true. But Vonne was hurt by both of them. How could neither woman want her? I mean, she had no control over her parentage. She just wanted someone to truly care about her. At least, her father loved her."

Margo nodded toward the ledgers. "Didn't you tell me that Afternoon Tea was doing really well until a few months ago?"

"Yes." She handed Margo one of the ledgers. "You can see for yourself that the first few months they were open were terrific. And then sales suddenly went kaput in October."

"Hmm . . . makes you wonder."

"Wonder what?"

"Well, it makes me wonder if that's when Vonne discovered the truth about her life."

Katie's eyes widened. "What? You mean, you don't think she knew all along?"

"Why would she? The three adults decided the child would be raised as Booth and Francine's child. They'd have no reason to ever tell Vonne the truth."

"Oh my gosh. You're right."

"And either one of those women could've killed Vonne," Margo continued. "Nancy didn't want Vonne to destroy her

new life. Maybe Francine resented Vonne for tearing down
the old one by wanting to reconnect with her birth mother."

But that wasn't uncommon. Many adopted children
longed to know their birth mothers, fathers, and any half or
full siblings. But Margo could be right. Katie had known
the women since they'd opened the shop and remembered
Francine's concern for "her daughter" when the murder at
Wood U had taken place the previous July. She'd done an
about-face since then.

Katie took a closer look at the envelope. Yes, it was post-
marked September 29.

Margo was right about the timing.

Poor Vonne. Poor, poor Vonne.

~~~~~~~

About an hour after Katie called him, Detective Schuler
arrived to retrieve the letter. He'd taken a page from Ray
Davenport's stylebook and was wearing a tan trench coat.
Had he been wearing a fedora, he'd have looked like he
came right out of a film noir.

"Did you find anything else of interest in the ledgers?"
he asked Katie as he perched on the edge of the armchair.

"No, but you're welcome to them."

He gave her a tight smile that came across more like a
grimace. "I was going to ask to take them anyway."

"How will I explain that to Francine?"

"Stall her for a while. Tell her you're still studying them,"
he said. "Or I guess you could tell her the truth."

Katie didn't want to do that, and she suspected Detective
Schuler knew it. She'd do as he'd suggested and tell Francine she hadn't yet made up her mind about the tea shop. At
least, that much was absolutely true.

"What about Carl Fiske?" Margo asked. "How much
time is he likely to serve for what he did to our Katie?"

Katie felt herself blush a bit at being called *our Katie*
by Margo, but it was also kind of nice. She wondered if

she might be growing fonder of her former mother-in-law or if she was simply still feeling the sting of Vonne's rejection.

"Yeah, that's something else I meant to talk with you about," Detective Schuler said rather sheepishly. "Fiske claims he didn't see you standing in the middle of the parking lot and that he bumped you—his words, not mine— completely by accident."

"That's not true," Katie cried. "He looked me straight in the eye when he steered his car *at* me!"

Detective Schuler spread his hands. "I believe you. In fact, no one believes Fiske, but that's the argument his lawyer used to get the judge to set bail when Fiske was arraigned this morning."

"Set bail?" Katie suddenly felt sick—and dizzy. "No. He's not going to get out . . . is he?"

Margo moved closer to the sofa and put her hand on Katie's shoulder, giving it a squeeze.

"He'll get out if he can raise the bail money," the detective said.

"But . . . but he tried to run over me. I have every reason to believe that man wanted to *kill* me."

"And you'll certainly get the opportunity to testify to that in court," Detective Schuler said.

"Yeah, if I live long enough."

"Now, Ms. Bonner, we're going to make every effort to step up security on Victoria Square. I'll make sure our patrolmen do a sweep twice as often."

Twice as often was never much to pin your hopes on.

"Isn't there anything else you can do?" Margo asked, her voice strained. "Can't you station a patrolman in the parking lot or something?"

"Nope. Not until Carl either threatens Ms. Bonner's life or attempts to harm her."

"Swell," Katie said sarcastically. "That makes me feel *so* much better."

~~~~~~

By the time Andy arrived with a pepperoni and sausage thick-crust pizza, Margo was livid. Katie had calmed herself by trying to reassure Margo that nothing was going to happen to her, but to no avail.

"Even if Carl does get out and knows where to find me, he wouldn't dare do anything with so many people around," Katie was saying as Margo opened the door for Andy.

"What's this about Carl finding you?" Andy asked.

"They're letting that maniac out on bail!" Margo cried.

"*If* he can make bail," Katie added. "We can't forget that concession of his release. There's no guarantee he'll be able to come up with the money."

"Either way, I'll run home after we eat and get my sleeping bag. I'm bedding down here on the floor until I'm certain Katie will be all right," Andy said. "And you, too, of course, Margo."

"Thank you, Andy. I'm sure we'll both feel safer having you here." Margo went into the kitchen and took plates from the cabinet. "Heaven knows, the Sheriff's Office isn't going to do much. Not unless the man comes here and either threatens Katie's life or harms her."

"Attempts," Katie stressed. "Attempts to harm me."

"Oh, right. Because he's already succeeded in harming you once and will be let go if he gives the court some money."

Margo had her there. She couldn't argue with that logic.

"Okay, but Andy doesn't have to sleep here on the floor." Katie looked to Andy for help, but he'd already taken the pizza into the kitchen and was helping Margo put slices on the plates.

"What do you want to drink, Katie?" Margo asked.

"Water is fine. Andy, please, be reasonable. You have a business to run."

"As a matter of fact, Erikka did a terrific job running the

place yesterday when I was with you. She'll have no problem filling in for me until I get there." He shook his head. "That woman is such a dynamo. I'm so glad you sent her my way."

That's right. Katie had suggested Erikka for the job of Andy's assistant manager. At the time, however, she didn't dream it would work out as well as it had. What had she been thinking? It was like inviting the fox into the henhouse. She felt an immediate pang of guilt for making the comparison. There was no indication that Erikka was actually trying to steal Andy away from her. Just because she was beautiful and funny and *a dynamo* was no reason for Katie to be so jealous of her.

Katie's phone rang. She looked at the screen and saw that it was Detective Schuler. Hopefully, he'd have good news for her, and everyone would settle down about Carl Fiske coming into the apartment to kill her as she slept.

"Hi, Detective Schuler."

"Hey, Katie . . . Ms. Bonner. I . . ." He sighed. "I wanted to go ahead and let you know . . . um . . . Carl Fiske coughed up that bail money. He's out."

Katie's stomach did a flip-flop and she wasn't certain she could finish her pizza dinner. "Oh."

"I want you to know that I'm—the entire Sheriff's Office is—doing everything we can to assure your safety. A patrol car will swing around every few hours at Victoria Square." He barked out a fake laugh. "In fact, I hope it won't scare off your customers at Artisans Alley to see so many officers hanging around."

"Yeah." Katie didn't even try to return the fake laugh. "Thanks. I appreciate your call and . . . and everything you're doing." As she ended the call, she refused to look at either Margo or Andy.

It didn't matter, though. They both read her body language as easily as if she'd had Detective Schuler on speakerphone.

Andy clapped his hands. "All right! So! Let's eat up, and then I'll go get my sleeping bag. It'll be fun."

Nobody believed for an instant that Andy sleeping on the living room floor because the man who'd run Katie down was roaming around free would be all that fun, but neither Katie nor Margo disputed him. And they all tried to choke down some more pizza.

Finally, Andy gave up. "Katie, call Vance and ask him to come over."

"Why?" she asked.

"I want him to stay with you until I get back."

"Andy, I don't need a babysitter. Besides, he went home hours ago."

"Fine." He turned to Margo. "Call Davenport. He'll be here Johnny-on-the-spot, if you call him," he said sarcastically.

Margo nodded. "All right."

Katie was surprised to learn that Margo had Ray's number. She supposed he'd given it to her in case she'd needed to back out on their lunch Saturday. But despite Katie's protests, Margo called Ray. Andy's assertion had been irrefutable— Ray came right over.

The first words out of his mouth when he barged into the living room were "I can't believe this. How dare they put that man back on the streets?"

"Isn't it terrible?" Margo asked. "And the Sheriff's Office isn't doing a thing to stop it."

Ray couldn't allow her to disparage his former colleagues, even if he was retired. "It was the judge who'd granted the cretin bail. There's nothing the Sheriff's Office can do about that. And, to be fair, there's a squad car in the Square right now . . . or, at least, there was when I came in."

"That's good," Andy said. "Thanks for coming over to stay here with Katie and Margo while I go home and get my sleeping bag. I'm staying here tonight." He'd said the words with a note of triumph in his voice. Ray seemed to ignore it.

"I'll be happy to stay until you get back."

Andy nodded and left, and Ray shrugged out of his jacket and sat on the armchair.

Katie met his eyes. "Thank you for this . . . and for driving me home yesterday."

"No problem. How're you feeling?"

"I'm not scared," Katie said adamantly.

"That's crap. You are, too." Ray wasn't quite able to hide a grin at her outraged expression. "You know how I know that for sure? Because you said nothing about your leg or the fact that the pain meds were helping or that you're sorer today than you'd expected you'd be. Instead, you said you weren't scared."

She huffed. "If my leg didn't need to be elevated on this pillow, I'd throw it at you."

At that, he did grin. "Sorry. I used to read people for a living. It's a skill you don't lose simply because you retire."

"I think it's an admirable skill," Margo said.

"Look, Carl doesn't know where I live. There's no way I can go out walking now, and even if I could, he has to know the deputies are watching him." Katie lifted her chin. "I have no reason whatsoever to be afraid of Carl Fiske."

"You keep telling yourself that, and we'll keep protecting you to make it so," Ray said, and winked.

Katie glowered at him. "Stop patronizing me."

"Fine." Ray leaned forward and placed his elbows on his knees. "Here are the facts, then. Carl might not know where you live, but it wouldn't take an Einstein to find out, especially in a town the size of McKinlay Mill. His aunt could have already told him. It's possible he's already killed one woman—Vonne—so what's another murder to him at this point? Especially if he can rid himself of the woman who can not only testify that he purposefully and maliciously hit her with his car but also tie him to his first victim—and don't forget him serving underage kids alcohol."

"Oh my," Margo murmured. "I'd never thought of that."

Neither had Katie. But she was determined not to let Ray freak her out.

"But we have another suspect in Vonne's death now," she said. "Maybe two." She told him about the letter Detective Schuler had taken.

He straightened and took a small notebook and pen from his pocket. Old habits certainly did die hard. "What's this Nancy's last name?"

"Parks."

"I'll see what I can dig up on her."

~~~~~~

Ray left as soon as Andy returned; then he, Katie, and Margo watched a movie on TV before Margo announced she was ready for bed. She'd tried to get Katie to sleep in the bedroom, but Katie assured her that the couch was easier to get on and off than the bed. The truth was, she preferred to be near Andy. One, because he was her boyfriend. But two, he and Ray had her terrified that Carl Fiske would find her and try to kill her in her sleep. Of course, if Margo hadn't been there, she would have just shared the bed with Andy.

Before sliding into his sleeping bag, Andy kissed Katie thoroughly.

"So . . . how are you feeling?" he asked, huskily.

She laughed quietly. "Not that well."

"Damn." He chuckled. "I'm only joking, you know. And, despite the seriousness of this entire situation, I had fun hanging out here with you and Margo tonight."

"Me, too. Well, maybe not fun, but it was pleasant."

Andy sobered. "Margo was right. We've let our relationship suffer by not making it a priority." He took both her hands in his and kissed them. "I promise I'll do better from now on."

"So will I."

"I love you." He kissed her again.

"Andy, I love you," she said, and hugged him.

I do . . . I love Andy. I mean, what's not to love, right? Andy's perfect.

Perfect.

Then what was that funny feeling that seemed to have taken root in the pit of her stomach?

Sixteen

The couch wasn't nearly as comfortable as Katie had hoped—not that she'd have been much more comfortable in her bed, given the pain she'd been in—and she'd had a restless night filled with bad dreams, some she remembered, and some she didn't. Andy had woken during the worst one. He must've had as hard a time falling back to sleep as she had because he and Margo were still asleep early Tuesday morning when Katie managed to get up, take a thorough sponge bath, and get dressed. She was proud of herself as she opened the bathroom door, then glanced over at the bed and saw that a formidable-looking Margo was sitting up with her arms crossed staring at her. It irritated Katie that even when the woman had just woken and wasn't wearing any makeup, she still managed to look terrific.

"Good morning?" Katie realized it sounded more like a question than a greeting, but she couldn't help it.

"I'd have been happy to help you," Margo said. "Why didn't you wake me?"

"I guessed I did enough waking up of my guests last night. Didn't you hear my middle-of-the-night shenanigans?"

"No. What happened?"

"I had a nightmare." Her crutches were getting hard to manage, so she hopped over to the bed and sat down. "Andy heard me and soothed me back to sleep."

"He's a good man."

"He is. I hate that he didn't get enough rest last night . . . and that he wasn't at home in a comfy bed."

"I'm sure he was happy to be here for you," Margo said. She changed the subject. "What's on our agenda today?"

Katie took a deep breath. "I need to go to work. If I sit around here all day, I'll do nothing but worry that we're about to be accosted by Carl Fiske. Every sound I hear will make me jump out of my skin."

"You're absolutely right." Margo grinned as her former daughter-in-law's eyes widened in surprise. "I'm serious. You do need to get out of this apartment today. So, if you'll go on out into the living room and check on your young man, I'll get dressed, feed the cats, and make breakfast."

"Wow . . . thank you." Katie stood up, positioned the crutches under her arms, and strode carefully to the door.

As she entered the living room, she could see that Andy was up and was already working on breakfast, breaking eggs into a skillet.

"Good morning, Sunshine."

She went over to the stove, balanced her crutches against the counter, put her arms around Andy's waist, and hugged his broad back. "I'm sorry I woke you last night. I feel like an idiot."

"Nonsense. If someone had tried to k—" He stopped abruptly. "Tried to crash into me with his car, I'd have nightmares, too." He moved the skillet off the burner, turned, and kissed Katie. "I'm just glad you're okay."

"Thank you for staying."

"You're welcome. I'll be here tonight, too, unless the deputies are able to lock Fiske back up."

"You don't—"

He put his index finger on her lips. "I know I don't have to. I want to. And I'm going to." He bent and picked her up. "Let's get you onto that sofa with your two fur balls so I can finish breakfast."

"Have I told you lately how wonderful you are?" Katie asked.

"Not often enough," he said, with a grin.

~~~~~~

Ensconced in her office at Artisans Alley, Katie began to second-guess her haste to return to normal. Not that she'd admit that in a million years to anyone else. Finding a comfortable position was an impossibility, her leg throbbed, and she refused to take her prescription medication until she returned home because she needed to keep a clear head while at work.

"Oh, goodness me," Rose clucked as she brought Katie a cup of coffee from the vendors' lounge. "You know you shouldn't be here yet. Why, if I was recovering from a broken bone, I'd sit at home and watch romance movies all day long."

"Somehow I doubt that." Rose was here at Artisans Alley more than almost anyone. She'd hate it if she couldn't come to work.

Rose smiled. "So do I."

Katie looked up to see Vance standing in the doorway. He held a bright pink faux-fur pillow.

"Janey sent you this." He brought the pillow over to where Katie's foot was propped on the chair beside her desk. "She said it has memory foam and will help." He gingerly picked up Katie's foot and slid the pillow beneath it.

"That's much better! Thank you. And thank Janey," Katie said. "No, wait. I'll call and thank her myself. And thank you, Vance, for being the deliveryman."

"No problem. If you need anything else, just holler."

"Actually, would you check to see if Dana Milton is in her dance studio? I need to speak with her when she has a minute."

He hid a grin. "Surely, you haven't heard reports about our angelic ballerinas causing trouble?"

Katie groaned. "What have they done to you?"

"Aw, nothing too major. They're just kids running around unsupervised. You've got to expect they'll be a nuisance to somebody."

"Or to everybody. Rose said they were even jostling the customers."

"Jostling is a nice way to put it," Rose said.

"Yeah." He nodded. "I'll send Dana over."

Vance nearly bumped into Godfrey Foster on the way out.

"Hey, Vance. Just wanted to check on the patient."

"I'd better get back to the cash desk," Rose said. "Like Vance, I'm here if you need anything."

Katie thanked them both and greeted Godfrey.

"I'm sorry you had such an awful weekend," Godfrey said. "I know you'd been looking forward to the tree-lighting ceremony and . . . and everything."

"Actually, I did enjoy the tree lighting," Katie said. "It was later that night—or, rather, Sunday morning—that things got hairy."

"Yeah . . . what were you doing walking around the Square at that time of night, anyway? Worried about your figure after drinking too much hot chocolate at the ceremony or something?"

The man could never say the right thing. "No. I had insomnia and felt like it might do me good to take a walk and clear my head. Apparently, I thought wrong."

"I can see where you'd think that, though." Godfrey

looked at some point to Katie's left. "It's so peaceful at that time . . . between midnight and dawn. It's beautiful to be out when the rest of the world is asleep."

Katie wondered if Godfrey was often prowling around at night while the rest of Victoria Square was dreaming. It was an unsettling thought.

"It is beautiful." Katie barked out a mirthless laugh. "I only wish Carl Fiske had been asleep."

"I'm sure you do. Well, I'll be seeing you. Like everybody else has said, let me know if you need anything."

"Thanks, Godfrey."

He smiled at her and left. Maybe Godfrey wasn't such a bad guy after all. She reprimanded herself for calling him obnoxious all those times in her mind. Not that he wasn't obnoxious.

The parade of well-wishers continued with Erikka, who "popped in" to see how Katie was doing.

"Andy told me he slept in a sleeping bag on your floor last night." She put her well-manicured hand to her ample breast. "Isn't he a dream? He's like a knight in shining armor or something."

"He certainly is." Katie pretended to get a sudden thought. "I know that when you took the job at Angelo's, you weren't looking to make it your career. I saw in the newspaper earlier that the Greece school district is hiring administrative assistants. A couple of the jobs don't require a civil service test. It would be good pay and excellent benefits."

"Oh, gee, thanks for thinking of me. I'll check into that . . . but . . ." She bit her lip. "I don't know what Andy would do without me."

"True." Katie managed a tight smile. *I don't know, either, but I'd like for him to find out.*

"Hot tea coming through." Francine Barnett all but muscled Erikka out of her way.

"I'll get back to our guy, then," Erikka said, winking at Katie. "Feel better!"

Our guy?

"Ugh, that one bears watching," Francine said, when Erikka had gone.

To avoid agreeing with her, Katie asked, "What's this?"

"It's ginger tea. It's good for pain. I brought over a thermos full." She poured the brew into one of the teashop's take-out cups.

"Thank you." Katie took a sip of the tea and was happy to find that it wasn't half-bad.

"Have you had a chance to look through those ledgers?" Francine asked pointedly.

"I have." *Please don't ask for them back.* "I couldn't help noticing that everything appeared to be terrific until October. Did anything traumatic happen to Vonne around that time?" she fished.

"Well, you know Booth died in September. But October . . ." She looked up toward the ceiling and tapped her chin with her index finger. "I believe that's about the time that she and Charles broke up. I told you about that."

"Right. At least, Vonne and Charles were still a couple when her dad died. I know that had to have been terrible for her."

Francine met Katie's eyes. "It was hard on both of us. Booth was . . . well, he held our family together."

"Had Vonne always known that you weren't her biological mom?"

"Vonne never knew!" Francine's face flushed, and she put her fingers to her temple as if the outburst had pained her. In a calmer voice, she continued. "Well, she wasn't *supposed* to ever have known that I wasn't her birth mother. But after Booth died, Vonne was snooping around in some of his old papers and . . . she discovered . . ." Francine's eyes filled with tears, and she quickly lowered her head. "She found out the truth."

"I'm sorry."

Francine batted her tears away. "There was just no satisfying her then. She wanted to meet Nancy. I told the girl that Nancy didn't want anything to do with her, but she wouldn't listen. That only made a bigger rift between Vonne and me."

"Did Vonne ever get to meet Nancy?"

"Your guess is as good as mine. After we had our blowup about the whole thing, we never discussed it again." She cleared her throat. "I'd best be going. When you take a break, think about how wonderful it will be for you to own and operate Afternoon Tea. You won't regret it."

Katie looked down at her cup. She was already regretting Francine's visit. Not for the first time, she wished she'd realized what Vonne had been going through. The woman's entire world had turned upside down during the fall—her father died, her boyfriend left her and married someone else, and she learned that Francine wasn't her biological mother. How different things might have turned out for Vonne if she'd had a friend she'd felt was a trusted confidante.

Katie didn't have much time to dwell on Vonne before Cheryl, not the owner, but one of the other dance instructors, came prancing into her office. Cheryl never simply walked anywhere. She pranced, glided, or sashayed. Katie supposed it was a by-product of being a graceful dance instructor. Today, she wore a pink leotard, a pink knit skirt, nude dance shoes, white leg warmers, and a pink fleece jacket. Her blonde hair was in a neat bun on top of her head.

"Vance said you wanted to talk with Dana. Unfortunately, her daughter, Bella, had an appointment with the pediatrician this morning. I can take care of anything you need." Cheryl placed her back against the wall and slid down into a sitting position. "This is excellent for your core, your thighs, and your glutes. You should try it after your leg has mended."

Katie merely nodded. No way was she going to sit on an invisible chair when she had plenty of seating alternatives. "I need to speak with you about your middle school class."

"The sugarplum fairies?" Cheryl smiled. "Aren't they precious?"

"They are, but even though I spoke to Dana about them last week, I'm afraid I've been getting reports that they're still running wild throughout Artisans Alley."

Cheryl rolled her eyes. "By some of these old fuddy-duddy vendors, I'm sure. What are their complaints?"

"I understand they've been giving Godfrey Foster a hard time."

Cheryl rolled her eyes. "Can you blame them? I mean, really—lint art? I saw their chewing gum picture." She giggled. "I know it was kinda mean, but it was kinda funny, too. I had no idea they were going to leave it for him. I tried to tell him he should be flattered—the girls wouldn't have done it if they didn't like him."

Katie felt certain the girls didn't make the picture because they *liked* Godfrey, but she didn't want to debate the matter with Cheryl. "So, you and Godfrey have discussed this?"

"Yeah, he brought it to my attention." She straightened. "I basically told him to chill, that they were just playing. I told him they admired his art and were trying to emulate it. And then he asked me to have coffee with him, I told him to get bent, and I'm guessing that's when he came to complain to you."

"Even so, Godfrey isn't the only one who has complained."

"Let me guess—the old lady with the wart who tats lace?" Cheryl scoffed. "If she doesn't want anyone touching her precious lace, she should keep it locked up."

"I don't want to go into detail, but suffice it to say that several of the vendors have said that the girls aren't being properly supervised and that they're exhibiting some destructive behavior."

"Oh, good grief. Tell everybody to chill. It's the Christmas season, they're excited, and they're getting ready to perform *The Nutcracker*. Everything will go back to normal in a couple of weeks. In the meantime, I'll try to keep the girls corralled in the dance studio, since Artisans Alley seems to be full of grinches and scrooges."

"Thank you, Cheryl," Katie said stiffly.

"Yeah. Hope you feel better." With that, Cheryl sashayed out of the office, leaving Katie to wonder if everyone was being too hard on the little darlings . . . or if the little *darlings* were being even worse than her vendors were letting on.

One thing was obvious. Katie and It's Tutu Much's owner were going to have a much more serious conversation in the not-too-distant future.

~~~~~~

At a little past noon, Ray knocked lightly before opening the door to Katie's office. "Hi. How are you feeling?"

"A bit useless," she groused.

"Never. I'm on my way to get the girls and me some lunch. May I bring you something?"

"No, thanks." She motioned him inside. "Do you have a second to talk?"

"Sure." He came inside and leaned against the wall. "The girls want to come by and check on you sometime today. I've told them not to stay too long when they visit, so don't let them wear you out."

"They could never wear me out. Do you have any news about Carl?"

Ray frowned. "He's lying low and trying to stay out of trouble as far as I can tell."

"He . . . he hasn't been seen . . . you know . . . in the Square?" she asked.

"He has not. You'd also asked me to check up on Nancy Parks, but since you gave that letter you found to Schuler, he was already on it." He whipped out his notebook. "Nancy Parks has a serious problem with alcohol. She has one DUI and two drunk-and-disorderlies on her record."

"Any history of violence?"

He put the notebook back in his pocket. "Nothing yet, but in light of that letter she wrote, I'm not putting anything past her. Drunk, disorderly, and angry often go hand in hand with violent behavior."

Katie nodded. The fact that the woman lived out of state made it less likely she'd arrive in the area to commit fili-cide. And yet . . . stranger things had happened. Someone had bashed Vonne in the head and tried to make it look like an accident.

Katie wished the list of suspects wasn't quite so long.

~~~~~~

Katie lifted her right hip and prayed the action would al-leviate some of the soreness in her rear end, but wasn't hopeful. The ache made it that much harder to review the previous week's master sales spreadsheet. And then, with-out so much as a greeting, Ida Mitchell moved to stand in front of her office door.

"Margo Bonner is a nice person," Ida announced. "You should be terribly thankful for her."

Katie let out a breath slowly. "I am." And, to Katie's sur-prise, she realized she truly was thankful for Margo. She needed to be sure to tell her that. Margo had been wonder-ful to stay and fuss over her, something she hadn't ex-perienced since childhood, before Great-aunt Lizzie had succumbed to the ravages of age. "Thank you, Ida. By the way, I spoke with Cheryl, one of the dance instructors over at It's Tutu Much, earlier. Hopefully, the tiny terrors won't have their fingers in your lace anymore."

Before Ida could say anything in response, Nona Fiske brushed past her and stormed into Katie's office.

"Excuse us, please. I need to speak with Katie alone."

"Well!" Ida huffed, turned on her heel, and stalked off.

"Wait—" The word fell on deaf ears. Katie glared at

Nona, her least favorite of the merchants on Victoria Square. "You need to apologize to Ida. We were in the middle of a conversation."

"Sure, fine. But there's something *we* need to discuss that's much more important. Do you realize the deputies are saying that Carl hit you with his car on purpose?"

"Yes . . . because he did."

Nona shook her head adamantly. "Oh no, he did *not*! Carl would *never* do that. Sure, he made a mistake in serving alcohol to one or two girls who'd made themselves up to look older at The Pelican's Roost," she blustered, "but I blame their parents. Why were they allowed to go to a bar in the first place? Why weren't their parents keeping better tabs on them?"

"I don't know."

"Neither do I. Anyway, they tricked poor Carl into thinking they were old enough to drink, and since he was so busy, because goodness knows the cheap management at that joint don't have enough staff, he didn't check their identification. But he would never purposefully harm anyone. Did you look at the artistry on your repaired cup? Is that the work of a violent young man? I hardly think so. The man who restored your teacup has patience and precision. He doesn't act impulsively or hastily."

Katie realized Nona was waiting for her to say something, but she had nothing to say and was happy the cup now resided in her apartment on the shelf she'd commissioned Vance to make just weeks before.

Eyes blazing, Nona leaned across Katie's desk. "You have to tell them!"

"Tell who what?"

"Tell Detective Schuler that Carl did not hit you on purpose! If anything, he was trying to *avoid* hitting you. How could he know that anyone would be idiotic enough to be walking across the parking lot on Victoria Square after midnight? What on earth were you thinking?"

There was no opportunity for Katie to answer because Margo and Rose were suddenly on the scene to come to her rescue.

"Nona, you need to leave and stop pestering Katie," Rose said. "She has work to do."

"You're being terribly rude, Rose." Nona lifted her chin so she could look down her nose at the other woman.

"Really? Tell that to Ida, whom you made leave Katie's office a few minutes ago." Hands on her hips, Margo was not in HR executive mode. She wasn't trying to placate Nona in the least.

Nona turned and made one last effort to make Katie see things her way. "You need to call off the dogs, Katie. Carl is being persecuted for something he didn't do."

"As I understand it, your nephew is being prosecuted for a number of things he did do," Katie corrected.

The tiny woman glared at her. "You won't get away with this. None of you! I'll make sure of that!" And with that, Nona stormed off.

Rose and Margo turned to gaze after the woman.

Could Nona's words really be considered a threat? Katie hoped not. But what kind of influence did Nona have over Carl—and vice versa?

Seventeen

Katie hated to admit it, but Nona's visit had rattled her, and once again she was grateful she'd left the newly repaired Black Magic teacup in her apartment for safekeeping. Nona had been so angry she might have deliberately smashed it, and this time with no promise of a repair.

Katie's nerves were still jangled an hour or so later when Seth stopped by with flowers. He set the bouquet of sweet-smelling yellow roses surrounded by baby's breath on her desk before stepping around to give her a kiss on the cheek.

"I just heard," he said in sympathy. "I go out of town for one weekend . . ."

She laughed. "Let's not talk about the trouble I got into. Tell me about your great time."

"It was wonderful." Seth actually blushed. "I really like this guy."

"I'm glad."

It was apparent Seth wasn't going to go into details when he changed the subject. "Are you doing all right? Is there anything you need?"

Katie frowned. "I'm a little miffed that Carl Fiske made bail." That was certainly putting it lightly. "But his story is that he didn't see me in the middle of the Square."

"And you know better?"

"Yes. He looked right at me."

"You know I have to ask." He grinned. "When you—" He put the words to music. "Went out walkin' after midnight . . ."

Katie laughed again. "Patsy Cline, you're not. To make a long story short, I couldn't sleep and went outside to clear my head. Now, would you mind if *I* change the subject?"

"Of course not."

"Okay, this is a really personal question, but I hope you'll bear with me."

Seth sobered. "Okay."

"How did it affect you when you learned that Rose was your biological mother?"

It had come to light the previous year that Rose Nash and the late Ezra Hilton were Seth's biological parents. Rose had given Seth up for adoption, and he and Ezra's legitimate son were dead ringers, which had caused all kinds of speculation.

"Actually, the news didn't affect me much at all. I already knew Rose and liked her; and while I care about Rose, she's not my mom. You know what I mean? I had a great childhood, and I loved my parents. Why are you asking about this?"

Katie explained the note she'd found from Vonne's birth mother.

Seth let out a breath. "Yeah, that's rough." He seemed about to expound further, when Nick poked his head around the door to the office.

"Seth! Hey!"

The two men hugged, and then Nick embraced Katie.

"I see great minds think alike," Nick said, pushing some files aside so he could sit on the corner of Katie's desk.

"Seth and I were talking about the letter I found," Katie said.

"You told him?" Nick pursed his lips. "You swore me to secrecy about that."

"I know, but—"

"I'll fuss at you later. Since Seth is in the know, I can tell you what I really rushed over here to get off my chest. After you told me about Nancy, my inquisitive mind wouldn't let it go and I started digging." He grimaced. "That didn't thrill Don, let me tell you. He went so far as to accuse me of not doing my fair share of the work today."

"And yet there you were, working for the greater good," Seth said, unsuccessfully trying to suppress a grin.

"That's what I told him! Anyhoo, I discovered that Nancy's husband is mayor of Ballarat, Ohio. Granted, it's not like he's the mayor of a great metropolitan area or anything, but a scandal—à la Vonne—could easily derail any further political aspirations he could ever hope to have."

"So other than the fact that Nancy didn't want any old chickens coming home to roost simply because she didn't want her family to know about her past, she was well aware that the revelation that she had a daughter—by a distant cousin, no less—could jeopardize her husband's career," Katie said. "Interesting."

"Very interesting," Nick said. "You have to wonder how far Nancy would have gone—or how far she did go—to keep Vonne out of her life."

"Then she should have done her drinking at home," Katie said, and filled them in on what Ray had told her. "Seems that would be scandal enough for a small-town political family."

Nick nodded.

"But enough about that," Seth said. "Why don't we get

you out of here for a little fresh air? We can walk over to
Angelo's and get a cinnamon bun."

"That's a good idea," Katie said. "Andy has been working on a couple of new recipes—apple cinnamon and pumpkin cinnamon—and has been urging me to give them a try."

"Pumpkin cinnamon?" Nick stood and raised his hands.
"I'm there. Just don't tell Don. No, wait, I'll take one back
for Don . . . then all will be forgiven."

Seth grabbed Katie's coat off the peg by the door and
helped her shrug into it. She was glad she hadn't bothered
with the Dickens outfit today but instead wore a simple
maxi skirt, a calf-high riding boot on her right leg, and a
white shaker-knit sweater.

Nick handed Katie her crutches, and they left Artisans
Alley by the side door. Nick and Seth hovered by her sides
as they traversed the salt-bleached asphalt, but Katie knew
they had nothing to worry about as far as ice was concerned. Both Vance and Andy were great about keeping ice
melt on the tarmac around Artisans Alley and the pizzeria.

Seth opened the door to Angelo's and permitted Katie to
go through first.

Andy smiled and came to greet the trio. "This is a nice
surprise!"

"Nick and Seth talked me into getting some fresh air,"
Katie said. "And, of course, when I told them you were
experimenting with new cinnamon bun flavors, I couldn't
have kept them away from here if I'd tried."

"I'm all about that pumpkin cinnamon," Nick said. "Have
you got some made up?"

"I have some of both flavors," Andy said. "Have a seat,
and I'll bring some over."

A seat was about right. Angelo's was primarily a pizza
take-out business, but Andy had provided one small table for
those who came in too soon to pick up an order or couldn't
wait to get home to eat it.

Nick held a chair for Katie while she handed her crutches

to Seth and lowered herself into the hard metal chair at a small table.

"This business with the crutches is tricky," she said, "but I believe I'm getting the hang of it."

Seth chuckled. "I broke my right ankle when I was in junior high. At about the time you get really good with the crutches, you won't need them anymore."

Andy brought a tray of cinnamon buns over to the table. There were two apple cinnamon, two pumpkin cinnamon, and two regular cinnamon buns. He also brought three forks and a stack of napkins. The buns were warm from the oven, and they smelled heavenly. Andy hovered over the table to gauge their reactions.

Thinking that, like Nick, she'd probably like the pumpkin cinnamon best, Katie saved it and tried the apple cinnamon first. She cut a small piece and lifted it to her nose. The scent was almost intoxicating. She took a bite and found that the bun's taste was even better than its aroma. Maybe she was wrong about which would be her favorite.

Nick was already halfway through one of the pumpkin cinnamon buns and had asked Andy to give him half a dozen to go.

"And I'll take two of the apple cinnamon," Seth said. "I want one for breakfast tomorrow morning, and I'm afraid I'll end up eating it tonight if I get only one."

Andy beamed, delighted that his new creations were going over so well. "Katie, what do you think?"

"I think the apple cinnamon is divine." She cut off a piece of the regular cinnamon bun. "This will cleanse my palate before I try the pumpkin spice."

Nick rolled his eyes. "Oooh, we've got a connoisseur in the house!"

"Aren't you going to try the apple cinnamon?" Seth asked Nick. "I think you'll love it."

"All right. But you haven't tried the pumpkin yet."

"I'm not a big fan of pumpkin."

Nick and Katie both looked at Seth as if he'd just insulted their mothers.

Seth spread his hands. "Sorry, but not everyone loves pumpkin."

Katie cut off a portion of the pumpkin cinnamon bun, savored its scent, and then popped a bite into her mouth. She moaned. "This is fantastic."

Andy inclined his head and raised his eyebrows. Katie could tell he wanted to say something provocative but was restraining himself because they were in his pizzeria with their friends.

Before Katie could further expound on the deliciousness of the pumpkin cinnamon buns, the door flew open, and ten little giggling girls raced into the pizzeria. They were followed by their teacher, Cheryl.

With a deep breath, Andy muttered, "I'd better take this situation in hand because I've got a feeling it could get out of control pretty quickly." He stood and jovially greeted the group. "Hi, and welcome to Angelo's. Are you celebrating a special occasion today?"

"No." Cheryl gave Katie a pointed look. "Apparently, there have been some complaints about my little angels here disturbing some of the mean old vendors at Artisans Alley, so I thought it might help to feed them a snack before rehearsal." She turned back and looked up at the menu high above the counter. "Um . . . let's have two orders of plain bread sticks with no dipping sauce, please." She glanced over her shoulder at one of the girls. "Can't get our tutus messy, can we?"

"All right," Andy said. "I'll get those out to you as soon as possible. What are you drinking?"

"We've got water back at the studio," Cheryl said, saving herself a good ten or twelve bucks.

Katie was just thinking that maybe giving the girls a

snack would help curb their rambunctious behavior when one of the girls let out a high-pitched squeal.

"My frog prince!"

The group erupted in screams, shrieks, and laughter.

"Don't anybody step on him!" the first girl cried.

Katie, Seth, and Nick exchanged glances. Nick's eyes widened and he placed a hand over his mouth as he nodded at a spot to Katie's right.

She whipped her head around just in time to see a large green bullfrog land in the middle of their table.

The amphibian rolled his head back, peered at Katie, and made a sound like *rum-rum.*

Katie leaned back in her chair, eager to put some distance between herself and the bullfrog.

"Catch him!" another girl squealed.

No way was Katie going to attempt to grab the frog. She looked at Nick and Seth, both of whom gave slight shakes of their heads. Nick was laughing so hard he was almost breathless.

The little girl who'd apparently brought the bullfrog with her into the pizzeria flung herself onto the table just as the frog leapt onto the window ledge. The remainder of their cinnamon buns were crushed beneath the girl. This, however, didn't deter her in her quest.

"For goodness' sake, who brought a frog in here?" Cheryl cried. "You girls had better catch him."

"Yeah," Andy shouted above the din of the croaking frog and the squealing girls. "I'm pretty sure some of my patrons would enjoy frog legs."

It was absolutely the worst thing Andy could have said, as it sent the little girl into an immediate crying fit. Andy ran a hand over his face.

Andy's protégé, Jeremy, who'd been busy filling Nick's pumpkin cinnamon bun order, took off his plastic gloves and tossed them into the trash can. "Let me see if I can help." The lanky boy scanned the tiny waiting area until he'd located the frog. "Ladies, if you'll quiet down for just a minute, that would help."

"You heard him," Cheryl barked. "Quiet!"

While the girls didn't exactly become still, the noise level diminished to the point that Jeremy could both see and hear the frog. Within seconds, he'd cornered and caught it. He handed it back to the grateful ballerina, who hugged the bullfrog to her chest and who looked at Jeremy as if he were her hero.

"I'll go get cleaned up," Jeremy said to Andy. The bullfrog had peed all down the front of his shirt. Thankfully, Andy kept clean uniforms on hand for—well, not *this* type of emergency, but for more pizza-related mishaps.

Frog prince indeed.

Katie poked at her smooshed bun and found that she'd lost her appetite.

~~~~~~

After the excitement at the pizza parlor, the men walked Katie back to Artisans Alley. Nick had his pumpkin cinnamon rolls and a fantastic story to tell Don. Seth had his apple cinnamon rolls, and Katie had a fear that she hadn't seen the last of that bullfrog.

The men had barely been gone five minutes before there was a knock on Katie's office door. Assuming one of them had forgotten something, she called, "Come on in!"

A thin man wearing a red hoodie, a bulky black jacket, and sunglasses entered the office, carrying a small box wrapped in brown paper. "Got a package for Katie Bonner."

"That's me." Something about the man caused the hair on the back of Katie's neck to prickle. "Just put it there on the desk please."

The man nodded toward the flowers. "You must be popular. Know who else was popular? Vonne Barnett."

Katie froze. *Is this Carl Fiske?*

"She even let me take her home a time or two," the man

said. "Guess that makes me popular, too, huh? But popular people often find themselves in a world of trouble. Just ask Vonne." He leaned closer so Katie could smell the foulness of his breath. "Oh, wait. You can't, can you?"

"Wh-who are you?" Katie whispered.

The man simply smirked and darted out the office and through the building's rear exit.

"Help! Somebody help!" Katie yelled, unable to get up fast enough to follow. She grabbed her crutches but lost sight of the so-called deliveryman as Vance raced into the vendors' lounge.

"What is it?" he asked.

"Carl Fiske was just here! Go after him!"

Vance barreled out the back door after Carl as Margo hurried into the lounge. "Katie, what's happened?"

"That . . . that deliveryman. It was Carl Fiske!"

Margo brought a hand up to her mouth. "I'm calling the police."

"No, I'll do it. I have Detective Schuler's number on my phone." With a trembling hand, Katie picked the phone up off the desk.

Margo pointed at the box. "What's that?"

"I don't know. He brought it."

Margo took a step back from the innocuous-looking box, as though it might explode at any moment.

Detective Schuler answered his phone promptly, and Katie had to force herself to remain calm.

"I found Carl Fiske for you."

"Oh yeah?"

"He just left my office at Artisans Alley. Not only that, but he left me a present—something I haven't had the courage to open. I thought maybe you might. You or the bomb squad."

"I'll be right there," Schuler said tersely. "Whatever you do, don't open that box. See if you can get someone to carefully place it outside and well away from the building until I arrive."

As Katie ended the call, Vance returned.

"I'm sorry, Katie. He got away."

"That's okay," Katie said, although her voice was shaking.

Katie pointed to the box. "Would you mind putting that outside and away from the building until Detective Schuler can get here?"

"Of course not," Vance said. "What is it?"

"We don't know." Katie blew out a breath. "Carl brought it in here. You might want to be very careful with it."

"Well, I don't think the man would be carrying around a bomb." Vance looked the package over before picking it up. "And it's pretty small. I'd say it was just a ruse to get in here." Still, he gently lifted the box and carried it out the building like it was as fragile as a soap bubble.

Katie backed up to her chair and allowed Margo to take the crutches from her. As Margo rested the crutches against the file cabinet, Katie let out a breath and glanced at the clock. It would be at least an hour before Schuler could arrive from across the county, but if there was a sheriff's cruiser nearby, maybe one of the deputies would be willing to stand guard over the terrible little box.

Vance returned and seemed determined to protect Katie from anything or anybody that threatened. One by one a dozen or more vendors made a point to drop by Katie's office, some curious, some demanding to know what was going on. She let Vance do most of the talking, while Margo kept bringing her cups of coffee. At this rate, she was never going to get to sleep that night.

Through her office window, Katie saw a sheriff's cruiser arrive. The deputy came inside and briefly spoke with her, and then when the second car arrived, that deputy guarded the box while the first one interviewed Katie, Vance, and then Margo.

Finally, a third cruiser showed up and Schuler got out just as a big boxy van pulled into the lot. She watched as, between vendor interrogations, deputies with face guards and heavily padded clothing exited the truck. She couldn't see what they were up to, but she had a good idea. At about the same time, an angry Ray arrived.

"What the hell is going on? I just heard Carl Fiske was here. What kind of security do you have here?" he demanded.

"Will you pipe down!" Katie whispered harshly. "The customers will hear you."

Ray lowered his voice but continued his rant. It felt like the old days when they'd first met and everything she said and did irritated him.

"I'll tell you what kind of security you have here—*none*! You're at the mercy of Carl Fiske or whoever else decides to storm in here!"

Vance and Margo had backed away at Ray's arrival and stood in the middle of the vendors' lounge taking turns whispering and casting furtive glances in Katie's direction.

Katie was glad when Detective Schuler came in through the back exit and strode up to her office door carrying the box. "The bomb techs went over this thing before opening it, but it's only a dead mouse. We'll photograph it for evidence and then dispose of it."

Thoroughly grossed out, Katie merely nodded.

"That is a death threat!" Ray stabbed the air with his index finger. "It's obvious that Fiske is telling Katie that if she rats him out, she'll end up dead . . . just like Vonne Barnett!"

"This is between Ms. Bonner and me," Detective Schuler said with authority. "I'd appreciate it if all of you excused us." He shut the door on the outraged faces of Katie's friends.

Katie didn't know whether to admonish or thank him.

Schuler ran his hand over his chin. "I hate to tell you

this, Ms. Bonner, but it's a matter of your word against Fiske's. The guys dusted the box for prints—"

"Carl was wearing gloves," Katie admitted.

"—and apparently no one else saw him in here . . . at least, no one who can positively identify him."

"Right. I understand."

"Unless he'll cop to it, or we can somehow find someone to corroborate his being here—they saw his car, they recognized him leaving here—then it's not enough to revoke his bail. I'm sorry, but that's how it is."

"I know," Katie said quietly, feeling defeated.

Detective Schuler started to say something else, but Katie said, "I get it. There's only so much you can do."

Andy burst into the office. He was pale and out of breath. "What the hell? Somebody just came into Angelo's and said there was a bomb over here."

"Not a bomb, Mr. Rust. A mouse. A dead mouse." Detective Schuler flicked his wrist toward the box.

Andy's eyes flew to Katie. "Are you all right?"

She nodded.

"I'm going to find that Carl Fiske, and I'm gonna beat the—"

"If you do that," Schuler interrupted, "you'll go to jail, and Carl Fiske will still be out on bond."

Andy blew out a breath and ran both hands through his hair.

"Would someone please take me home?" Katie asked.

Andy, Margo, Ray, Vance, and even Schuler immediately volunteered.

"Sophie is at the shop," Ray said to the group at large. "I can stay with Katie until Andy gets there after work."

"All right," Andy said. "I can be there as soon as Erikka comes in for the evening shift. We'd already planned on that anyway."

"Then I'll stay here and help Rose and Vance hold down the fort," Margo said. "Everybody will be all up in the air about this situation, and they'll need someone to help the vendors as well as the customers keep their heads about them."

"And we need to keep an eye out to make sure Fiske doesn't come back," Vance said.

Despite the fact that she resented everyone talking about her as if she weren't even in the room, Katie was glad that she was going to go home. She wanted her sofa, a blanket, and her cats. And maybe . . . maybe a very large dish of ice cream.

~~~~~~

If Ray had had his way, he would have carried Katie into her apartment and deposited her on the sofa. Instead, she allowed him to hold on to her left arm while she held on to the railing with her right and sat on the second stair leading to her apartment. She might not have looked dignified, but she was damned if she was going to let Ray coddle her. Of course, her much warmer posterior melted some of the caked-on snow and by the time she reached the landing, her butt was pretty damp. She allowed Ray to help her stand and waited while he fetched her crutches.

She practically fell back onto the couch, hoisted her injured leg up onto the coffee table, and allowed Ray to place her foot on a pillow.

"Thanks," she said wearily.

He sat down beside her. "Hey, you need a hug or something?"

"Something." But she didn't take him up on the offer. "Carl Fiske back in jail is what I need."

"It's okay now. You're safe."

"No, I'm not. Not as long as Carl Fiske is out there waiting to get me." She drew a long breath, thought about crying in frustration, and decided against it. She was, however, glad that Margo had stayed behind to help Rose and Vance close the Alley for the day. She glanced at her broken leg, angry that it had reduced her to a proverbial woman in jeopardy and dependent on others to save her.

Ray was still looking at her, waiting.

"If Carl had drawn a gun on me this afternoon, there wouldn't have been anything I could do to save myself."

"Well, that's true had your leg been broken or not," Ray said reasonably. She gave him a sour look. "Sorry."

She shook her head. "No. You're absolutely right. I'm at that man's mercy."

"No, you're not. We're going to protect you, Katie."

"There was no one to protect me today."

"I know. Damn it, I know. I should've been there."

Katie raised her gaze and looked into Ray's dark eyes, taking in the depth of his concern.

"I'm so sorry," he whispered.

She couldn't handle Ray's guilt, and she couldn't stand the thought of wallowing in self-pity. She was going to have to either let Carl get away with what he'd done to her—which she was adamant she wasn't going to do—or find a way to deal with his bullying until he was brought to trial.

"Prove it."

"What?" Ray asked softly.

"I said prove it."

Ray raised his hands as though in surrender. "I'll do anything you want."

"Good. Get me some chocolate peanut butter swirl ice cream—it's in the freezer—and add whipped cream and chocolate syrup."

He grinned. "Yes, Your Majesty. Anything else?"

"Peanuts," she said, raising her fist. "We require peanuts."

"Queen Victoria, is it?" He got up and headed into the kitchen.

"But of course. Just don't expect me to do a British accent," she said. "You can have ice cream, too, provided you do not object to the goofiest movie I can find for us to watch while we eat it."

"That's a deal."

Katie picked up the remote and began flipping through the channels. "Hey, *Elf* is on—and it just started!"

"Cool. I haven't seen that one."

"You haven't seen *Elf*? Where the heck have you been?"

"I don't know," he said as he dipped their ice cream into bowls. "I've never been that into Christmas movies."

She groaned. "Hurry up and get over here."

"How much whipped cream do you want?"

"A lot."

Finally, he brought their heaping bowls into the living room.

Katie skootched around so she could better see the television.

He handed her a bowl and sat down beside her.

Will Ferrell's silly antics didn't seem as funny that day, and neither of them laughed. During a commercial, Ray took their bowls into the kitchen, rinsed them out, and put them in the dishwasher. And just in time, because Sadie and Sasha knocked on the door.

"Wow, we heard there was some real excitement over at Artisans Alley this afternoon," Sadie said.

"Seems like the whole world knows," Katie muttered. "The real excitement happened earlier today when a bullfrog got loose in Angelo's Pizzeria."

Katie had both girls' rapt attention as she described—and maybe exaggerated the teensiest bit—the story of the ballerina's bullfrog. "She called it her frog prince. And I think she might've fallen in love with young Jeremy right on the spot when he caught it and returned it to her."

"Yuck," said Sadie. "Who'd want a frog as a pet?"

"I suppose that depends on whether you thought it was a prince or not," Katie said.

"I think it's sweet," Sasha said. "Oooh, what an adorable little tree!" She went over to admire the two-foot artificial spruce that sat atop a table by the window.

"Petite is sweet," Sadie agreed, and both girls giggled.

"Oh, look—*Elf* is on. Can we watch the rest of it with you?" Sasha asked.

"Of course."

The girls settled on the floor by the sofa, too close to Della, who streaked off into the bedroom, but Mason allowed Sadie to pick him up and cuddle him.

The girls were positively enchanted when Buddy the Elf showed Jovie the "big" Christmas trees until she showed him the one in Rockefeller Center. Ray seemed resigned to suffer through the rest of the movie as Buddy entered the conference room to interrupt a meeting with the elf-sized Mr. Finch. But before spotting Mr. Finch, Buddy declared his love for Jovie.

"That's like Dad and Katie," Sasha said. "They're in love, and they don't care who knows it."

"What?" Katie asked, nearly choking on her question, but nobody seemed to be paying attention. Ray kept his gaze firmly trained on the TV.

"Shut up! They are not!" Sadie said. "Dad and Katie are *friends*, and that's it. Not everybody is in love, Sasha. Dad still loves Mom!"

"He can love them both," Sasha insisted. "Mom is gone, and he can love Katie now, too. Right, Dad?"

Ray cleared his throat, but his voice was husky when he spoke. "Sadie's right. Katie and I are only friends . . . really good friends."

"But that's how love starts, right, Katie?"

Katie offered a wan smile, hoping they didn't notice her cringe.

Eighteen

The movie had just finished and Katie not only wondered where Margo had gotten to—she'd have thought her former mother-in-law would've jumped ship on Rose and Vance long before now—but hoped that Andy might soon arrive to relieve Ray of his guard duties. Then someone knocked on the apartment door, and Katie's gaze flew to Ray's. She hadn't heard anyone come up the steps.

"It's okay," he said firmly. "I've got this. Girls, go into the bedroom and stay there until I tell you it's safe to come out."

Sasha stood and moved closer to Katie. "What's wrong?"

"What's going on?" Sadie asked. "You're scaring me, Dad."

"Do what I told you to do." He grabbed Katie's crutches, handing them to her. "Go with the girls."

"I will not," she said defiantly. "I'm staying right here." She raised her voice. "Who is it?"

"Nona Fiske."

Ray raised his index finger and pointed to the bedroom. "Girls, do what I said. Go into the bedroom and close and lock the door." This time his tone and their fear caused them to obey.

"Are you alone, Nona?" Katie called.

"Of course I am. Now let me in. I need to speak with you."

Ray looked out the living room windows, checking the parking lot, before he moved to the back of the kitchen to open the door slightly, leaving the security chain in place.

"What are you doing here?" Nona sneered.

"The question is what are *you* doing here? Do you know that if you were to help your nephew gain entrance into this apartment, you'd be liable for any illegal acts he might commit?"

Nona bristled. "Carl is not with me. Are you going to let me in or not?"

Ray turned and looked at Katie, who nodded.

He unlatched the security chain, opened the door, and allowed Nona to step inside, then quickly checked to ensure that she was telling the truth about Carl not being with her.

Nona marched over to the end of the sofa to stand with her hands on her hips and glare at Katie, who was glad she still held her crutches. "How dare you make false claims against my poor Carl? Again! Why do you have it in for him?"

"I don't have it in for Carl, and I've made no false claims against him."

"Oh really? A couple of deputies just questioned him about someone delivering a dead mouse in a box to your office at Artisans Alley, but I'll have you know that Carl was at The Quiet Quilter with me putting up a shelf in my storeroom."

"Is that right?" Ray asked, coming to tower over Nona. It wasn't that he was all that tall but that she was that short. "Are you certain Carl was there the entire time?"

Nona jutted out her chin. "Yes."

"Did either of you leave The Quiet Quilter at any time?"

"I didn't, and as far as I know, neither did Carl. You have no idea what that dear boy has been through. His father is dead, he lost his nice job restoring porcelain and ceramics because he was attacked in a bar . . ."

"And he was arrested?" Ray asked.

"Yes! For merely defending himself!" She shot a baleful glare at Katie. "And now he's having to defend himself against yet another bully."

"You think I'm bullying Carl?" Katie placed her palm beside her broken leg. "Did *I* hit him with *my* car?"

"Had you not been where you didn't belong—sticking your nose in other people's business like you always do— that never would've happened." Nona raised her chin and folded her arms across her chest, a feat Katie was surprised she could manage given the thickness of her wool coat.

Katie wasn't sure if Nona meant Carl never would have hit her if she hadn't been walking on the Square or that he wouldn't have hit her had she not mentioned that he was serving liquor to underage girls. Either way, the fact remained that Carl purposefully hit her with his car. If he'd had his way, a broken leg might've been the least of Katie's problems.

"Are you aware, Ms. Fiske, that if your nephew violates any of the conditions of his bail at any time—including harassing Ms. Bonner—his bond will be revoked and whoever put up that money will suffer the loss?"

Katie couldn't help being impressed. Ray sounded as lawyerly as Seth.

Nona blanched, and Katie surmised—as had Ray, apparently—that it was she who'd paid Carl's bail. She glared at Katie. "I don't know why you're out to get Carl, but you'd better be careful. That's all I've got to say."

"Are you threatening Ms. Bonner?" Ray asked.

"I'm not threatening anybody, Ray Davenport, so stop being all high and mighty with me!" She uncrossed her arms and flung them by her sides, her bulky purse banging against Ray. "All I'm saying is that people who make trouble for others often find themselves in a big pot of hot water."

"Like Vonne Barnett did?" Katie asked.

Nona's eyes narrowed. "Exactly like her."

"It's time for you to leave." Ray walked over and opened the door.

With one last venom-filled look at Katie, Nona turned and stalked out of the apartment.

Ray shut and locked the door behind her before coming to sit by Katie on the sofa. "Are you all right?"

"I'm not sure what to feel. Do you think Carl sent Nona here to further threaten me, or did she come on her own? And why is she so sure Carl is innocent?"

"I can't answer your first question, but people never want to think ill of their family members."

"I wonder where he was the night Vonne died."

"Humph. I wonder where Nona was. Maybe she directed the same threatening attitude toward Vonne that she's taking toward you. I'll certainly look into it and find out where they both were."

"Thank you." Katie took his hand. "I appreciate everything you've done for me."

"I'm glad to do it."

"I wish I could wake up and find this was all just a nightmare."

"I know." He reached over and squeezed Katie's hand. "Girls, you can come out of the bedroom now."

Sadie opened the door and poked her head out. "Is it safe?"

"Would I have told you to come out if it wasn't?" Ray asked.

Sasha brushed past her sister and hurried to sit between Katie and Ray. Ray kissed her forehead. "Everything's okay." Sadie snuggled against Ray's other side. He kissed her, too.

"Is Katie gonna be all right?" Sadie asked. "That lady sounded really mean."

"I'll be fine." As Katie smiled reassuringly at the girls, she wished she felt as confident as she sounded.

This time Katie did hear the clatter of footfalls on the stairs. Margo and Andy had arrived. The key rattled in the lock, but the security chain held fast.

"Open up," Andy announced, "we've got bags of groceries."

Ray let them in, along with another rush of cold air, and Margo set her bags on the counter. "Gosh, it's frosty out there. The perfect weather for meat loaf and mashed potatoes. I thought, given the day we've had, we need something hearty to help us buck up," she said. "Ray, will you and your lovely daughters join us?"

"No, thank you," Ray said. "We appreciate the generous offer, but I'm guessing Sophie has something in the works by now." Not likely, as she'd been holding down the fort at Wood U all afternoon. He turned to Katie. "Do you plan to return to Artisans Alley tomorrow?"

"Of course."

"Then I'll be here to collect you and Margo around eight. Would it be okay if I worked in the vendors' lounge outside your office?"

"That's a great idea, Ray," Andy said. "I'll talk with Vance and see if he can relieve you every so often."

"I don't think it's necessary to take Ray away from his shop." Katie gave both men what she hoped was a stern stare. It did her no good.

Ray placed his hand over his heart as if wounded. "During this busy season, maybe I'll get a few more customers if

I hang out in Artisans Alley. You wouldn't take that chance from me, now, would you?"

Katie scowled in frustration. "I know what you're doing!"

Margo walked over to Ray and put a hand on his arm. "He's being wonderful, that's what he's doing. He's a trained officer of the law providing you protection for a brief change of venue. Now, how could you turn down such a fabulous offer, Katie?"

Katie threw up her hands in defeat. "I give up."

Ray grinned at Margo. "You'd have made one heck of a police interrogator."

"Yes, I know." She winked at him and then headed for the kitchen to get dinner started.

Sasha went to give Katie a hug. She'd already put on her coat and as she bent over, a small box fell out of her pocket. She quickly hugged Katie, palmed the box, and shoved it back into her pocket. The girl looked to see if Ray had seen. He hadn't. But Katie had. The box contained diet pills.

~~~~~~~~

It had been a really long day, and Katie was ready to hit the sack—but it wouldn't be fair to make Margo and Andy retire so early. They had finished dinner, and the dishes had been rinsed and put in the dishwasher when Andy suggested they watch TV. Katie would have preferred to read for a while, but before she could voice that alternative, more footfalls pounded up the stairs to her apartment. A knock sounded.

Andy went to the door. "Yeah."

"It's me, Erikka!"

Andy opened the door, and Erikka breezed into the apartment in a full-length faux fur coat. "I hate to interrupt, but it is my break time," she said, "and I need to speak with you for just a second."

"Sure," Andy said. "Is everything all right downstairs?"

"Oh yeah, everything's great. No need to worry about

that." She smiled, her perfect white teeth gleaming. "Did Katie tell you she turned me on to a terrific job opportunity?"

Andy looked down at Katie. "No, she didn't." His voice was so cold Katie felt the need for an additional sweater.

"Yeah, so anyway, I applied for the job and had an interview today," Erikka said.

"So, you're submitting your notice?" Andy asked, turning away from Katie and looking at Erikka with irritation.

"Oh, no way!" Erikka stepped forward to put her hand on Andy's arm. "I adore working with you. Even if I get the other job, I'll still work nights at Angelo's . . . that is, if you'll have me."

"You've got a job for as long as you want it."

Smiling, Erikka hugged Andy. "Thank you! I really need the extra cash. But you know if I had to choose, I'd choose you over money any day." She stepped back. "Thanks again for understanding. I didn't want there to be any secrets between us and definitely didn't want you to feel like I'd gone behind your back to apply for the other job."

"I don't feel that way at all," Andy said.

Erikka smiled sweetly. "How's that leg treating you, Katie?"

"Oh, it's hanging in there," she said.

"It's too bad you had to have an accident right before the holidays. It must really be curtailing all your really fun activities." She eyed Andy and then winked.

"It was so nice of you to stop in," Margo said, in a tone that let everyone know that short as her visit had been, Erikka had already overstayed her welcome.

"Back to work I go. But if you need me, Andy, I'll be right downstairs."

As soon as Erikka left, Andy whirled to face Katie. "What the hell?"

"If you'll excuse me, I believe I'd like to go read for a

while," Margo said. Behind Andy's back, she gave Katie a thumbs-up. "I'll be in the bedroom if anyone needs me."

After Margo closed the bedroom door, Katie said quite innocently, "It appears you're upset with me."

"Upset? That's the understatement of the year. Why would you undermine my business? Do you want to find jobs for all my other employees while you're at it?"

"This isn't about your business, Andy. This is about Erikka. You have to know that she's barely making enough to get by."

"How do you know what she makes?" He placed his hands on his hips. "You know what? I don't think this job hunt for Erikka was motivated by concern for her at all. I think you're jealous of her."

"Don't be silly."

"Oh, now I'm being silly? Tell me the truth. If I hadn't taken Erikka home the other night, would you have been trying to find her a job?"

"Okay, no, I wouldn't have." Katie pulled herself up as tall as she could while still sitting on the sofa. She wished she could stand toe-to-toe with him. "Had you not driven Erikka home and stayed with her for hours sharing a bottle of wine, I wouldn't have been looking at job sites for her. But, hey, what're you worried about? Your precious Erikka isn't going to leave you. She adores working with you. You'll still get to see her every day, working side by side, being the dynamic duo of pizza."

"You're a hypocrite! How dare you throw my friendship with Erikka in my face while Ray Davenport is always at your heels like a lovesick puppy?"

"Ray feels responsible for what happened to me, and he's trying to protect me from Carl Fiske. I thought you were on board with that."

"I'm on board with it because I'm willing to do whatever it takes to protect you from Fiske, too! But don't sabotage my friendship with Erikka unless you're willing to give up yours with Ray."

Katie considered arguing the point, but then thought again. Weren't they both worried about the same thing? It bothered her that he spent far too much time with Erikka, and he stewed about her spending too much time with Ray.

It seemed neither of them had anything more to say on the subject.

The rest of the evening was a silent night in Katie's apartment.

Nineteen

<hr />

True to his word, the next morning Ray arrived bright and early to escort Katie and Margo to Artisans Alley. Vance had already opened the place for vendor restocking. Margo kept Katie company in her office while Ray set up his carving tools and prepared to start a new project. The one disappointment came when Katie quizzed Vance and found that, despite his promise, Andy had neglected to call and give him some warning—not that it really mattered. Vance was Katie's trusted lieutenant, for which she was grateful.

Margo toyed with the pretty gold wristwatch on her left wrist. "I tried not to listen to your argument with Andy last night, but I couldn't help overhearing some of it," she said, her voice low so as not to be heard by others in the vendors' lounge.

"That's okay. It wasn't like we were whispering." Katie sighed. "Andy's right. I was—am—jealous of his relationship with Erikka. But I don't want Andy interfering with my friendship with Ray, either."

"I understand completely. You'll eventually have to choose between them, you know."

Katie dodged that statement. It was ridiculous. She had different relationships with the men. Andy was her lover, and Ray was her friend. "I miss Chad. And I'm not saying that because the world is so complicated without him. I just miss him. We started off as friends. You never get over the loss of such a good friend."

"I miss him, too, darling—every minute of every day." Margo glanced toward the door and then extended her leg, pushing the door until it was almost closed. "I need to tell you something, and without an audience."

Katie tensed but tried not to convey her sudden anxiety. "What's on your mind?"

"Yesterday I walked over to Afternoon Tea and had a long conversation with Francine, after which I made an offer for the shop."

Katie felt as though she'd been sucker punched. "I . . . I didn't realize the idea of going into business interested you."

"It doesn't. But you want the tea shop . . . and Chad would want you to have it."

"No, Margo. That . . . it's too much," Katie managed. "I can't allow you to do it."

"Let it be a Christmas gift . . . from me and Chad. He'd want you to be happy. Besides, I feel badly that Chad left you with this—" She spread her arms to take in the shabby office, her expression glum. "This burden."

"Artisans Alley isn't a burden. Or, at least, it isn't anymore," Katie said. "I have to admit that when I first took over after Ezra's death, I hated it. It was a mess, the vendors were behind on their payments, and I resented the fact that I was stuck with this hulk of a potential firetrap rather than the English Ivy Inn. But this place is Chad's legacy. If nothing else, I was determined to turn it around to prove him right. He always said with the proper management it would prosper." She smiled. "And I made it work."

"You certainly did. But now it's your turn, Katie. It's time to do something for *you*."

"I am. I've come to love it here."

"I realize that, but Artisans Alley was never your dream. It was Chad's." Margo took a deep breath. "And I realize I was pretty much the mother-in-law from hell."

"Oh, of course you weren't. You—"

Margo shook her head. "Don't even try to deny it. I just refused to accept how much you loved Chad and how much he loved you. I thought the two of you were mismatched and that you couldn't possibly make him happy. I was wrong." Katie's mouth dropped and Margo shrugged. "Anyway, I'm in a position to do something potentially life-changing for you . . . and I want to do it."

The rising bustle of activity outside Katie's not-quite-closed door alerted the women that Ray had attracted an audience of other crafters who were interested in the block of wood he intended to turn into a reindeer.

"At least, think it over," Margo said, before getting up. She patted Katie on the shoulder. "How about I get us both another cup of coffee?"

Before Katie could reply, she'd already left the office, pausing to listen in on the lively conversation around the old chrome-and-Formica table that occupied most of the vendors' lounge.

Katie sat back in her chair, a new worry hanging over her head. Should she accept Margo's generous offer? It would solve her financial worries in one way, but it would keep her beholden to a woman she wasn't sure she could trust. What was that old saying about a leopard not able to change its spots? What price would Katie pay to dabble in the teatime trade? Would Margo move to McKinlay Mill to keep an eye on her investment? Would she want to help run the place—which would be a constant source of friction? Katie could foresee all kinds of unpleasant possibilities that could doom the budding relationship they might be forging.

She needed to think long and hard before she could accept such an offer. And have several lively discussions not only with Seth but with her financial adviser as well.

Yes, a proposition such as Margo offered could be full of pitfalls. But it would also give Katie back at least part of the dream Chad had stolen from her. Despite her triumphs at Artisans Alley, she wasn't sure she would ever be able to forgive him for betraying her trust. And yet it hadn't diminished the longing she still felt for him. Had she jumped into her relationship with Andy in order to fill the void Chad had left? Or was Andy truly the one with whom she wanted to spend the rest of her life?

She wasn't up to pondering that question, either, at least not then.

Christmastime was supposed to be the Joyous Season. If that was so, how come Katie felt no joy in any aspect of her life?

~~~~~

The rest of the morning passed quietly, and Katie was proud of the amount of work she'd been able to accomplish. Margo seemed content to spend her time in Chad's Pad, which was a bit of a relief for Katie.

Her stomach grumbled and a glance at the clock told Katie it was past noon. Not only was she thinking about sustenance, but she realized she hadn't packed a lunch. Not only was she hungry, but she was antsy, too, and decided to stretch her legs with a walk around Artisans Alley—the first floor, anyway—to see how things were going.

She reached for her crutches and stood, but as she grasped the door handle, she heard a woman's raised voice.

She nudged the door open a crack and saw Godfrey Foster sitting alone at the far end of the big Formica table. The other end was still littered with wood chips, but no sign of Ray. He must have stepped out to give the couple some privacy. Godfrey's wife, Lucy, stood over him—her face twisted in anger.

"How many times did you go out with that Barnett tramp?" Lucy grated.

"Once. I went out with her only once, I swear!"

Lucy looked around. "Keep your voice down," she ordered. "Did you know she was pregnant?"

Katie took a step back. She really shouldn't intrude on such a personal conversation.

"So what if she was?" Godfrey asked. "Why would that have anything to do with us?"

"I'd hoped the two of us could find our way back to each other," Lucy said. "But there's no way we can reconcile if you got another woman pregnant."

Godfrey groaned. "Honey, that woman was seeing a lot of men, whether they were free to date her or not. It seems like you're simply looking for a reason to give up on our marriage. Who cares whether or not a dead woman was knocked up when she died?"

Katie was about to retreat into her chair when Ray reentered the lounge. Lucy glared at him, and he backed up a step. "Uh, I was just going to see Katie."

Katie scrambled to get away from the door before he could burst in and run her over. Sure enough, he knocked before entering and closed the door behind him.

"What's going on in the lounge?"

Katie laid her index finger against her lips, then spoke in a whisper. "Godfrey's wife is giving him the third degree over Vonne. He was telling her he only went out with Vonne once, but Lucy asked if he knew Vonne was pregnant. I thought the police were keeping the pregnancy under wraps."

"They are."

"Then how do you think Lucy found out?" Katie reached for her candy jar and took out a peppermint. She offered Ray one, and he accepted. "Have you heard if Nona made threats to Vonne?"

"Not yet," Ray said. Katie chomped on her peppermint, causing Ray to wince. A lot of people reacted the same way. "Uh, it's occurred to me that neither of us has had our afternoon break. Why don't I buy us both a cup of tea and a sandwich over at the tea shop?"

"Our afternoon break? Since when is that a thing?"

"Since we need to get out of here before Lucy Foster kills us all."

Katie grinned. He was pandering to her or else he'd have chosen somewhere else to take their break . . . like Angelo's, which was much closer. A gruff old guy like Ray didn't seem the type to drink tea from a delicate china cup, but she wasn't going to let him off the hook, either.

"That sounds delightful." He took her coat from a peg on the wall and helped her with it. He peeked out the door. "Huh. Guess I must have scared them off. They're gone." He helped Katie to her feet and exited her office, grabbing his trench coat and hat before they headed for the Alley's front entrance.

Katie didn't fully appreciate how far Afternoon Tea was from Artisans Alley until she'd traversed the parking lot using crutches. When Ray opened the door to the shop, Katie gratefully sank onto a chair at the first table she saw.

"Katie! How wonderful to see you!" Francine grabbed a couple of menus and hurried out from behind the sales counter. "And, Ray, how nice of you to help Katie get here." She placed the menus on the table. "What can I get the two of you?"

"Um . . . I'm not sure yet," Katie said.

"Neither am I."

"Well, I'll brew a fresh pot of tea and give you a few minutes to make up your mind. You like Earl Grey, right?"

Katie nodded. "Is that okay, Ray?"

"I'm fine with whatever."

"Splendid. I'll be back to check on you in a few minutes. Oh, and just to let you know, I've got blueberry muffins, pecan scones, shortbread cookies, pumpkin bread, and cherry tartlets, if you're interested." Francine smiled broadly before going to check on a middle-aged man in a dark tweed jacket sipping a cup of tea at the back of the shop, and then she slipped into the kitchen.

"What's up with her?" Ray asked under his breath.

"I'll explain later."

Ray picked up the menu and scrutinized it. Instead of dainty pastries, he'd probably rather have a cinnamon bun from the pizza parlor. But she had no sympathy for him, since he'd been the one to suggest this place. Had there been some other reason he'd chosen Afternoon Tea over Angelo's or Tanner's Café and Bakery? Maybe he'd wanted to check the place out for Sophie, in case Katie bought it and allowed his daughter to do an internship there.

"Sophie wanted me to let you know she scoped this place out so you could have a professional's take on its viability."

So Sophie had already checked Afternoon Tea for herself.

"Professional?" Katie asked skeptically. So far, Sophie had spent only one semester at the Culinary Institute of America learning her trade. Katie was pretty sure that didn't qualify the young woman as a professional.

"Of course. She *did* frost cakes and cookies at Wegmans for more than a year. She told me to mention that to you," Ray said with amusement.

"I'll take your word for it," Katie said, and smiled. "And what was her professional opinion?"

"She pretended to mix up the doors for the kitchen and ladies' room so she could see how the operation worked. No sign of mouse droppings or other vermin, but the kitchen was untidy to the max."

That didn't surprise Katie, considering the tea shop was now a one-person operation, but she was impressed that Sophie had taken the initiative to check it out. Naturally, should Katie choose to assume ownership of the operation, she'd go over every inch of Afternoon Tea with a fine-tooth comb. "Anything else?"

"No thermometers in the refrigerated cases means Francine has no idea if temperature-sensitive items, like cannoli, are safe to eat. That's a health-code violation."

"But not enough to shut Francine down," Katie countered.

"No."

"Anything else?"

"She thought the menu was stodgy."

"Was that her description?"

Ray nodded.

"But overall, what did she think?"

"That you should go into hock, snap it up, and hire her the minute she graduates from the CIA."

Katie grinned. She could have predicted that. "That would be in three years?"

"There's always summers," Ray countered.

When Francine returned, she poured the tea and took their orders. Katie decided that life was short and ordered a couple of slices of pumpkin bread. Ray settled on a pecan scone, but he didn't look entirely happy about it.

Francine retreated to the kitchen once again.

"Nice place," Ray commented, eyeing the precious decor and looking uncomfortable. "But Francine really needs to have someone in the front at all times. The shop is rife with security problems. Just anybody could walk in and empty the till."

Katie shook her head ruefully. "Once a lawman, always a lawman. I'm afraid she couldn't afford to replace Vonne. In fact, she'd already let Janine—the girl who usually worked weekends—go even before Vonne died. Janine was great. As a matter of fact, if I do buy the shop, I'm planning on asking her to manage it for me."

Francine returned with their food in no time, and once she'd emptied the tray, she took the seat next to Katie.

"I'm simply delighted to see you up and about," Francine burbled. "Are you still in much pain?"

"Uh, not bad," Katie said.

"I'm so happy to hear that. It still rankles me that you could be run down right here on Victoria Square. Another reason why I'll be glad to—" But then she didn't finish the sentence.

Katie could guess what she meant, however. "Speaking of my accident, do you know Carl Fiske?"

Francine's enthusiasm seemed to falter. "No, I don't believe I do. I mean, I know who he is, but we're not exactly acquainted."

"I was under the impression Vonne had some sort of relationship with Carl," Ray said matter-of-factly.

Francine took a moment before answering. "Vonne was trying to have relations with all sorts of men, Ray. I don't know whether one of them was Carl Fiske or not."

"Carl led me to believe that Vonne might've been blackmailing him, but I don't know whether or not that's true." Katie cut into her pumpkin bread with her fork. "I don't have a high opinion of Carl, and I'm totally convinced he isn't above lying."

"If Vonne was getting money from somewhere, she certainly wasn't funneling it into the tea shop." Francine said flatly.

"I imagine she was saving it for the baby," Ray suggested quietly.

Francine got up from her chair and looked across the dining room. "I need to check on my other customer. If you'll excuse me." She scooted out of her chair and over to the man in the tweed jacket.

Katie was glad Francine was no longer in earshot when

Ray leaned over the table. "I wonder where Godfrey's wife got her information about Vonne's pregnancy. Do you think Francine could have told her?"

"Based on her reaction to the mere mention of a baby, I'm guessing not. I wonder if Carl knew Vonne was pregnant."

"We can't very well ask him," Ray said.

A shiver ran up Katie's spine. "I hope I never see that man again. That goes double for talking with him." She sipped her tea. "I suppose it's possible Nona knew. As Francine once pointed out to me, not much stays a secret on Victoria Square."

"You're not planning on talking with Nona, are you?"

"Not me," Katie said. "But maybe Rhonda Simpson might be persuaded to ask."

Ray merely scowled.

"But for now, there's something else I need to tell you." Katie took a deep breath. She'd been dreading talking with Ray about this all day. But now that the opportunity had presented itself, she couldn't simply let it pass. "Yesterday, when she hugged me, a box of diet pills fell out of Sasha's coat pocket."

"Diet pills? Are you sure?"

"Positive. Ray, I'm only saying this because you enlisted my help and advice concerning your fear that Sasha might be developing an eating disorder, but I think it's time to call in a professional . . . before Sasha's condition becomes more serious."

"So . . . what?" He stiffened. "You think I should take her to a shrink?"

"Nothing that drastic . . . not yet, anyway. Right now I believe your best bet might be the school counselor. I imagine he or she is well equipped to deal with these kinds of problems. Plus, the school has Sasha's records on hand."

"You're right." He sighed. "I asked all the girls if they needed to talk with someone—you know, a professional—after their mother died, but they all said no. They said they were fine." He ran a hand over the lower portion of his face. "They weren't *fine*. None of us were fine. We still aren't."

Katie patted his hand.

"Do you think Rachel's death could have anything to do with what Sasha is going through now?" he asked.

"I don't know," Katie said. "That's why Sasha needs to talk with someone better qualified to help her."

"Yeah." He blew out a breath. "Thanks, Katie."

They finished their food and tea and headed back to Artisans Alley. They stopped at cash desk one, where Rose was ringing up a sale for a customer. "And have a merry Christmas!" Rose told the woman, her voice filled with good cheer. Then she turned to Katie, who'd leaned against the counter to stabilize herself. "What's up?"

"Is Rhonda in today?"

"She's walking security upstairs."

"Great," Ray said. "Come on, Katie, I'll get you settled in your office and then—"

"I am not a china doll. I can walk the length of the Alley by myself and go to my office."

"Yeah, but can you hang up your coat?" Ray asked.

Katie glowered at him.

Once she was ensconced behind her desk, Ray hurried upstairs to ask Rhonda to come down to talk with him and Katie.

Katie had just fished a peppermint out of her jar when Ray and Rhonda returned. Ray pulled the chair he'd been using into Katie's office and offered it to Rhonda. He sat on the chair beside Katie's desk.

"Am I in trouble for some reason?" Rhonda asked, her blue eyes wide with concern.

"Not in the least," Katie said. "I was wondering how things are going between you and Nona Fiske."

Rhonda groaned. "What now? She's not complaining and threatening to sue me again, is she?"

"No. This situation has nothing to do with you and

Nona." Katie told Rhonda about Nona's two unpleasant visits the day before.

"Wait," Rhonda said. "I thought Carl hit you by accident . . . or I did until I heard about his bringing that dead mouse to you in a box yesterday. Ewww. That's disgusting."

"Not only is Nona denying that Carl hit Katie on purpose, but she's denying that the man who delivered that mouse yesterday was Carl, too," Ray explained.

"Feel free to say no to what we're about to ask you," Katie said. "I promise there won't be any hard feelings."

Rhonda's lips curved into a smile. "What do you need?"

"We'd like to know how Nona felt about Vonne Barnett." Katie unwrapped the peppermint and put it in her mouth. "Anyone else care for a mint?"

Ray and Rhonda both declined. Katie crunched the candy and the others cringed.

"Vonne is the woman who was killed in the car accident, right?" Rhonda asked.

"Yes." No need to go into all the specifics of Vonne's death with Rhonda at this point. "I believe Carl and Vonne knew each other and quite possibly had a relationship," Katie said. "I'd like to find out if my guess is right."

"I'm sure I can discreetly ask Nona a few questions," Rhonda said.

"Throw Katie to the wolves," Ray suggested.

Both women looked at him in surprise.

"What?" he asked, with a shrug. "It's what I'd do. She's angry with you, Katie. If I were interrogating Nona, I'd offer her some sympathy and say something along the lines of 'I realize Katie was hurt in that accident and that she's angry about it, but what would make her think that Carl would ram his car into her on purpose?' Then you could take it a step further and point out that Katie's physical wounds will heal, but her testimony could destroy Nona's nephew's life."

Katie grinned. "I see what you're saying. Make like Nona

and pretend I'm being unreasonable and that Carl Fiske is not a maniac."

"Precisely," Ray said. His eyes narrowed and he turned on Katie. "Couldn't you at least sit down and have a civil conversation with darling nephew Carl? What has he ever done to *you*?"

"Um . . . tried to kill me and then frightened me with threats and a dead mouse in a box?" Katie asked.

Ray spread his hands wide. "Well, if you're going to be picky."

Rhonda laughed. "You guys are hilarious. But, sure, I'll be your undercover operative. I'll go see Nona now and find out as much as I can. I've got some new pillowcases that complement one of her patchwork quilts to show her anyway. That will be my in."

"Be careful," Katie warned. "You know as well as any of us that Nona isn't a nice person."

"I'll stay on my toes," Rhonda promised.

Ray opened the door and checked the vendors' lounge to make sure it was clear of Nona or anyone who might report back to her that Rhonda had had a secret meeting with him and Katie. Assured that the coast was clear, he allowed Rhonda to carry out her mission.

Once again, he closed the door and sat on the chair Rhonda had vacated. "What do you think? Will she bring back solid intel?"

"I hope so." Katie looked down at her desk pad. "I just hope we haven't painted a target on her back. Maybe we should call her back, Ray."

"She'll be all right."

"Rhonda has kids. What if Carl decides to go after her next?"

"He won't. If I thought that, I wouldn't have agreed with your suggestion to send her over to The Quiet Quilter to go all Jane Bond on Nona." He frowned. "I appreciate your high opinion of me."

"I do have a high opinion of you. I'm just concerned about Rhonda. I wish there'd been another way to find out what we needed to know."

"You said it yourself," Ray said. "Rhonda has kids. She has to be able to think on her feet. And, if she takes my advice and trashes you, Nona will believe every word out of Rhonda's mouth."

"I'll be glad when she gets back." Katie bit her lip. "I'd be even happier if Carl was back in jail. Or do you think maybe I am being too hasty in my judgment of him?"

"Is that a joke? Because if it is, it's a dumb one."

"Well, you indicated that he and I might be able to sort things out with a civil conversation."

Ray slapped his hand to his forehead. "I was simply prepping our undercover detective. Don't you recognize sarcasm when you hear it?"

"Normally, I can, but . . . why would Carl have intentionally aimed his car for me that night? What if I *did* imagine it? Maybe I jumped to the conclusion that he hit me on purpose because he believes I ratted him out for selling drinks to underage girls."

"Carl Fiske is a psycho. You talked to me, and that discussion eventually got Carl caught serving liquor to minors. He's been arrested and has lost his job. I don't think he intended to give you a little love tap with his front bumper."

"All right, all right," Katie acquiesced.

Ray stood. "Back to work. Maybe I can finish my carving before I turn my guard duty over to Andy."

Katie nodded. "Oh, and thank you for . . . afternoon tea." She laughed.

Ray merely shook his head and left her alone.

Katie woke her computer and glanced at her list of things to do. Considering where to place ads for the Alley for Valentine's Day had finally made it to the top of the list. Strawberry tarts would work well at the tea shop. Red, juicy berries smothered in whipped cream. Or maybe chocolate-dipped cherries. Heart-shaped scones.

She shook her head. She was jumping the gun. Still, it was fun to think *what if*?

Twenty

A leg encased in a fiberglass cast was as effective as the lock on a jail cell. Katie never realized how often she left her office during the day to get coffee, stretch her legs, or seek a few minutes of conversation with an ever-changing assortment of vendors. Being stuck in her cell-like office for hours on end began to feel like solitary confinement. So when Susan Williams came barging into Katie's office late that afternoon her mood lightened—until she saw that Susan was angrier than Katie had ever seen her.

"Susan, what's wrong?"

"I went upstairs to check on my booth, and one of my Bitty Baby dolls was naked."

"Naked?"

The older woman nodded. "The doll was tossed aside, and her bonnet and dress were gone. Who would *do* that? I mean, my first thought was that Arthur Henderson had been in my booth with his sticky fingers again, but he'd have just taken the entire doll like he did the last time. He wouldn't have left her like that."

Katie had a sneaking suspicion of where the doll's clothes might be. "Let me do some checking around. Then I'll let you know what—if anything—I've learned."

"Thank you." Susan turned and stalked out into the vendors' lounge.

Grabbing her crutches, Katie hoisted herself out of the chair and made her way to the door. She was grateful that Susan had left it open so she didn't have to deal with that.

Ray looked up from his carving. "Going somewhere?"

"Just stretching my legs. I'll be back in a few minutes."

Ray nodded and went back to work.

It was a long, aggravating trek to get past the thicket of customers in the main showroom and through the lobby to the dance studio. Outside its door she saw the owner of the bullfrog holding him up proudly for all to see. The frog was wearing a blue gingham dress and a white bonnet.

"Hello," Katie said.

The girl turned her bland face up to her. "Hi."

"I see Mr. Bullfrog has a new outfit."

The frog's owner nodded as the girls around her giggled. "He's in disguise. He's a prince, you know. Prince Lamar. And he's hiding from his enemies."

"Did you ask Ms. Susan if you could borrow the dress?" Katie asked.

The girl's eyes narrowed. "There was nobody around to ask."

Dana Milton seemed to glide from the studio into the hall with a water bottle in her hand. "Hey, what's going on?" she asked, taking in the gaggle of girls and Katie on crutches.

"It seems one of your students took something from one of my vendors' booths without paying for it." Katie turned her gaze on the offender.

"Madison?" Dana inquired.

The girl rolled her eyes and blew out a breath. "Fine. Take the dumb old dress back to her. Prince Lamar says we have much prettier things at home for him to wear."

She pulled the Velcro apart, took the dress and bonnet off the frog, and handed them to Katie. Thoughts of getting warts made Katie shudder, but she also wondered if Prince Lamar was content with his current station in life. She highly doubted that he was. "You know, Prince Lamar might be happier down by the lake."

"Don't be stupid," Madison said. "This time of year, he'd die of the cold—besides being eaten by something." She took a small plastic aquarium out of her tote and placed the frog inside it.

"Madison, it was extremely rude of you to insult Mrs. Bonner. You need to apologize," Dana demanded.

The girl thrust out her bottom lip. "Sorry."

"Like you mean it!"

Madison's head dipped. "I'm sorry, Mrs. Bonner."

"And nothing like this will *ever* happen again, will it, girls?"

All the children's heads bowed. "No, Miss Dana."

"Now, I want everyone to go to the barre and practice plié. We've got some wobblers in the third movement."

"Yes, Miss Dana," they said in unison, and shuffled back off into the studio.

Dana turned to Katie. "I'm so sorry this happened. Cheryl told me there had been complaints, but I haven't had a chance to address this with my staff or students. I hope you can accept my sincere apology."

"Of course."

"As it turns out, for some of these girls, my classes are the only place where they're expected to behave like civilized people instead of spoiled brats. I've made it clear to both my students and their parents that if they can't follow my rules, they're out. I'll remind Cheryl of that, too."

"How many pupils do you lose per year?"

Dana's smile was somewhat crooked. "So far, none. Contrary to what some believe, kids actually *crave* structure. Dancing is structure. Discipline. I demand it from all my students. It's a little life lesson they can apply to every aspect of their lives."

Katie couldn't help smiling, knowing her decision to lease the space to Dana had been correct. "Keep it up," she said, and turned to leave.

Holding the tiny garments between her palm and her left crutch handhold made it hard to navigate, but Katie managed to get back to her office without dropping them. She set them on a piece of scrap paper, squirted some hand sanitizer on her palms, and worked it in. Then she called for Susan via the public address system. Her vendor showed up in record time.

"Where were they?" she demanded. "One of those little ballerina brats took them, right?"

"Yes. You'll want to take them home and wash them." She lowered her eyes. "They were on a . . . a bullfrog."

"A *bullfrog*?"

Katie looked up to see that Susan's own eyes were bulging. Might she be a member of the amphibian family herself?

"They put my darling doll clothes on a *frog*?" Susan repeated, horrified.

"Yes, but it's all right now. There doesn't seem to have been any harm done, but as I said, you might want to wash the clothes."

"You'd better believe I'll wash them. What was the kid thinking? Did you at least put the owner of the dance studio on notice? What's her name—Dana?"

"I spoke with Mrs. Milton about the girls," Katie said. "She assured me that nothing like this will happen again."

Susan drew herself up to her full six feet in height. "If it does, I'll take it up with her myself."

"Please don't. She has a lease with me. *I* need to be the one to deal with her."

"If those kids step out of line one more time—lease or not—I *will* speak with her."

Katie merely nodded and watched as Susan stalked off. It was then Katie realized the situation had caused her to break out in a sweat. After patting her glistening face with a tissue and taking a long drink of water from the bottle she'd left on the corner of her desk, she unwrapped a peppermint and popped it into her mouth.

Maybe Susan *would* speak with Dana. But Katie believed the dance instructor when she'd said she demanded discipline from her students. She just hoped she wouldn't have to swallow her pride if mindful little Madison pushed her boundaries and Cheryl allowed her to act out once again.

The day was winding down when a pink-cheeked Rhonda showed up at Katie's door. Once again, Ray joined her in Katie's office.

"Nona is *so* mad at you," Rhonda told Katie with relish. "Whatever you do, don't find yourself in the path of *her* car. I'm afraid she might finish you off."

"Wow. That's not comforting," Katie said, disconcerted.

"I know, right? Nona is crazy about Carl, I can tell you that. She looks at him as the son she never had." Rhonda settled deeper in her chair, apparently eager to dish the dirt.

"So, is Carl her brother's child?" Katie asked.

"No. Carl's father—now deceased—was Nona's husband's brother."

"Carl's dad is dead? That's interesting," Ray said. "Nona's husband is dead, too."

"Yeah. Apparently, weak hearts run in the Fiske family," Rhonda said. "That was something else Nona went on a tirade about—she's afraid Katie will cause Carl to have a heart attack and die too young just like his father and his uncle."

"Oh, poor Carl." Katie threw up her hands. "It's not like I'm trying to run him down with my car, though!"

Rhonda laughed. "I know, Katie. But you don't realize what a sweet, delicate guy you're dealing with."

"Did Nona say anything about Vonne?" Ray asked.

"It seems that Nona did know at least a little about Carl's relationship with the late Vonne Barnett. His mother told Nona that something had been going on between Vonne and Carl. From what I could gather from Nona's account of the situation, Vonne and Carl had been seeing each other but Carl got bored and moved on. That's when Vonne began threatening to have him fired from The Pelican's Roost."

"So, no mention of blackmail," Ray murmured.

"Not exactly. But Nona said Vonne started causing all kinds of trouble for Carl simply because he threw her over. First, she tried to extort money from Carl—and according to Nona—on more than one occasion. Nona said Vonne even went so far as to tell Carl she was pregnant, but Nona said she knew for sure that was a bald-faced lie."

"What made her so sure it was a lie?" Katie asked.

"Nona didn't say, nor did she admit to ever confronting Vonne about her trashy behavior. After that, a customer came in. By the time she left the shop, Nona didn't want to discuss Carl and Vonne anymore." Rhonda shrugged. "We discussed our mutual business endeavors, and then I came straight back here."

"Thanks for your help, Rhonda," Katie said, not quite able to keep the disappointment from her voice.

"I don't know what good it did, but I was happy to help. If you need me to try to find out anything else, just let me know." Rhonda retied her Dickens capelet before leaving the office, and scooted up the back stairs.

"Well, good try," Ray said with a shrug, and returned to his temporary workstation in the vendors' lounge.

Katie grabbed one of her crutches, nudged the door completely closed, and then called Andy.

"Is everything all right?" was his first question. After their unpleasant conversation the night before, he was sweet to worry about her.

"Yes. I'm calling to see if you might accept an apology calzone or cinnamon roll."

He laughed softly and said, "I can have those things anytime I want. What else have you got?"

"I'm sure I could find something that might tempt you."

"Yeah . . . you probably could. But then . . . you've got a houseguest."

It was then Katie realized Margo had been absent most of the day after offering to buy the tea shop for her. Maybe Margo was giving Katie some space to think over her proposal. She sighed. What she needed to say would be difficult.

"You were right to call me a hypocrite last night. I was—I am—jealous of your friendship with Erikka. The two of you seem so close. Ray and I aren't like that."

"I understand your being jealous," Andy said. "I'm a hot guy. All the babes want me."

"Oh yeah?" Katie asked skeptically, but then what he said about being hot was true.

"Oh yeah."

She could hear the smile in his voice.

"So, how are things going today at Artisans Alley?"

"Mostly normal."

"Mostly?"

Katie sighed. "Mostly. This morning Margo offered to buy the tea shop for me." Katie let her sentence lie there a second to see what Andy might say. He didn't say anything, so she continued. "I think it's wonderful of her to offer, but I'd prefer to have her give me a loan. I don't want to feel indebted to my former mother-in-law for the rest of my life."

"I see your point, but don't approach it that way with

Margo, Sunshine. She only wants to help, and if you ask for the loan, it's almost guaranteed to hurt her feelings."

"I don't want to do that," Katie said. "I'd just feel guilty taking a gift of that size from Chad's mother. She never showed me much generosity when Chad was living—much less, generosity of *this* magnitude—so why now?"

"She wants to help you, and she wants to remain in your life. She cares about you. Anyone can see that. Do you want her to remain a part of your life?"

"I guess that's the question I have to ask myself."

"Definitely," Andy said. "If you don't want Margo hanging around, then you should completely refuse the offer, even if that means forfeiting ownership of Afternoon Tea. If you do want her in your life, then either accept the gift or gently suggest to Margo that you have Seth draw up either a loan or a partnership agreement."

Katie nodded. "Andy, you're a genius."

"What can I say? It's another reason all the babes love me."

~~~~~~

It wasn't much later when Katie shut down her computer for the day and Margo showed up at her office door. "Have you had enough for one day?"

"Definitely," Katie agreed.

Out in the vendors' lounge, Ray was instantly on his feet. "Give me just a moment, and I'll walk the two of you over to the apartment."

"That's okay, Ray," Katie said. "Since Margo and I are together and it's such a short distance away, I believe we'll be safe. Thanks, though."

Ray seemed disappointed. "Sure."

Margo gave Katie a disapproving look. Yes, Katie could hear the frustration in Ray's voice as well as Margo could, but she wanted to speak with Margo privately. She shrugged into her coat, grabbed her crutches, and headed out.

"Thanks again, Ray," Katie called.

"You don't know how much we appreciate everything you do," Margo added.

"Not a problem."

They exited through the vendors' lounge, and Katie knew good and well that Ray would shadow them until he knew they were safely behind locked doors. And, nice though it was, it wasn't necessary. She wished he'd get over his guilt trip already. If it was anyone's fault—besides Carl's—that the lunatic had hit her with his car, it was hers. She took full responsibility for that.

Katie said good night to Vance, who'd been taking care of locking up since her accident.

The frosty air was like a slap in the face as Margo held the lobby door for Katie to exit. "Look out for black ice," she warned.

Katie sure would. She was terrified of falling and perhaps breaking the other leg.

They headed across the bone-dry strip of asphalt. Katie knew it was time to talk turkey with her mother-in-law. "Margo, I've been mulling over your offer. I can only accept your more-than-generous offer if you'll agree to be my partner in the shop."

"Oh goodness, I can't be a partner. I'd have to relocate to McKinlay Mill to do that." Apparently, the idea had little appeal, which boded well for Katie.

"No, you wouldn't. But it *would* give you an excuse to visit more often."

"That's sweet, but let's get real. You just don't want to accept the shop as a gift."

Katie grinned. "I've always prided myself on my independence—you know that—but I'd like you to be a part of this venture. If you don't want to become a partner, then I'd like to have Seth draw up a loan agreement so I can pay you back."

Margo paused and waited for Katie to do the same. "So,

as far as you're concerned, it's a partnership or a loan, or it's nothing."

"Please don't say it like that," Katie said.

Lips pursed, Margo nodded. "Tell you what. Call your attorney friend, and we'll talk with him as soon as he has time for us. Then we'll take it from there." She nodded toward Angelo's door. "Can you give me a second?"

"Sure."

Margo stepped inside and called for Andy. Katie saw Andy wipe his hands on the apron tied at his waist and nod. He came outside, trying to hide a smile.

"Margo asked me to carry you up the stairs." Andy took Katie's crutches and handed them to Margo. "If you'll agree to let her borrow your car, she's decided to go shopping this evening." He picked Katie up as though she were as light as a feather and whispered close to her ear, "I think I just figured out how you can make last night up to me."

Katie laughed and felt secure in his arms, but her elation dimmed when she caught sight of Ray standing in the Victoria Square parking lot with a frown on his face and his shoulders slumped. She was sorry if he felt slighted because she hadn't let him carry her up the stairs when she arrived home from the hospital. But, surely, he understood the difference. Andy was her lover. His carrying her up the stairs was a romantic gesture, not one born of a sense of duty and guilt.

Twenty-one

With Erikka managing the pizzeria below, and Margo absent for more than three hours, Katie and Andy were able to reconnect in a very personal way for the first time in what seemed like forever.

It was after nine, and they were snuggling on the couch, with a cat on each of their laps, when Margo returned from her shopping trip laden with bags from a myriad of shops and department stores.

She held up a fancy bib apron with a strand of fake pearls for Katie and Andy to see. "Don't you think these are perfect for Sophie?"

"A definite Julia Child vibe," Katie agreed.

"And look at these." Margo pulled out a couple of funky leather-bound journals. "Do you think Sadie and Sasha will like these?"

"They're crazy if they don't," Andy said.

"Being laid up like this," Katie said, glancing at her broken leg as a pout pulled her mouth, "nobody is going to get any presents from me this year."

"Don't worry, dear. You just concentrate on recovering. That's all any of your friends would wish from you this year," Margo told her.

Her words made Katie feet even more uncomfortable. She'd already had a lot of attention lavished on her. The idea of getting gifts and not being able to reciprocate weighed on her soul.

Andy cleared his throat. "Did you get anything for Ray?"

"Not yet," Margo said with a frown. "I couldn't find anything that corresponded to his carving or his love of the piano. I did have an interesting encounter at the mall, though. Godfrey Foster was there. He apologized to me for the scene his wife made today. I had no idea what he was talking about. I must've been in Chad's Pad at the time." She gave Katie a pointed look. "He said you would know all about it."

"Not really. I was going to take a walk—or maybe a lurch—around the Alley when I heard the two of them arguing, so I retreated into my office."

"Godfrey told me that before their separation, he and his wife had been trying to conceive a child. Apparently, they had reproductive problems. That man has no sense of propriety. Like I wanted to hear about his sex life! Anyway, in an attempt to make his wife jealous, Godfrey had told her about his going on a date with Vonne."

"That was stupid," Andy observed.

"Terribly." Margo settled on the armchair. "Even worse, Godfrey said he'd embellished the so-called date to be more than it was. But when Nona Fiske told Godfrey's wife that Vonne was pregnant when she died, she went berserk."

"So, Nona told Lucy Foster about Vonne's pregnancy?"

Katie said. "Rhonda said Vonne had told Carl she was pregnant but that Nona thought it was a lie. Why would Nona mention it to Lucy?"

"To cause trouble, more than likely," Andy said. "Sounds like it got the job done."

"Godfrey said he thought his wife's behavior was ridiculous, and, naturally, he tried to get me to go along with him," Margo said. "He said that even if he'd been having a torrid love affair with Vonne and she'd been carrying his child when she died—which, he said, was definitely not the situation—what bearing would that have on anything now? Seriously, he asked me that question and demanded an answer."

"What did you say?" Andy asked.

"That as a male of the species, he had no clue about women. He followed up by asking me why women dwell in the past so much." Margo stiffened her spine. "I didn't care for that attitude at all. Lumping all us women in together. I took the opportunity to point out that he was the one who appeared to be living in the past and that he was a fool to tell his wife about his dalliance with Vonne."

"What did he say to that?" Katie asked, eyes wide and a smile hovering.

"He didn't deny it. I figure he either intended to hurt his wife or made an abominably stupid move to try to win her back. I suggested he try to repair the relationship or move in a new direction. Either way, he and his wife need to make a decision—and probably with the help of professional counseling—to stop hurting each other and move forward."

"That's awfully sound advice," Katie said. "Still, I can't get my head around the fact that Nona knew about Vonne's pregnancy. Does it make sense to either of you that a nephew would tell his aunt that he'd gotten a girl—woman"—she corrected herself—"pregnant?"

"Makes no sense to me," Andy agreed. "Maybe Francine or Vonne told her. I mean, their shops are side by side. How neighborly are they?"

"After all the problems Nona has caused for them, I can tell you for sure there were no positive feelings among them. But Nona told Rhonda just today that she knew for a fact that Vonne was lying about the pregnancy."

"Vonne wasn't lying . . . was she?" Margo asked.

"Not according to Seth's friend in the medical examiner's office." Katie thought it best to leave Ray's name out of the conversation, at least for the time being. Andy was still stung over Katie's jealous reaction to Erikka. She didn't need to add any fuel to that fire. "But why would Nona lie to Rhonda?"

"I can think of only one reason," Andy said. "To cover for Carl."

"Yes . . . it's pretty obvious that Vonne was desperate to get her hands on some money," Margo said. "It looks as if she was willing to blackmail Carl Fiske, and we know what a dangerous idea that was. Maybe Vonne asked Nona for money and told her about the baby then."

Katie frowned. "I can't see anyone asking tight-fisted little Nona Fiske for money . . . with the possible exception of Carl. You guys should've seen the expression on her face when she learned that if Carl forfeited his bail, whoever put up the money for him would lose it."

"We're doing a lot of speculating here," Andy said. "We have no facts. We don't know the reason Vonne was attempting to get her hands on some cash. She could've been trying to save the tea shop. Or she could've wanted to use the money to visit her birth mother."

"How far along in the pregnancy was she?" Margo asked. "She might not have been aware of it yet."

"I don't know. I can't imagine she was past her first trimester, or everyone in Victoria Square would have been speculating long before Vonne died." Katie sighed. "Everything you're both saying is true. I just can't help but think that if we discover why Vonne was so desperate for money, we'll find out why she died."

"Based on Carl Fiske's behavior toward you, Katie, I'm betting he murdered Vonne . . . either because she was blackmailing him or because she told him he'd fathered a child—which would be an eighteen-year financial commitment, if not more." Margo grimaced. "That man is a menace."

"He'll regret it if he ever threatens Katie again," Andy said.

Margo patted her lap. "Let's put this unpleasantness behind us for tonight and do something fun. Why don't I make us some popcorn and then we'll play a game?"

"I have to warn you." Andy put up his hands. "I *am* the Boggle king."

~~~~~~~

For Katie, sleep came in fits and starts. Her leg had throbbed that evening before bed, but she'd taken only half a dose of her pain medication, afraid that if she took a full dose she might oversleep the next morning. And she could well imagine Andy and Margo letting her sleep in and thinking they were doing her a kindness. In reality, nothing could be further from the truth. Thanks to her injury, her unfinished daily tasks had been piling up. Hard as it would be, she might have to ask for more help from Vance and Rose. Once she was back on her feet, she'd find a way to reward them handsomely.

She heard a hissing noise. Della? But why would she be hissing? She and Mason got along so well.

Mason emitted a low, rumbling growl. From the direction of the noise, Katie knew he was standing near the kitchen door.

Oh no, guys. Please don't fight, she thought wearily.

Della hissed again. The sound was close. The poor cat must be hiding under the sofa. What in the world was going on? Why were they so scared?

Katie raised herself up on her elbows and tried to allow her eyes to acclimate to the darkness. Although she still couldn't see what was upsetting the cats, amid their growls and hisses, she heard the doorknob rattle.

Someone's trying to get in!

"Andy!" she whispered harshly.

"What?" Andy answered sleepily, and fumbled to throw back the sleeping bag as he scrambled out of it. "What is it? What's wrong?"

"Someone's trying to get in the house! Someone's at the door!"

A nightgown-clad Margo stumbled from the bedroom, looked around, and then raced to the kitchen. She turned on the light.

Andy nearly ran her over as he hurried toward the door. They could all hear feet pounding down the stairs. Andy went to the door and grappled with the lock.

"No!" Katie cried. "Don't open that door! What if he's got a gun?"

"She's right, Andy. Lock that door and call the police."

Andy stalked back to the living room and snatched his cell phone off the coffee table, punching in 911. Katie and Margo listened to the one-sided conversation.

"I want to report an attempted break-in at Two Canning Street, in McKinlay Mill. The deputies should be on the lookout for someone speeding away from Victoria Square."

Andy listened to the dispatcher, then mouthed, *There's a cruiser nearby.* "We've had trouble this week and believe Carl Fiske, who's currently out on bail, might be responsible." He listened. "Uh-huh. Uh-huh. Yes. Thank you." He pressed the "End Call" icon.

Noticing that Katie was trembling, Andy sat down on the sofa, threw an arm around her, and pulled her close.

"I'm so grateful you're here," she said breathlessly. "Both of you. If I'd been alone, I might've wound up like Vonne."

They looked at one another with doomed expressions, and then Margo snapped fully upright. "Well, now that we're all wide-awake, this is the perfect time for a nice, comforting cup of cocoa."

"With lots of whipped cream?" Katie asked rather timidly.

"How else?" Andy asked. He braved a smile, and Katie felt infinitesimally better.

They pretended to enjoy their cocoa, not saying much, each one absorbed in his or her own thoughts. Margo was collecting the mugs to rinse when Andy's phone rang, startling them all. He answered it, stabbing the speaker button so they could all hear.

"This is the nine-one-one operator. I wanted to let you know that the deputy on duty called in. They have Carl Fiske in custody."

"Did he admit to trying to break in?"

"Mr. Fiske denies any wrongdoing with regard to trying to break into the Canning Street address or to any other offense involving the occupant," said the woman on the other end of the line, "but he was picked up for speeding and a possible DUI. Mr. Fiske will be detained until a judge determines whether or not to revoke bail."

"Thank you for following up with us. Good night." Andy hit the "End Call" icon. He turned to Katie, beaming. "So, there you go, we're all safe. Why don't we try to get some sleep?"

"I'm all for that," Margo agreed, and retreated to the bedroom once more. "Good night."

"Good night," Katie echoed.

Andy turned out the light and went back to his sleeping bag.

I could have used another good-night kiss, Katie thought as she pulled the covers up to her chin once more.

Soon, Andy was snoring softly, but Katie was still restless.

We're all safe . . . for now. But who knows how long it will last?

Twenty-two

Katie had lain awake for torturous hours after the attempted
break-in and was only vaguely aware of Andy kissing her
on the forehead and muffled conversation between him and
Margo sometime the next morning. But her heavy eyelids
closed and she drifted off again, simply too exhausted to
rouse herself out of her slumber. The next sound she was
aware of was Ray's voice. She opened her eyes and became
aware that Ray and Margo were talking in the kitchen.

What's Ray doing here so early? What's going on?

She heard the name ". . . Carl . . ." and struggled to sit
up. "What about Carl?"

Ray and Margo hurried into the living room.

"Hey, sleepyhead. How are you feeling?" Ray asked.

Katie waved a hand as though to shake away the question. "What's going on with Carl?"

"Fiske is back in jail, and it's likely his bail will be revoked and he'll be staying there until his trial."

Katie sagged with relief. "That's great news. Did he confess to trying to break into my apartment last night?"

"No. He still denies that, but the DUI is enough for a judge to keep him out of circulation, especially given the fact that he was originally arrested—in part—for vehicular-related offenses." He gave Katie a sympathetic smile. "I heard you had a rough night. You should stay home and rest today."

"Yes," Margo agreed. "I'm sure Artisans Alley will be okay without you for only one day."

"Well, Artisans Alley might not need *me*, but I need *it*," Katie said. "I need to feel at least some small bit of normalcy after last night. And knowing that Carl Fiske is in jail, I can finally feel safe."

"All right, then," Ray said. "I'll wait until you're ready and then I'll carry you down the stairs."

"Thanks, but no, thanks. I've gotten pretty darn good with these old crutches."

"Are you sure? It would do my ego good to know I can still carry a woman around. It gives me street cred with the younger crowd."

Katie merely laughed and shook her head. "I need my own street cred letting people know I can take care of myself."

"While Katie gets ready for work, why don't I make us all some lunch?" Margo asked.

Ray gave Katie a wistful smile before turning to Margo. "Only if you let me help."

~~~~~~

With Ray back at Wood U and Margo either upstairs in Chad's Pad or helping out at the cash desks, Katie sat back in her office chair and found herself humming along with the Christmas music being piped throughout the building.

Rose gave a brisk knock before opening the door. "I brought you coffee."

"Thank you. You must be a mind reader."

"I'm glad to see you looking so cheerful today."

"Not as much as I am to be feeling it," Katie said. "I'm beginning to believe that the entire nightmare is finally over—or, at least, almost over. Carl Fiske is off the street, and that does wonders for my peace of mind."

"Who'd have thought Nona would have a nephew who'd be so downright nasty and scary?"

Laughter bubbled up in Katie's throat. "Um . . . have you met Nona Fiske?"

"You do have a point there," Rose said, and joined in her laughter. "Seriously, though, do you believe Carl killed Vonne Barnett?"

"Based on his behavior toward me, I'm sure of it," Katie said. "I was truly frightened for my life last night when someone tried to get into my apartment. I can't say definitely that it was Carl, but the police caught him speeding away from Victoria Square . . . and he'd been drinking."

Rose shook her head. "That's terrible. I hope they can convict him."

"I hope so, too, Rose."

"What about Margo—how's everything going there? I know you weren't looking forward to her extending her stay so she could play nursemaid."

"I wasn't, but things have gone better than I'd ever expected. I honestly don't know what I'd have done without her these past few days. I owe her a lot." She motioned for Rose to close the door. "Do you have a minute? I'd like your opinion on something."

"Sure." Rose pushed the door closed.

"Margo made me a very generous offer to buy Afternoon Tea outright."

Rose blinked. "Yes, I'd say that's generous."

Katie nodded. "The problem is, I don't feel comfortable

receiving a gift of that value. I'd much rather she float me a loan or become my partner in the business."

"She doesn't want to go for that?" Rose asked.

"Not so far. What do you think?"

Rose looked thoughtful. "Fabulous as she looks, Margo is not getting any younger. If it makes her feel good, perhaps you ought to let her do this for you."

"Oh, Rose, I don't know."

"Put it this way, what if she'd offered to help you and Chad buy the Webster Mansion a few years back? Would you have accepted her gift?"

"In a heartbeat," Katie admitted. "But the situation was different then. Her son was still alive. And besides, he probably would have preferred she invest in Artisans Alley—that's where Chad's heart was."

Rose straightened. "Well, then—we could use a sprinkler system, expand the heat and air-conditioning in the back of the building, and—"

Katie held out a hand and cut her off. "I'm well aware of all the Alley's deficiencies."

The older woman shrugged. "All right. But think about what's going on right now. It's our busiest time of year, you've got a houseguest with no timetable for leaving, your leg has got to be hurting, and the threat from Carl Fiske—and his pain-in-the-butt aunt. And who says you have to make a decision today?"

"Francine."

"You can't rescue the world, Katie. You need to look at everything with a clear head."

"I'm pretty sure I was in full control of my faculties when I made the counteroffer."

"Does that mean Margo will be moving to McKinlay Mill?"

"No," Katie said, "but she'll probably be visiting more often."

"And that's a good thing?"

Katie nodded. "Yeah, I think it is."

Rose tilted her head, her blonde curls bobbing. "Just make sure that isn't the pain meds talking."

There was a woodpecker-like knock at the door. Rose opened it and stood aside so her fellow vendor Edie Silver could venture inside. The poor woman had her clasped hands beneath her chin, and her gray eyes were almost as wide as her oversize glasses.

"Vance needs you in the lobby." Edie's voice was barely above a whisper.

"All right," Katie said. "Tell him I'm on my way."

Rose handed Katie her crutches and they exchanged puzzled glances. Edie scurried away before she could say anything more about what was going on.

"What now?" Rose asked.

"The universe is punishing me for believing all was right with the world since Carl Fiske is back in jail." Katie struggled to the door, which Rose pulled shut behind them.

Katie could tell Rose was impatient to get to the lobby, but she slowed her steps to match Katie's labored strides. A crowd had gathered—vendors and customers alike—and they parted to allow Katie to see what was happening.

Arthur Henderson was standing slumped against cash desk three holding a bloody tissue to his nose.

"Oh my goodness!" Katie exclaimed, inching closer to the man. "What happened?"

Ed and Vance, who stood on either side of Arthur, looked at each other and then at Katie.

"We did just like you told us to," Ed said, glancing at Vance to see if he was going to corroborate Ed's story. "Arthur came by and took a little unicorn from my booth. He put it in his pocket and walked away. I called Vance and told him about the theft."

Vance picked up the account. "I told him to keep Arthur in sight but to be nonchalant about it and that I'd stand just outside the Alley to see if Arthur did, in fact, leave the building without paying for the unicorn."

"Just like you told us to," Ed reiterated. "But when Arthur went out the door, I guess I got kinda jumpy, and I—"

"He tackled me! That's what he did!" Arthur cried. "The idiot tackled me!"

"Mr. Henderson, I'm sorry," Katie said. "Are you all right?"

He shoved the tissue at her. "Does this look like I'm all right?"

"No, sir," she said, "but you *were* stealing from Artisans Alley, and our vendors did have the right to stop you."

"I wasn't stealing anything. I was going out to see whether or not my ride was here—my daughter-in-law was coming to pick me up—and then I was going to pay." He took the broken unicorn out of his pocket and glared at Ed. "I'm not buying it now, though. You caused me to break it."

Katie looked at Vance. "Have you called the police?"

"I did," Margo said from where she stood at cash desk two.

"Thank you," Katie said. "Do you know when they should be here?"

Margo shook her head.

"Well, whenever they get here, I'm pressing charges against that guy"—Arthur jerked his thumb in Ed's direction—"for assault. My son will be here in a few minutes. He's an attorney, you know."

Katie didn't know anything about Arthur Henderson or his family. His son could be a State Supreme Court judge for all she knew. She just wished this whole nightmare wasn't happening. Yes, Ed and Vance had the right to detain Arthur. But the man was *old*. What on earth had compelled Ed to tackle him?

The entire crowd stood there until the sheriff's cruiser arrived. It was the same patrolman who'd been the first on the scene when they called about Carl Fiske coming into

Artisans Alley disguised as a deliveryman leaving the dead mouse. The officer had probably never dreamed how much excitement occurred at an artisans' arcade before. Katie certainly hadn't before she took on the role of managing the place.

"What's going on here?" the deputy asked.

When everyone started to explain at once, the deputy asked them all to be quiet. He nodded at Arthur Henderson. "Sir, you seem to be hurt. Let's start with you."

Oh brother . . .

Arthur pointed at Ed. "That one right there knocked me down right out there on the sidewalk. He attacked me, and I want to press charges for assault . . . and battery, too! I was assaulted and battered."

"All right. Your name?" the officer asked, taking out a notepad and pen.

"Arthur Henderson."

"Address?"

Arthur's face went blank. "I . . . uh . . . I can't recall it offhand. But my son will be here any minute. He knows what it is."

"I see." The deputy looked at Ed. "Is it true that you assaulted this man?"

"No! I mean, yes, I . . . I . . . accidentally . . . knocked him down . . . but I wouldn't say I *assaulted* him!" Ed looked at Vance for confirmation.

"Sir, Mr. Wilson"—Vance jerked his head in Ed's direction—"called me earlier this afternoon and told me that Mr. Henderson had stolen something from his booth. Mr. Wilson creates blown glass figurines and ornaments."

"It was a unicorn," Ed supplied. "He stole a unicorn."

"We know that we can't accuse a customer of shoplifting until he or she has left the store," Vance continued. "I waited outside and asked Mr. Wilson to follow Mr. Henderson to make sure that it was, in fact, his intention to steal the item . . . the unicorn."

"And did Mr. Henderson leave Artisans Alley?" the officer asked.

Ed and Vance spoke at once. "Yes."

"I was looking to see if my ride was here yet," contended Arthur. "My daughter-in-law was picking me up, and I was just peeping out the front door to see if she was waiting for me."

"He was almost to the parking lot," Ed said. "I was jogging to catch up to him."

"That's when he tackled me!" Arthur exclaimed.

"You stopped, and I ran into you. I wouldn't exactly call it 'tackling' you." Ed again looked to Vance to back up his story, but this time, Vance merely lowered his eyes.

Oh no . . . Ed really did tackle an elderly man, and Artisans Alley is going to be sued, Katie thought. *So much for that loan from Margo going toward Afternoon Tea.*

"How much is the item in question worth?" asked the deputy.

"Fifteen dollars," Ed answered.

"Can anyone testify that you did not use excessive force when attempting to detain Mr. Henderson?" The officer looked around at the crowd. No one immediately came to Ed's defense. Not even Vance, which was obviously distressing for Ed because he continued to stare at Vance.

"It wasn't just the unicorn." Ed finally dragged his eyes away from Vance to look at the deputy. "This man has been stealing from Artisans Alley for a while now."

"Is that true?"

Katie felt the deputy's eyes on her and realized he was asking her the question. She chose her words carefully. "Mr. Henderson has exhibited some suspicious behavior lately."

"But no one had caught him in the act of any wrongdoing . . . at least, not until today."

"Correct," she said.

As the deputy continued scribbling away in his notebook and the tension in the lobby showed no sign of abating, a middle-aged man wearing a beautifully tailored suit and a calf-length coat rushed through the door.

"I'm Philip Henderson," the man said. "My father called and said I was needed here." He rushed over to Arthur and put an arm around the older man's shoulders. "Pop, what's going on? Are you okay?"

Arthur managed a brief nod before burying his face against his son's shoulder. Katie was glad his nose had stopped bleeding because she had the perverse thought that it would be a shame for Arthur to get blood on his son's expensive coat.

Philip Henderson looked at the officer. "What happened here?"

"It's my understanding that this vendor—Mr. Wilson— believed your father stole something from him—"

"He *did* steal something!" Ed cried. "It's right there in his hand!"

Arthur opened his hand to show Philip the broken unicorn. "I'm sorry."

Philip hugged his father. "It's all right. Everything is fine."

"I'm very sorry I knocked him down," Ed said.

Ignoring Ed for the moment, Philip examined Arthur's face. "Are you hurt, Pop?"

Arthur shook his head.

"Why don't we take you by the emergency room just to make sure?" Philip asked.

Arthur nodded.

"I'll pay for your emergency room costs," Ed said.

"All right. If you'll do that, then we won't press charges against you or Artisans Alley." Philip turned to Katie. "You're the one in charge here, right?"

"Yes, sir."

"Pop is in the beginning stages of dementia, and we have observed some kleptomania on his part." Philip looked around the lobby. "He loves this place—who knows why?—but I'll make sure he doesn't come in here unattended again."

"Okay," Katie said. "Thank you."

"So, are we good?" asked the deputy. "No charges filed by either party?"

Philip looked at both Ed and Katie.

"No charges," Katie said.

Ed nodded.

"No charges, Bill," Philip said to the deputy. "Good to see you."

"You, too, Mr. Henderson."

The Hendersons and the deputy departed and the crowd disbursed. Katie was relieved to get back to her office and off her leg. By the look on Ed's face—and the fact that he was going to have to pay Arthur Henderson's emergency room fees—she didn't think she'd need to caution him or any of the other vendors about using excessive force with suspected shoplifters again. At least, she hoped she wouldn't. She also hoped that Mr. Henderson's injuries wouldn't turn out to be more serious than a few bumps and bruises and that Philip wouldn't change his mind about suing Artisans Alley.

But hope was tenuous. She'd much rather have something in writing . . . like a loan agreement with Margo?

Katie had way too many things to think about.

~~~~~

Francine arrived later that afternoon with a box of scones and muffins "made fresh this morning" at Afternoon Tea. That made Katie slightly concerned about all the things that might not have been made fresh that morning at Afternoon Tea. She made a mental note to put as much money as her budget would allow into public relations. Then she tore her mind away from thoughts of the future and concentrated on Francine's visit.

"Margo and I have discussed scheduling a meeting at Afternoon Tea sometime tomorrow to nail down the terms of this acquisition," Francine said. "I want to make sure the time and location works for you. I fully realize that mobility is an issue for you right now, so we can meet here at Artisans Alley if that's better."

"Whatever the two of you decide should be fine with me," Katie said. "By the way, did you know that Carl Fiske is in jail again and that his bail has been revoked?"

"Really? I imagine Nona is beside herself. She's the one who put up all that money for Carl, you know."

"Have you and Nona ironed out your differences?" Katie asked.

Francine shook her head. "Not a chance. But Vonne and I bent over backward to try to placate the old bat. Having our shops located so close together rather dictates that we treat each other as well as possible. I even went so far as to buy a quilt from Nona. If nothing else, she does beautiful work."

"She does," Katie agreed. "How well do you know her nephew, Carl?"

"I don't know him at all."

"Do you think he could have been the father of Vonne's baby?"

"I have no clue." Francine sighed. "Vonne was so out of control these last few months that her baby could've belonged to any number of men."

"You don't think it's possible that Carl killed Vonne?"

"As much as it pains me to say this, Katie, Vonne ultimately killed herself. Her destructive behavior destroyed her. What possible reason could Carl Fiske have had to kill her? They didn't have much of a relationship, from what I gathered, so I doubt he was heartbroken if she's the one who moved on. More than likely, though, he was the one who grew tired of her, just like Charles did. Men don't respect desperate women who throw themselves at men, hoping to be loved."

Katie felt sick to her stomach. How could Francine talk

that way about her only daughter, even if Vonne wasn't her biological child? Had Booth's betrayal damaged Francine that much?

"I really must be going. I have a lot of work in the kitchen to do. If the health inspector dropped by, I might receive a citation because I'm falling behind," Francine said.

So, Sophie Davenport had been right about that.

"Thank you so much for your thoughtfulness in bringing me goodies from the shop."

"Well, without customers, they were going stale anyway."

So, not quite as thoughtful a gift after all.

"Let me know when you want to go over the details of the sale. I'll be glad to shut down the shop if I have to." And with that, Francine turned to leave.

Katie looked down at the wrapped goods on her desk. Should she risk sharing them with her vendors, or just toss everything in the trash?

Right then the idea of owning the tea shop didn't flare quite so bright.

Twenty-three

The day wasn't getting any younger when Gwen Hardy, Artisans Alley's resident weaver, entered the vendors' lounge—probably to get one of the water bottles she left in the fridge while she worked—and Katie called her over.

"Hey, Katie. How's the leg?"

"It's still there. Listen, I've got this box of baked goods from the tea shop. Would you like something?"

Gwen wrinkled her nose. "Last time I visited, there was a small piece of mold on the scone I was served."

Katie cringed. "I tried the pumpkin bread yesterday. It was really good." Gwen didn't look convinced. "Anyway, with this bum leg, I can't put it out on the counter. Would you mind carrying it over for me?"

"Sure thing." She bent down to read the note Katie attached. "'Help yourself. If it's a little stale, you might want to nuke it for a few seconds to freshen it up.' Wow. At least you're honest."

Katie shrugged. "I try to be."

Gwen removed the box, and Katie immediately picked up the telephone on her desk and called Seth's personal number and was happy he wasn't with a client and she got right through.

"Always happy to talk to my little pseudo sister," Seth said, and laughed.

"Any chance you have a break in your schedule soon— like tomorrow would be good."

"What for?"

"Legal advice. Margo has offered to give me Afternoon Tea."

"Wow. That's generous."

"Yes. Overly so. I would much prefer for you to draw up a loan agreement or a partnership arrangement."

"Ah, I see. Let me look at my calendar."

She heard him humming for a long ten or twelve seconds.

"How about four this afternoon? I can even come to Artisans Alley."

"Even better. I'd love for the three of us to sit down and talk this through," she said. "Maybe you can help us decide what would be our best solution."

"Sounds good. I'd planned on bringing Rose a poinsettia today anyway, so I'll meet with you and Margo then."

"You're such a sweetheart. I think it's wonderful that you and Rose have developed a friendship. I wish Vonne and Nancy could have had a cordial relationship. Poor Vonne must've felt so betrayed by everyone she'd ever cared about."

"Hey, I feel sorry for Francine, too. Nick and I discussed the situation yesterday over lunch. Francine sacrificed her pride and dignity to raise her husband's love child as her own. I understand why it was hard for Francine to love

Vonne, especially given the doting relationship Vonne had with her father." He blew out a breath. "Francine had to wonder if Booth loved the child so much because Vonne was his only child or because Vonne reminded him so much of Nancy—possibly, at least in Francine's eyes, the only woman Booth truly loved."

"Whew, I'd never thought of it like that."

"And then Vonne found out the truth and—once again, I'm speculating on Francine's behalf—Francine was no longer good enough. Vonne wanted Nancy, whom she considered her real mother, forgetting that it was Francine who had done the dirty work of raising and caring for her all her life. I can't imagine how bitter and frustrated Francine must feel."

"I'm understanding more and more why you're such a terrific lawyer."

He laughed. "Seeing things from every angle is something I do well."

"That is true. By the way, do you know Philip Henderson, Esquire?" Katie asked.

"I do," he said, his voice flat. "Why do you ask?"

Katie's hackles rose. "Why do you sound so grave?"

"It's just that Philip is known as a pit bull," Seth said. "I mean, he's a great guy, but I'd never want to have to face him in court. I sat in on one of his cases when I was interning for Judge Wilkins, and Philip is one of the most brilliant attorneys I've ever witnessed in the courtroom."

"Hmm . . ."

"Hmm? Katie, please tell me you haven't run afoul of Philip Henderson."

"Well, I hope not." She went on to explain to Seth what had happened with Arthur Henderson earlier in the day.

He blew out a breath. "Ed Wilson had better pray he didn't injure Arthur."

"He did agree to pay the emergency room costs."

"I suppose he meant that as a gesture of goodwill, but it can also be construed as an admission of guilt. Plus, if I'm understanding you correctly, Vance didn't corroborate Ed's account of accidentally knocking Arthur down."

"No, he didn't. Vance is an honest man, and I believe Arthur was telling it correctly—that Ed tackled him."

"This could be bad, Katie. If Philip Henderson sues Ed personally, as well as Artisans Alley, it could devastate the business."

"But he said he wouldn't press charges."

"Pressing charges and suing are two different things. Plus, he can always change his mind about taking a warrant out against Ed for assault if he learns that his father is injured worse than anyone realized."

Katie put a hand up to her forehead and rubbed her left temple, which was beginning to throb.

"I'm sorry to have frightened you," Seth said. "We'll hope for the best and try to get a report on Arthur Henderson's physical assessment as soon as possible. Don't worry too much just yet. Philip is fair—if Arthur isn't hurt, then you have nothing to worry about."

"And if he *is*, I could lose everything."

Seth blew out a breath. "You might want to reconsider Margo's generous offer, just in case. I'll see the two of you soon."

"Okay. Good-bye, and thanks."

Katie hung up the phone. She had a lot to think about before Seth arrived. Vonne, Carl, and even Francine were now the least of her worries.

~~~~~~

Katie stared at the computer spreadsheet she'd created to run some purely hypothetical numbers through. Thanks to her graduate degree in marketing, she had a good idea of what Seth was likely to tell her. But she also needed to consider another aspect of the equation: Artisans Alley, if it survived the attack on Arthur Henderson.

Sure, the argument could be made that he was a shoplifter and that Ed was behaving within reasonable limits, but all the jury would see should Philip Henderson sue was an old man with dementia who was knocked down on a parking lot and roughed up simply because he'd made a mistake. What a nightmare it would be if the Hendersons should file suit. Even if Artisans Alley could weather the financial layout of legal fees and a judgment, its professional reputation would be destroyed. And would Ed Wilson be the only individual sued?

Katie considered what Seth had said about taking Margo's offer; and while it would probably be good to get all her eggs out of one basket, she was just one person, and it would be a big gamble to take on Afternoon Tea. For that business, she'd need someone to manage the shop and greet customers and serve—plus, she needed someone in the kitchen. She loved to bake, but she'd never made large-volume recipes.

Her pupils were about to spin like pinwheels when she heard a noise at the door and looked up to see Sasha Davenport standing before her.

"Are you busy?"

Katie smiled, relieved there was finally a glimmer of sunshine in her otherwise dark day. "Never too busy to talk to you. Come on in and sit down."

The young girl took the chair beside Katie's desk, sitting stiffly, her gaze traveling all around the tiny room. She'd been in Katie's office on more than one occasion, so Katie realized she was avoiding saying what she'd come to Artisans Alley to say.

"What's on your mind?" Katie prodded gently.

Restless, Sasha got up and leaned against the big green file cabinet. "I thought you were my friend." Her blue eyes blazed even as they filled with tears.

"Of course I'm your friend." Katie struggled to stand and raised her arms so she could hug the girl.

Sasha held out a hand. "Don't bother. Just let me say what I came here to say."

Katie eased back onto her chair. "All right."

"You acted like you were my friend, but you were only lying to me and spying for my dad the whole time."

"Sasha, that's not true."

"You know what happened to me today? I was at school minding my own business when I got called into the office. That scared the ever-loving crap out of me, even though I knew I hadn't done anything wrong. And guess what they wanted?"

Katie had a good idea what they wanted, but she just shrugged.

"They told me I had to talk with Ms. Dornan, the school psychologist. And guess who was sitting on the bench next to me when they told me that? Bitchy Brianna Titus, who heard everything and spread it all over the school by the end of the day that Sasha Davenport is crazy!"

"Oh, sweetie, I'm so sorry."

"Save it! I knew the instant those pills fell out of my pocket that I was in trouble. But then I thought, 'No, Katie's cool, she won't rat me out.' Man, was I wrong!"

"Sasha, I told your dad about those pills because I care about you. You don't realize—"

"I realize that what I do is none of your business! Maybe Sadie was right—you don't belong with our dad. So stop pretending you're our friend. Leave my dad alone and just stay out of all our lives!" She turned and slammed the door on her way out.

Stunned by what had just transpired, Katie fought tears.

Seconds later, someone knocked on the door and it opened. Rose popped her head into the office. "I saw your visitor storm out of here. Is everything okay?"

"I'm not sure. I told Ray something that Sasha thought I shouldn't have mentioned."

"Well, I'm sure you told him for his daughter's own good. Right?"

"Yes, but now I'm afraid she'll never trust me again."

"I know you, Katie, and I'm positive you did the right thing."

"Thanks, Rose."

"Will you be okay?"

"Of course," Katie said, and sat straighter in her chair.

Rose nodded. "Well, call if you need anything."

"I will. Thanks."

After her friend had pulled the door closed, Katie briefly succumbed to tears. She truly cared about the Davenport girls, and now two of them couldn't stand her. There'd be no more homey dinners and piano sing-alongs for her.

But did it really matter all that much? What if she lost Artisans Alley thanks to Ed Wilson's stupidity and the deal to buy Afternoon Tea fell through? Would she even have a reason to stay in McKinlay Mill? Other than Andy, of course. She heaved a heavy sigh before trying to push aside her depressing thoughts and return to her work.

She turned back to her computer screen. If she took over the tea shop, she was going to have to officially recruit an assistant manager for Artisans Alley. Ezra hadn't wanted to bother with payroll and taxes, so he had set up the Alley so that the people who rented space were required to work a certain number of days, depending on the square footage of their booths. For the most part, it worked—mostly thanks to vendors who were retired—like Rose and Vance—who enjoyed being on the premises more than their time requirement. She gave them special perks as a thank-you. But she would have to do more for a real employee.

Katie picked up her phone and pressed the button for the public-address system.

"Vance Ingram, please come to the manager's office. Vance Ingram to the manager's office, please." She set the phone down and closed the program.

Vance must have been nearby, because he was there within a minute. "What's up?"

"Sit down," she encouraged, and Vance took the seat by her desk.

"I spoke with Seth Landers a little while ago. Have you heard anything about Arthur Henderson's condition?"

"No. Ed called the hospital to ask, but they wouldn't tell him anything because he isn't a family member."

Katie nodded. "Did they at least say whether he was still in the emergency room or if they'd admitted him?"

Vance shook his head. "Did you call Seth or did Seth call you?"

"I called Seth about the tea shop—I'll get to that in a minute—but while I had his ear, I asked him about Philip Henderson. Apparently, Mr. Henderson is a formidable attorney."

"I didn't get the impression he was going to cause trouble for us." He blinked. "Did you?"

"No, but Seth made an excellent point. If, after Arthur was seen at the emergency room, it was discovered that he suffered any significant injury, then the Hendersons could sue Artisans Alley as well as Ed personally."

Vance puffed out his cheeks and slowly expelled a breath. "This is awful. All this trouble over a fifteen-dollar glass unicorn . . . that wound up broken, no less."

"I suppose I should call a meeting of the Merchants Association to address this matter, but I don't feel I can adequately do so until I know what we're facing."

"I'll do my best to find out about Mr. Henderson's condition." He shook his head. "I knew Ed shouldn't have been so rough with him, but I couldn't get to them in time to stop Ed."

"It's all right. I know you did your best. This is such a weird situation. We all did what we thought was best to stop a shoplifter . . . and now we could be facing financial ruin because of it."

"Katie . . . are you saying Artisans Alley might have to be shut down?"

"Not yet. I don't want you or anyone else to be alarmed. I need to talk to my insurance agent to see what we're covered for. Worse, this could be a PR nightmare for us." She lifted her hands. "But no lawsuit has been filed yet. And, if it isn't, I'll have to talk with the Merchants Association and see if we can come up with a better way to deal with shoplifters in the future."

They sat in silence for a moment before Vance said, "You mentioned something about the tea shop?"

"Yes. You know I've been thinking of taking Francine up on her offer to sell it to me," Katie began.

"Is that a done deal, then?"

"Not yet, but I'm becoming fairly confident it will be. Today's episode has taught me that it might not be wise to have all my eggs in one basket. If anything happened to Artisans Alley, I don't know what I'd do."

"Well, whatever caused you to come to your decision, congratulations." Vance offered his hand and gave her a hearty handshake.

"Thanks, Vance. Ideally, I'll be involved with renovating the tea shop and getting it off the ground, and then I want to pass the day-to-day management on to my employees . . . That is, if I can find some who are half as competent as you are."

"Don't make me blush," he said, but did anyway.

"I know when I first took over the Alley you weren't interested in running the place, but I'm going to need an official assistant manager if I take this one. I can't even begin to make that decision until I know the Alley will be in good hands when I'm not available."

Vance nodded.

"I know you spend a lot of your time here anyway, and now you'd get paid for it. But the big question is—would you be at all interested in taking on that kind of responsibility?"

"Janey and I kinda thought you might be thinking along those lines, and we've already talked it over. I'd be honored to take on whatever you need to keep this place going strong . . . provided that's still an option once the dust settles on this Henderson mess."

Katie let out a pent-up breath and smiled. "I'll be talking to Seth Landers about business requirements before the end of the day—and if and when the sale of the tea shop goes through, we can talk about salary, et cetera."

Vance nodded, his eyes bright with eagerness. "Assistant manager. I like the sound of that."

Katie grinned. One problem down, just a million more to solve.

~~~~~~~

The sky was already beginning to darken when Seth arrived. After removing his dark wool topcoat, he looked dapper in his dark three-piece pin-striped suit. Katie asked him to bring in another chair from the vendors' lounge while they waited for Margo to arrive. It was a tight fit, but Katie didn't want to discuss business in the vendors' lounge where they could be overheard by anyone.

Margo breezed into the office looking pretty in the dress she'd been wearing the day she first arrived on Victoria Square, and Seth—like everyone else—was immediately charmed.

"Mrs. Bonner, I've heard such wonderful things about you." He stood and shook her hand. "I'm delighted to meet you."

"The pleasure is all mine," Margo said. "How sweet of you to come here and meet with us."

"I'm happy to do it." He grinned. "Since we're all crammed in here like sardines, let's get started. I feel we should work out a partnership agreement prior to discussing the tea shop purchase. A partnership would be in both your best interests."

He took a legal pad and a pen from his briefcase. "Now, will this be an equal partnership with each of you holding a fifty percent stake?"

Both Katie and Margo nodded.

"I suggest the partnership be made a limited liability corporation so that any claims against the company are confined to cash and assets owned by the partnership. This is to protect your personal equity."

"Personal equity?" Margo slid forward in her seat, her brow furrowing. "You mean, if someone should sue the tea shop, I could lose everything I have?"

"Not if we draw up the paperwork properly." Seth gave her a reassuring wink, but Margo did not seem comforted.

"I didn't realize this would be such a serious undertaking. I must admit, I find the whole thing a little scary." She turned to her former daughter-in-law. "Katie, won't you please reconsider simply accepting the funds to purchase Afternoon Tea as a gift from me?" She turned to Seth. "Wouldn't that be the simplest way to approach this?"

Katie realized Seth and Margo were looking to her for the answer. On the one hand, if she allowed Margo to gift her with the money, she could do exactly as she wished as far as the renovations were concerned. And, although she'd feel beholden to Margo for providing the money, she'd feel freer to operate the business as she chose.

On the other hand, if she and Margo were full partners, Katie would have someone to bounce ideas off and share the financial responsibility. Then she remembered how she and Margo had clashed during their visit to the antique shop. Would it be that way with every decision they made concerning the tea shop?

She took a deep breath. "Margo, would you reconsider offering me a loan rather than a gift?"

"I want to do something nice for you," Margo said, sounding frustrated. "Why is that so hard for you to understand? Was I such a nasty mother-in-law that you can't stand to allow me to do a kindness for you?"

"No . . . what? I . . . I only made the suggestion because it appears you're having second thoughts about the partnership."

Margo abruptly stood. "I need to be alone for a few minutes to think. Seth, it was a pleasure meeting you. I'm sorry we wasted your time today."

"No problem."

Margo hurried out of the office, the sound of her heels clicking on the vendors' lounge floor soon fading.

"That didn't go all that well," Katie said as Seth pushed the door closed once again.

He spread his hands. "It's obvious that you and Margo need to talk some more before either of you is ready to make any decisions."

"We're supposed to meet with Francine tomorrow."

"You might want to postpone that meeting."

Katie inclined her head. "You're a smooth talker. Couldn't you speak to Margo about making it a loan? Because if I'm going to have to hire an assistant manager for the Alley, it's occurred to me that I might be better off changing the business structure of Artisans Alley, too."

"You mean one corporate entity to cover both businesses?"

Katie nodded.

"It's a possibility. But then you definitely wouldn't want to draw Margo into the works."

"No." She wiggled the toes on her broken leg and winced. "This is all so complicated, and Francine is pushing hard. Margo thought buying me the shop would make a fine Christmas present, but I can see that the legalities are going to make this a long, drawn-out procedure."

"Things don't move all that fast at the state level, and that's where you'd be filing the paperwork. But there's so much more that needs to be done before the ownership transfer. Do you even know what Francine pays for rent on the building?"

"No," Katie admitted. "She loaned me some ledgers, but it was right after I got out of the hospital. Before I could study them, Detective Schuler confiscated them as potential evidence."

"Why don't I give him a call and see if I can't get them back for you? It sounds like you need to study them before you sink your time, money, and life into the business."

"I'd appreciate that. Thanks."

Seth stood, then bent down to give Katie a peck on the cheek. "What are pseudo brothers for?"

"By the way, Vance is supposed to be checking to see what he can find out about Arthur Henderson's condition. Hopefully, everything is okay on that front." She was aware of the uncertainty that crept into her voice.

"If you'd like, I'd be happy to call Philip."

Katie sighed. "Would that be wise? Wouldn't he maybe take that as a legal salvo on our part?"

"I won't call as your attorney. I'll call as your friend."

"You're the best," she said, with a smile.

Twenty-four

Katie heard Rose's announcement over the PA that Artisans Alley was closing, and she shut down her computer and tidied her desk. A couple of minutes later, there was a tap on her door. She called for the tapper to come in, figuring it was Margo.

Thank goodness. I was beginning to think she'd left the country.

Then again, she wasn't yet ready to have another conversation about the tea shop or partnership or any of that. She doubted Margo would be, either. Maybe she'd suggest they go out to dinner.

Whoever was at the door knocked again.

"Come in!" she called a bit louder.

The door slowly swung open.

Katie blinked, surprised to see that her visitor was a leering Godfrey Foster. "Oh . . . hi."

"Don't sound so happy to see me." His words were just a teensy bit slurred. Had he been drinking while at the Alley? Great—Artisans Alley already had the threat of one lawsuit hovering over its head. If the ballerinas' mothers found out there was a vendor drinking on the job, it could be disastrous.

"Sorry. I was expecting Margo."

"She's at Wood U with Ray." Godfrey snickered. "Who knows when she'll be back?" He scrunched up his face. "I can't believe Margo likes that guy. She seems so classy and sophisticated. Ray Davenport is anything but."

And Godfrey was?

"I wouldn't say that," Katie stated, feeling the muscles in her arms tighten.

Godfrey stumbled into the office and perched on the chair most recently vacated by Seth. "You know who I think is classy?"

He's drunk as a skunk! But now wasn't the time to tell him his time as an Artisans Alley vendor was over . . . again. She'd do that after he'd sobered up, and this time she wouldn't be talked out of it.

He pointed a finger at her. "You. You're classy, Katie Bonner."

"Thank you. Godfrey, you . . . you don't seem to be . . . feeling well. Have you been drinking?"

He held up his index finger and thumb to indicate he'd been drinking "a wee bit." Well, from where Katie was sitting, it looked like a heck of a lot more than "a wee bit."

"Why don't I call someone to take you home?" she asked.

"I'm happy where I'm at, thanks." He leaned back in the chair. "So . . . what's the deal with Andy? Do you love him? Does he say he loves you?"

Katie's cheeks grew hot. "My relationship with Andy is not open for discussion."

Godfrey put up his hands in a defensive gesture. "I just don't want you to get hurt. Have you seen the way Andy looks at that girl he's got helping him manage the pizzeria? Not that I can completely blame Andy—she's gorgeous . . . no offense—but I think Andy might just be stringing you along until he can get it on with her."

"That's enough," Katie said, and would have stood if she'd had access to her crutches. "I won't sit here and listen to you criticize relationships you know nothing about."

Godfrey stood and put one hand on Katie's desk and the other on her chair, effectively blocking her in. "Why are you women all alike?"

"Why do men like you make such sweeping generalizations? Look, I'm trying to cut you some slack, Godfrey, because I know you're going through a rough time. But you need to back off immediately."

"Why?" He pouted like a spoiled little brat. "Aren't I good enough for you?"

Was he out of his mind? "You know I'm in a relationship with Andy."

Godfrey scowled. "You're just like her . . . just like Vonne."

Katie felt an icy chill creep down her spine.

"You want somebody who'll end up breaking your heart," Godfrey said. "Even when Vonne got pregnant— pregnant with *my* baby—"

Katie drew in a breath.

"Yeah, you heard me. It was my baby Vonne was carrying. But even then, she wanted that stupid Charles—Charles, who'd long forgotten her and had married someone else."

Katie could feel and smell Godfrey's hot, alcohol-laden breath in her face. She swallowed the bile rising in her throat. "Are you sure the baby was yours?"

"Of course I'm sure. We only had one night of passion, but it was enough. Despite my wife never being able to conceive for all those years, one night with Vonne . . . she and I hit the jackpot." He frowned. "But was she grateful? No. She came to me to ask for money for an abortion. She wanted to kill my child! She said she thought I'd want that, too. Can you believe that?"

Not having a clue how to respond to any of this, Katie merely shook her head.

"I told her I was willing to step up and be a man . . . to take care of her and our baby. But she didn't want us . . . didn't want *either* of us." He slammed a fist onto Katie's desk. "What's the matter with you? You don't want a decent man. You want the man you can't have . . . the one who treats you like garbage . . . the one who's stringing you along until he can have someone better!" Godfrey drew back a hand to slap Katie.

"Godfrey, I'm not Vonne!" she hollered.

His arm froze in midair before he lowered it and sank back into the chair. His face crumpled and he began to sob. "Why? Why couldn't . . . she . . . love me and . . . our baby? Why wouldn't . . . she listen?" He drew in a gulp of air. "Why did she have to laugh at me?"

He killed her, Katie realized with a jolt, leaving her feeling numb. It was as if her brain had shut down in order to help her process what she needed to do to get out of this dangerous situation.

Godfrey had nearly struck her seconds before merely because she was a woman and he was projecting his feelings for Vonne onto her. If he decided she was going to call the police and report what he'd done, he'd kill her, too. He might anyway. She decided to change tack.

"You're right," she said. "Why don't we women realize when we have a great catch in a man? Vonne would've been so lucky to settle down and raise a family with you."

"You think so?" He blinked rapidly. "Really?"

"I know so. She was foolish."

"What about you, Katie? Do you think we could make a good life together?"

Ewww . . . no. "Uh, yes. Yes, I do."

His expression turned thunderous again. "Liar! You're patronizing me, that's all this is!"

"It isn't. But, Godfrey, tell me the truth. Did you kill Vonne?"

"No! N-not really." He raked his hands down his face. "She made me angry. She was standing there laughing at me like I was some kind of idiot—like the very suggestion that I could provide a happy life for her and our baby was ridiculous. When she turned to leave, I was holding a cricket bat I use to keep my dryer lint lying flat."

"You hit her with the bat?"

He nodded. "I hit her. Brought the bat up and smacked her right in the back of the head. I didn't realize I'd hit her all that hard until she didn't get up. All that blood . . ." He brought his watery eyes up to meet Katie's. "I didn't mean to."

Katie's breath caught in her throat, but she had to placate this idiot. "I—I know you didn't."

"Are you going to keep my secret?"

"Of course I will," Katie said softly.

Godfrey seemed satisfied with her response, but only for a second. He leapt out of the chair and fenced her in again. "You women are all deceivers! You're just like Vonne and all the rest!"

Katie pushed her chair away from the desk, swiveled to face Godfrey, and in an instant brought her cast up hard between his legs.

Godfrey doubled over in pain, letting out a wail that could curl hair. That's when Katie bashed him on the head with her stapler. When he crumpled to the side, she scrambled around him, hopping on her right leg to get to her crutches, which were leaning against the file cabinets behind the door.

Once she was out of the office, Katie pulled the door closed.

"Help! Somebody—help me!" she hollered, and she could see Margo running down the showroom's main aisle toward her. "Call nine-one-one!"

Vance passed Margo and ran to help Katie keep the door closed. "Who's in there?"

"Godfrey. He killed Vonne Barnett. We have to make sure he doesn't get out of there until the police get here."

"Godfrey . . . a murderer?" Vance breathed. "Why, that horrible little twerp. Are you okay?"

Though Katie's heart was pounding, she nodded. Meanwhile, Godfrey still wailed behind the door, pounding on it.

"What did you do?" Vance asked, holding on to the door handle.

"I—I used . . . used my cast as a weapon and . . . and hit him . . . where it counts."

Vance just stared at her for long seconds, and then he laughed. "Please remind me to never make you angry."

When Detective Schuler arrived at Artisans Alley half an hour later and opened the door to Katie's office, Godfrey was sitting on the floor, leaning against the file cabinet sobbing. He was docile as the deputies handcuffed him and led him away.

Andy and Ray arrived almost simultaneously.

"Katie, are you all right?" Andy asked, enfolding Katie in his arms.

"I'm fine. Can you believe it?" She looked up into his dark eyes. "It was Godfrey. Godfrey killed Vonne."

"Godfrey? Why?" Ray asked.

"Because he wanted a family," Katie said, "and Vonne didn't. She didn't want Godfrey or their baby. That fact apparently drove him over the edge."

Margo lurched forward to give Katie a hug, but since she was still clinging to Andy, she ended up embracing them both. "Katie, I'm so proud of you. You were brave and kept a much clearer head than I could have."

Rose, who'd trailed up after all the action had subsided,

smiled at Margo. "That's our Katie. Godfrey isn't the first killer she's faced down. Have her tell you about her other adventures sometime."

Margo blinked, astounded. "I'll—I'll do that."

Twenty-five

Given the day she'd had, Katie agreed to allow Andy to carry her up the stairs to her apartment once again. Margo clucked over her like a mother hen as well, and Katie let that slide, too. Maybe Rose had been right—Margo needed the opportunity to be a mom, to take care of someone, and to feel needed for a little while. Tomorrow, all bets were off with her babysitters, but tonight, Katie decided she would be a gracious recipient of their ministrations.

After getting her settled onto the sofa, Andy bent and kissed her forehead. "What else can I do, Sunshine?"

"Dinner," she said, tiredly. "I'd love one of those Yule logs."

"And I haven't gotten to try the new flavors of cinnamon rolls yet," Margo said.

Andy grinned. "Done. I'll go down and make us some

dinner, and I'll be back in a jiffy. Margo, give me a yell if either of you need anything."

"Will do." She went behind him and locked the door. Even though Vonne's killer had been caught and Carl Fiske was in jail, Margo still seemed apprehensive.

"Are you all right?" Katie asked her gently when she'd returned to the living room and perched on the armchair.

"Oh, I'm fine, darling." Her pallor belied her words. "Don't concern yourself about me."

"Margo . . ."

The older woman brushed tears away with a trembling hand. "Really. I'm just . . . overexcited, I guess. That wretched little man . . ."

"It's okay now, Margo. He's in jail. He can't hurt us now."

"I know that . . . I do. It's only . . . Well, it was *frightening*. Weren't you frightened when he had you cornered in your office?"

"I was," Katie admitted, "but I suppose my survival instinct took over." She shrugged.

"I don't believe mine would have. I think I'd have been too afraid to do anything."

Katie shook her head. "I doubt that. You're stronger than you realize."

Margo managed a brief smile. "Why don't I make us a cup of tea? Maybe that will help us relax."

"That sounds wonderful." Katie didn't particularly want a cup of tea, but she realized that Margo did and also that her former mother-in-law needed to busy herself.

"I want to hear about those adventures Rose mentioned," Margo called from the kitchen. "But I think my nerves will fare better with the news if we wait a few days before you tell me about them."

Katie chuckled. "All right. G—" She caught herself before she mentioned that Godfrey had told her what she was about to say. "I understand that you were at Wood U this afternoon. Sasha came in earlier today and was furious with me. Did Ray happen to mention anything about her?"

"Not to me. Why was Sasha angry with you?"

"She blames me for her father asking the school counselor to talk with her about her eating disorder."

Margo returned with the tea and handed Katie a cup. "The only girl he mentioned to me was Sophie. It seemed she was upset because she'd run into some girl named Janine who used to work for Afternoon Tea, and Janine told Sophie that you'd offered her a managerial position if you took over the shop."

"Well, yeah, I did, but I don't know why that would upset Sophie. It wouldn't keep me from hiring her to work as an intern in the shop over the summer."

"Ray said they were on rival teams for high school volleyball or something. I took it that the two girls didn't get along at all." Margo inclined her head. "I wouldn't worry too much about it, though. These things tend to sort themselves out."

Sure, they do. And now all *the Davenport girls hate me.*

Before they could further discuss the matter, there was a knock at the door. Margo put her teacup and saucer on the coffee table and went to answer the door. "If that's Andy, we'll have to give him the prize for speedy dinner preparation."

Katie doubted it was Andy, unless he'd forgotten his key.

Margo opened the door and Katie felt a trickle of dread when she heard Margo demand, "What're *you* doing here?"

"I came to speak with Katie." The voice was that of Nona Fiske.

"She isn't taking visitors right now," Margo said.

"It's all right," Katie called. "Come on in, Nona."

A reluctant Margo unlocked the door and Nona tramped into the living room and stood at the end of the sofa glaring at Katie. Her wool coat was tightly closed, and her purse was fisted against her stomach. "I guess you can apologize to Carl now. I'll be happy to deliver the message for you, if you'd like."

"Apologize to Carl for what? Not being a good enough speed bump in the Victoria Square parking lot?"

"For accusing him of killing Vonne Barnett. I've already learned the truth—that Godfrey Foster murdered Vonne by hitting her in the head with some sort of club."

"I don't believe I did accuse Carl of murdering Vonne," Katie said. "Although he certainly did make me believe he was capable of doing the deed."

"Well, he didn't, and now you know the truth." Nona pursed her lips as she looked down at Katie disdainfully. "You were wrong about him."

"Not in my opinion," Katie said.

"Nor mine," Margo asserted. "He might not have killed Vonne, but I wholeheartedly believe he attempted to murder Katie."

"He most certainly did not! Katie was wandering out in the middle of the parking lot like some sort of lunatic . . . and it was after midnight, for goodness' sake!" She scoffed. "I have to wonder if they did a blood alcohol test on you at the hospital that evening, Katie. Perhaps that's something Carl's attorney should look into."

"If Carl wants to waste money on attorney fees by having someone check my medical records for any indication that I was intoxicated, he may certainly do so, but I assure you that I hadn't been drinking that evening and the hospital can and will confirm that."

"And I can vouch for that, too," Margo said. "Andy took the two of us out to dinner at a steak house after the tree-lighting ceremony, and none of us had anything alcoholic to drink."

Nona rolled her eyes as if Katie and Margo had made up that entire scenario. "Whatever you say. I imagine the truth will come out in court."

"I imagine it will," Katie said. "I'll see you there, Nona. Thank you for dropping by."

"You love ruining other people's lives, don't you, Katie Bonner? Carl's, mine, Lucy Foster's—poor Lucy lost everything today. Little do *you* care."

"Please see yourself out." Margo silently dared Nona to ignore the challenge in her voice.

With a sniff, Nona turned, stalked through the kitchen, and slammed the door shut behind her.

"The nerve of that woman!" Margo dropped back onto the armchair and retrieved her tea. "And, if you ask me, you did Lucy Foster a favor. Godfrey might've killed *her* next! After dealing with Nona Fiske, maybe I should call down and ask Andy to bring up a pitcher of beer for us to have with dinner."

Katie laughed. "You? A beer drinker?"

"What?" Margo grinned. "Connoisseurs drink beer, too, you know."

"Unfortunately, Andy only sells canned soft drinks."

But then there was another knock at the door. Margo narrowed her eyes at Katie as she once again placed the teacup and saucer on the coffee table. "If it's that nasty little Nona Fiske again, I swear I'm going to push her down the stairs. Will you vouch for me and say it was an accident?"

Katie knew Margo was joking, so she went along with the gag. "It will probably wind up being your word against hers, but I can attest to the fact that the stairs get awfully icy in winter."

Despite the banter, Katie steeled herself against another verbal assault by Nona. She was relieved and delighted to hear Margo exclaim, "Seth! Am I glad to see you!"

"I hear I missed all the excitement down at Artisans Alley today," he said as he walked into the living room. He sat on the sofa beside Katie. "Are you okay, pseudo sis?"

"I'm fine."

"Good. From what I hear, if anybody suffered any"—he

cleared his throat—"pain during the incident, it was God-frey Foster."

Katie blushed. "I did what I felt was necessary for self-preservation."

"You did well."

"Seth, would you like a cup of tea?" Margo asked, picking up her cup and saucer and taking them to the kitchen. It appeared she'd completely given up on the idea of having a hot cup of tea.

"No, thank you, Margo. I only came by to check on Katie and to give her a piece of good news."

Katie's heart leapt. "Please tell me Arthur Henderson is okay."

"I spoke with Philip a few minutes ago. Other than a few bruises and a sore nose—which wasn't broken, but I'm sure it hurt when he hit and bloodied it on the pavement—Arthur is fine. Ed will still have fairly extensive medical bills to pay, even with Arthur's insurance paying the majority of the fees."

"I understand that. I dread getting my hospital bill," Katie said.

"The hospital took X-rays, performed an MRI, did an EKG to make sure his heart was okay, and even an EEG to check Arthur's brain activity . . ." Seth spread his hands. "I'm not sure how many tests they *did* do, but I know they did several and that they didn't allow Arthur to leave the hospital until they'd given him the all-clear. I imagine when Ed gets his part of the bill, it will serve as a serious reminder to him the next time he chases after a shoplifting suspect."

"Let's hope it will stop him in his tracks before he ever considers tackling someone else," Katie said.

Margo returned from the kitchen. "Still, I'm confident that Ed felt he was within his rights to detain Mr. Henderson. After all, the man had stolen an item from Ed's booth and he had left the building with it."

"Right," Seth agreed. "But there's a right way and a wrong way to detain shoplifters."

"I think I should invite a deputy to speak at our next Merchants Association meeting and to refresh our vendors on the proper way to apprehend a thief." Katie rubbed her temples. "What about filing suit? Did Philip Henderson mention his intentions in that regard?"

"Philip said that he isn't going to sue Artisans Alley or Ed, since Ed has already agreed to pay the amount of medical expenses not covered by Arthur's insurance."

Katie let out a breath and sagged back against the sofa cushions. "Thank goodness. I was truly frightened that incident might signal the end of Artisans Alley."

"Philip also told me that Arthur wouldn't be back into Artisans Alley without supervision," Seth said. "His dementia has taken a serious turn."

"I'm so sorry to hear that." Katie was glad, however, that there would be someone with Arthur the next time he visited Artisans Alley. Hopefully, an incident like the one that transpired today would never happen again.

"Seth, since you're here, I'd like to speak with you and Katie about the acquisition of Afternoon Tea," Margo said, once again sitting on the armchair where she could easily face them both. "I know Katie wants me to loan her the money, so I'm willing to compromise. I'll loan her half the money she needs if she'll let me give her the other half." She met Katie's eyes. "What do you say? We'll meet each other halfway."

Katie hesitated.

"Please . . . you've already given me the painting Chad made for me. He sank all your savings into Artisans Alley. You and I both know he'd want you to take at least half the payment as a gift from me—from him and me—to you."

Katie considered the offer and Margo's sincere expression. She smiled. "It's a deal."

"All right." Seth clasped his hands together. "I'll draw

up the paperwork and bring it to Artisans Alley sometime tomorrow."

"That sounds wonderful," Margo said. "Thank you."

Andy arrived and used his key to open the door. "Hey, Seth! I hope you're planning on joining us for dinner. I've brought plenty of food."

"I'm sorry—I can't." He winked at Katie. "I have other plans tonight."

"Have fun," she said.

Margo walked Seth to the door and then helped Andy set the calzones—or, rather, Yule logs—pizza, bread sticks, and all three flavors of cinnamon rolls on the coffee table, buffet style.

"Gee," Katie said, "do you think you brought enough?"

There was a knock at the door.

Katie let out a groan.

"Maybe not," Andy said as he went to see who their visitors were. "Hey!" he exclaimed when he threw open the door.

Katie let out her breath when she recognized the voices of Nick and Don.

"What've you got there?" Andy asked Don.

"A plate of my favorite homemade peanut butter fudge. I slaved over it for hours." He set the plastic-wrapped festive plate on the coffee table and took off his coat.

"Lies," Nick said, taking off his gloves. "He made it in the microwave."

Don ignored him. "Our guests are all out and about tonight, so we thought we'd come and check up on you guys."

"Yes," Nick said, pulled off his jacket, and squeezed in beside Katie on the sofa. "I heard you've been fighting crime again."

"She has," Andy said. "And then she fussed at me for bringing too much food, and yet here we have two more guests. Tell me I'm not psychic!"

"You're not psychic," Katie said.

"Okay . . . well, maybe I'm lucky."

"We'll give you that one," Don said.

Everyone grabbed a plate and helped themselves to the delicious fare.

Gesturing with a bread stick as if it were a magic wand, Nick entertained them with his tale of how he planned to memorialize Katie's adventures in McKinlay Mill in a novel. "And since Katie will be like our very own Nancy Drew, I suppose that would make Andy Ned Nickerson!"

"I refuse to be Ned Nickerson," Andy said, between bites of pizza. "He was so lame."

"He wasn't lame," Nick said. "He was dashing."

Don shook his head. "Too vanilla."

"I like vanilla." Nick bit the bread stick.

"I'd rather be a Hardy boy," Andy said.

"Oooh, Joe or Frank?" Margo asked. "I always loved Parker Stevenson when he was on that show."

Andy inclined his head toward Margo. "Then I'll be Frank Hardy. I always thought Nancy would end up with one of the Hardy brothers anyway."

"Or George," Nick said, with a wicked laugh.

~~~~~~

Finally, Nick and Don had gone back to Sassy Sally's, the dishes had been cleaned up and leftovers put away, and Margo had retired to the bedroom. Andy sat on the sofa cradling Katie in his arms.

"This was a good evening," he said. "We should host impromptu dinner parties more often."

"That sounds good to me." She nuzzled his neck.

"Any word on when Margo will be returning home?" he whispered.

"No . . . but I don't think she'll be here much longer. I'm doing well and, after today, I'm pretty sure she'll be eager to get back to her own routine."

"I'm eager to get back to *our* routine."

Katie kissed his neck. "So am I."

"If you keep that up, I'll be getting back to our routine whether she's in the next room or not."

Katie chuckled. "Sorry . . . you're simply irresistible."

"So are you, my love. So are you."

"When Seth was here earlier, Margo came up with a compromise on the Afternoon Tea acquisition."

"Which is?"

Katie explained about the offer Margo made to give Katie half the money and lend her the other half.

"And you accepted?" he asked.

"I did."

"Wow . . . You must be getting soft in your—"

"Don't you *dare* say old age," Katie warned.

"I wasn't. I was going to say . . . infirmity."

"Sure, you were. You know, I've got used to having you here these past few nights. It's going to be hard to go to sleep without you."

"I wasn't planning on leaving," Andy said. "Are you kicking me out?"

"But . . . there's no reason to stay now. Godfrey and Carl are both in jail, and I don't think either of them will be getting out soon."

He shrugged. "Still, it won't hurt me to sleep on your floor for one more night . . . right?"

She smiled broadly. "You're too good to me."

"I love you."

"And I love you." She gave him a kiss intended to wipe away any doubts either of them might have.

Twenty-six

The next morning, Katie was back at work wearing her Dickens costume. She felt that since she was doing so well with her crutches, she didn't have a valid excuse not to wear it. And, besides, she missed participating in the fun.

She was sitting in her office when she heard *rum-rum*. She was a little startled but not completely surprised when a large bullfrog jumped up to her desk and stared at her.

"Are you looking for a little girl wearing a tutu?" Katie asked the frog.

Rum-rum. Rum-rum.

"I'm sure your girl is looking for you, too." She picked up the creature and looked into its eyes. "Are you really a frog prince?"

Rose came around the corner and froze in the open doorway. "You aren't going to *kiss* that thing to try to find out, are you?"

Katie laughed. "No. Would you please take Mr. Bullfrog here over to the dance studio?"

"No, ma'am, I will not. I'm not about to touch that . . . that . . . creature."

"Oh, Rose. He's sweet. Look at him."

Rose took a step into Katie's office to peer at the frog.

Rum-rum.

At the sound, Rose squealed and backed away from the desk. "I'll call Vance." She spun around and dashed through the vendors' lounge calling Vance's name.

"I'm sorry about that, Your Highness. Some people are a little jumpy, you know . . . no pun intended."

A minute or two later, Vance came to the rescue.

"I understand I've been promoted to bullfrog delivery service," he said with a wry grin.

"Yes. I'd do it myself, but I can't carry him and hold my crutches, too."

"I'm on it. I'm surprised to see you sitting here holding him so calmly, though."

"Are you kidding? He's one of the best-behaved visitors I've had in my office all week."

"You've got a point there. He sure beats Godfrey all to pieces."

"Better-looking, too," Katie said. She handed the bullfrog to Vance. "Good-bye, Mr. Bullfrog. Mr. Ingram will return you to your princess now. I'm guessing I'll see you again . . . or, at least, hear of your exploits."

"It's not him I worry about—it's the princess . . . and her ladies-in-waiting." He chortled. "Oh well, the ballerinas' schedule will be back to normal in just a couple more days."

"That's a relief, Vance. I believe the vendors have had all of those little *angels* they can stand."

As Vance walked away, Katie took a wet wipe from her desk drawer and cleaned her hands.

A few minutes later, Margo arrived at Katie's office and closed the door. "How are you doing?"

"Thanks to over-the-counter pain relievers, good, and I'm feeling an unimaginable sense of relief now that both Godfrey and Carl Fiske are in jail. Who knew so many people would want to kill me in such a short amount of time?"

"Don't make light of it," Margo admonished. "You know, I always thought Godfrey was a strange man, but I'd never have pegged him for a murderer."

"It shocked me, too."

"Let's talk about something more pleasant. I like your bonnet."

"Thanks," Katie said. "It's part of the Dickens costume, but I haven't been wearing it. I thought it was too much trouble to take on and off throughout the day. But as we get closer to the holiday, I thought I should bite the bullet."

Margo sighed. "I've stayed far longer than I'd expected, and I still never got around to buying a costume. Sorry for that."

"Don't worry about it. I've got you covered." Katie reached under her desk and picked up an oblong box. "I ordered this a few days ago as a thank-you for taking such good care of me. It came yesterday . . . but I somehow forgot to give it to you."

Margo laughed. "Somehow." She opened the box and gasped with delight. She unpacked the maroon Dickens caroler costume, complete with a white faux-fur muff. "It's gorgeous."

"I hope it's the right size."

"May I run and put it on?" Margo asked.

"Please do."

When Margo returned, she looked fantastic. The costume could've been custom-made for her. "Thank you, Katie! I love it!"

"I'm glad you like it. You look wonderful, and of course, you know this means you must return next year."

Margo's eyes glistened. "I'd love to. I wonder if Vance's choir will let me sing with them."

"I'm sure they'd be delighted," Katie said.

There was a tap on the door.

Margo grinned at Katie. "Right on schedule." She opened the door to admit Seth.

"Margo, you look stunning!" he said, entering the office with a chair he'd pulled over.

She blushed and closed the door behind him. "Thank you. Katie just gave me the costume. I don't plan on being in McKinlay Mill for more than a few additional days, but she was terribly thoughtful to get me this gift."

"Yes, she was," Seth said, with a grin in Katie's direction. He handed both women a copy of the gift and loan agreements.

After carefully reading and ensuring that they understood all the details, Margo and Katie signed the documents.

"Are you going to keep the name *Afternoon Tea*?" Margo asked.

"No. That's a little too bland for me," Katie said.

"Ah . . . I'm guessing you'll want to call the shop English Ivy Tea, won't you? For the bed-and-breakfast you wanted so badly?"

"No. That dream is behind me now. What do you think about my calling the tea shop *Tealicious*?"

"Tealicious! I love it." Margo laughed. "Well, if you two don't need me anymore, I'll go see if Rose needs any help at the cash desks. To be honest, I'm eager to show off my costume."

"Go," Katie said. "And thank you again."

"My pleasure." She closed the door behind her, giving Katie and Seth some privacy.

"I'm happy things worked out so well between the two of you," he said. "I had my doubts when Margo first arrived."

"So did I." Katie sighed. "Am I doing the right thing in allowing her to give me half the money?"

"Yes," he said emphatically. "Don't second-guess your-self. You know you're doing the right thing. It's like Margo said last night, this is the perfect compromise. You both get what you want."

"But I end up with a tea shop, and she ends up with . . . what?"

"A relationship with her former daughter-in-law," Seth said gently. "She gets a chance to keep another part of Chad alive through you."

Katie smiled. "You're really special, you know that?"

"I merely call them like I see them."

"You seem happier these days. When am I going to get to meet the man responsible for that?"

"Soon, I hope. I'm hosting a Christmas party at my house next Saturday. I'd love it if you and Andy—and Margo, if she's still here then—could come."

Katie smiled. "I can't speak for Andy or Margo, of course, but I wouldn't miss it."

~~~~~~~

Katie was just about to call Margo to ask about going to lunch when Francine stopped by. She wasn't bearing gifts this time, and she looked both relieved and tired.

"Mr. Landers stopped by Afternoon Tea this morning," she said, easing into the chair beside Katie's desk. "He said he'd be handling the paperwork for the transfer of owner-ship of the tea shop from me to you. I'm happy to know it's going to be in capable hands."

"Thank you. I'm eager to get started on a new chal-lenge."

She smiled. "Seth said you were going to rename the shop Tealicious."

"That's the plan," Katie said. "Do you like it?"

"I do. It's cute." Francine ran a hand over the back of her neck. "I'm ready for a new challenge myself. It's as if one entire book of my life has ended."

"Every day is a clean page. Write something beautiful on each one."

"I will if you will. Don't work so hard you don't enjoy what you have."

"Is that what happened to you . . . and Vonne?" Katie asked softly.

"Maybe that was part of it. I believe Vonne and I both aimed too high in everything. With expectations as grand as ours, we could never be happy . . . with the tea shop, with each other, with our own lives." She smiled sadly. "I wanted to be supermom, to have Vonne adore me, for us to work together like a well-oiled machine to make our business this charming little shop where everyone in the community could come together and enjoy a cozy atmosphere, a hot cup of tea, and a delicious pastry."

"And what did Vonne want?"

"She wanted to be independent . . . wanted to find a man who'd love her as much as Booth did . . ." Tears welled in her eyes. "She looked so much like Nancy. Sometimes it was hard for me to look at her—even when she was a child—and see Vonne rather than Nancy. And I hated it."

Katie reached for the box of tissues she kept on her desk and handed it to Francine.

"Thank you." Francine took out a tissue and tried to dam the flood of tears, but it was no use. They fell unheeded down her cheeks. "I loved Vonne . . . I did. But I hated Nancy. And sometimes those lines blurred. Especially after Vonne learned the truth and wanted to meet her birth mother. I could barely stand to look at her after that."

"Did you tell her how you were feeling?"

"I tried. And maybe she tried to tell me what she was going through. But we couldn't say anything to each other toward the end without arguing." Francine covered her face with her hands. "And then that despicable Godfrey Foster murdered her. My girl died without knowing that I loved her."

Katie stood on her good leg and patted Francine's shoulder. "I'm sure she knew."

In a few moments, Francine regained her composure. She took another tissue from the box and dried her eyes before handing the box back to Katie.

"Thank you," Francine said. "I feel better now. I believe that once the paperwork is finalized for the sale of the tea shop, I'll go on a trip. I want to visit somewhere I've never been . . . create some new memories that are mine and mine alone."

"I think that will do you a world of good." Katie sat back onto her chair and returned the tissue box to the back of her desk. "We'll miss you here in Victoria Square, and we hope you'll come back to visit."

"That's nice of you to say so." Francine tossed her two used tissues into the wastebasket. "You've always been kind to me, Katie. That means more than you know."

Before Katie could reply, Rose tapped on the door briefly before popping her head into the office.

"Oops, sorry, Katie! I didn't know you had a visitor."

"That's all right, Rose. I was just leaving." Francine stood and glanced back at Katie. "I'll see you soon. And, again, I'm glad the tea shop will have a new life."

Katie smiled and said good-bye.

Francine left and Rose moved into the office and pushed open the door. "So, you've bought the shop?"

"Yep. I'm going to name it Tealicious."

Rose laughed. "That's fantastic."

"Thanks. I hoped you'd like it."

"This doesn't mean you're leaving Artisans Alley, does it?" Rose asked.

"Of course not. I'll still be an albatross around your neck every single day."

"You aren't a burden, dear. You're a blessing." Rose handed Katie her crutches. "Margo and I thought you might like to grab a bite of lunch with us. Are you up to it?"

"I am." Katie stood and took the crutches from Rose. "In fact, I was thinking about lunch before Francine came in."

"She seemed . . . different today."

Katie nodded. "She is, I think. I'm not sure what it is, but I believe Francine feels a sense of freedom. She's out from under the enormous responsibility of the tea shop, she doesn't have to strive for Vonne's affection anymore, she doesn't have to argue with someone day in and day out . . ."

Rose frowned. "You really think she was striving for Vonne's affection?"

"In her way, I believe she was. From what Francine told me about her relationship with Vonne, I feel like they loved each other but that it was as if they were on two separate mountain peaks. There was a valley between them that neither of them knew how to navigate, so they simply couldn't meet in the middle."

"That's sad. Poetic, but sad."

Katie giggled. "Maybe it's the hunger talking. Let's get Margo and go to lunch."

As Rose and Katie walked to the cash desks where Margo was waiting, the ballerina with the bullfrog ran to meet them.

"Hi!" she said. "Thank you for saving the prince this morning."

"You're welcome. Where is he now?"

"He's in his portable terrarium. He also says thanks, though, and that you're nice."

"I think he's nice, too," Katie said, with a grin.

"We'd like you to come to our performance of *The Nutcracker*." She looked up at Katie, all wide eyes and dimples.

"I'll do my best to be there. But for now, Ms. Nash and I have to run."

"You can't run, silly. You're broken." And to prove how very different they were, the imp sprinted off down the hallway.

"Are you really planning to go to their ballet?" Rose asked.

"Maybe. It would win me some brownie points with Cheryl. She and I have been clashing over the girls' behavior."

"Keeping those little terrors reined in would have made *her* some brownie points with *you*."

"True." Katie sighed. "Maybe I'm just feeling a little more generous today. Things are looking up, Rose."

~~~~~~~~

That afternoon, Katie was surprised to see Ray stroll into her office with a rather large and what looked like a professionally gift-wrapped box with green-and-red-striped paper, which he placed on the desk. He shut the door behind him and nodded at the bonnet perched on Katie's head. "That's new."

"Not really. I just don't like wearing it that much."

"You should. It suits you." He sat on the chair beside her. "I spoke with Schuler this morning. Godfrey gave a full confession."

"What did they charge him with?"

"Second-degree murder, since it wasn't premeditated, but there are additional charges stemming from the fact that he moved the body and staged the accident. Wanna hear something intriguing?"

"Sure."

"Schuler said that based on Godfrey's blood type, it's not possible for him to be the father of Vonne Barnett's child."

Katie's jaw dropped. "Then why would she tell him he was? And who was the father of her baby?"

"The Sheriff's Office's best guess, based on his blood type, is Carl Fiske. Of course, the DNA test is pending, but the blood type alone was enough to negate Godfrey. I figure Godfrey was Vonne's last hope at getting enough money for an abortion. She knew Godfrey was married and thought he probably wouldn't want her to be carrying his child."

"And it backfired on her because Godfrey wanted the baby. Huh. How sad that, basically, those two sad, lonely people actually wanted the same thing deep down but wound up destroying each other instead."

"Yep. That about sums it up." He indicated the box. "Open that. It might cheer you up."

"Christmas is still over a week away, and I haven't even started my shopping yet. I'll wait."

"Did I say this was a Christmas gift?" Ray asked. "This is a . . . glad-Godfrey-didn't-kill-you present."

She laughed. "Shouldn't I wait for the girls to be here before I open it, though?"

He lowered his eyes. "They . . . can't come by today."

"All three of them hate me, don't they?"

Ray spread his hands. " 'Hate' is an awfully strong word. They loved you last week. They'll probably love you again next week."

"And they might not."

"They might not," he admitted, and shrugged before once again indicating the box. "So, open it, already."

"All right." She removed the bow and placed it on her desk. Then she carefully unwrapped one end.

"What are you doing? You're not going to save the wrapping paper, so rip it off."

"Sometimes anticipation makes the gift all the better, Ray."

He grinned. "Good point."

Katie carefully removed all the paper and then opened the box, her mouth dropping open in awe. She carefully lifted a detailed replica of Sassy Sally's. But instead of Sassy Sally's, the sign read ENGLISH IVY INN. Tears sprang to Katie's eyes as she ran her fingers gently over the exquisite piece. She finally placed the house on her desk and pushed herself up on her good leg, so she could hug Ray. "Thank you so much."

He stood and returned her embrace. As she looked up at him, her eyes bright with unshed tears, he lowered his head and tenderly kissed her lips.

When he lifted his head, Katie merely stared at him.

"What? I had to. Isn't that mistletoe on your bonnet?"

"It's holly," she deadpanned.

"Oh, my mistake." He winked and eased her back onto her chair.

As he walked out of the office, he was whistling "You've Got a Friend in Me."

Recipes

Katie's Sugar Cookies

1½ cups (3 sticks) butter, softened
2 cups granulated sugar
4 eggs
1 teaspoon vanilla extract
5 cups all-purpose flour
2 teaspoons baking powder
½ teaspoon salt

In a large bowl, cream together the butter and sugar until smooth. Beat in the eggs and vanilla. Stir in the flour, baking powder, and salt. Cover, and chill the dough for at least one hour (or overnight).

Preheat the oven to 400°F. Roll out the dough on a floured surface ¼ to ½ inch thick. Cut into shapes with any shape cookie cutter. Place cookies 1 inch apart on ungreased baking trays. Bake 6 to 8 minutes in preheated oven. Transfer to wire racks and cool completely.

YIELD: APPROXIMATELY 60 COOKIES

Andy's Cinnamon-Pumpkin Buns

⅓ cup milk
2 tablespoons butter
½ cup canned pumpkin (not pumpkin pie filling)
¼ cup packed light or dark brown sugar
¼ teaspoon nutmeg
½ teaspoon salt
1 large egg
2¼ teaspoons (1 standard package) instant yeast
2⅔ cups all-purpose flour

Filling

6 tablespoons butter, softened to room temperature
½ cup packed light or dark brown sugar
1 tablespoon ground cinnamon
½ teaspoon ground nutmeg
½ teaspoon ground cloves
¼ teaspoon ground allspice

Caramel Icing

2 tablespoons butter
¼ cup packed brown sugar
1 tablespoon milk
¼ teaspoon vanilla extract
dash of salt
¼ to ⅓ cup confectioners' sugar

For the dough: Warm the milk and butter together over the stove or in the microwave until the butter is just melted. The mixture should be lukewarm (105–115°F). Set aside. Using a stand mixer fitted with a paddle attachment, beat the pumpkin puree, brown sugar, nutmeg, and salt together on medium speed. Add the warmed milk/butter and beat until combined, then beat in the egg and yeast. With the mixer running on low speed, add 1 cup of flour. Mix for 1 minute, scraping down the sides of the bowl frequently. Add 1¼ cups more flour and beat for 1 more minute. The dough will be very soft. Place dough into a greased bowl (cooking spray works well). Turn the dough around in the bowl so all sides of it are coated. Cover tightly with plastic wrap and allow to rise in a warm, draft-free environment until doubled in size, about 60 to 90 minutes. Gently punch the dough down to deflate it and turn it out onto a lightly floured surface. Knead the dough a few times so it is smooth. If it is too sticky, knead in a little more flour.

Add the filling: Combine the brown sugar, cinnamon, and spices into a small bowl. Roll the dough out into a 18-by-10-inch rectangle. Spread the softened butter evenly on top. Sprinkle all the filling over the top. Roll it up tightly. Using a very sharp knife, cut into 10 to 12 pieces, about 1½ inches each. Arrange the rolls into a greased 9-by-9-inch or 11-by-7-inch pan. Cover with plastic wrap and allow the rolls to rise again in a warm, draft-free environment until doubled in size. This takes about 1 hour. Preheat the oven to 350°F. Bake the rolls for 22–28 minutes, covering with aluminum foil at the 15-minute mark to prevent heavy browning. Remove from oven and allow to slightly cool while you prepare the icing.

Icing: Melt the butter in a saucepan; stir in the brown sugar and milk. Cook and stir over medium-low heat for 1 minute. Stir in the vanilla, salt, and ¼ cup confectioners' sugar; beat until well blended. Add more sugar, if necessary, to achieve desired consistency. Drizzle over the rolls.

YIELD: 1 DOZEN

Don's Ultra-Easy Peanut Butter Fudge

1 cup creamy or crunchy peanut butter
1 cup (2 sticks) unsalted butter
1 teaspoon vanilla extract
¼ teaspoon salt (optional)
4 cups sifted confectioners' sugar

Line an 8- or 9-inch square baking pan with aluminum foil, leaving an overhang on the sides to lift the finished fudge. In a microwave, melt the peanut butter and butter together in a large bowl, stirring the mixture every minute or so until completely melted and smooth. Remove from the microwave and stir in the vanilla extract. If you prefer a salty/sweet fudge, add the salt. Add the sifted confectioners' sugar and stir until completely combined. The mixture will be very thick, resembling cookie dough. Press the fudge into the prepared baking pan, smoothing the top with the back of a spatula or spoon. (The top will be somewhat oily.) Cover tightly with aluminum foil and chill for 4 hours or until firm. Cut into pieces. Store the fudge in an airtight container in the refrigerator for up to 1 week. Fudge may be frozen for up to 2 months.

YIELD: APPROXIMATELY 64 1-INCH PIECES

Ready to find
your next great read?

Let us help.

Visit prh.com/nextread

Penguin
Random
House